Praise for

MOMO ARASHIMA
STEALS THE SWORD OF THE WIND

"**THIS WILD RIDE OF A NOVEL** is simultaneously a hilarious adventure and a meditation on fear, anger, bravery, friendship, and the ties of family and love." —Sayantani DasGupta, *New York Times* bestselling author of the Kingdom Beyond series

"With vivid descriptions, relatable characters, and colorful figures from Japanese mythology, **MISA SUGIURA TAKES READERS ON A GRAND ADVENTURE.**" —Brandon Mull, #1 *New York Times* bestselling author of the Fablehaven series

★ "Sugiura's wonderful series starter is **A PAGE-TURNING, EMOTION-PACKED ADVENTURE** that draws on Japanese-inspired folklore to explore themes of family, friendship, and identity. . . . **HIGHLY RECOMMENDED FOR FANS OF THE ARU SHAH BOOKS.**"
—*Booklist*, starred review

"This hilarious, high-spirited tale blends Japanese legends, mythical creatures, and deities. . . . **FUNNY, RELATABLE, AND FULL OF ADVENTURE.**" —*Kirkus Reviews*

"Culturally specific details imbue this **ROLLER-COASTER-FEELING MAGICAL PLOT WITH AUTHENTICITY AND INTRIGUE,** while Momo's smart, funny narration and slowly reforming relationship with Danny ground their adventure in a thoughtful friendship tale."
—*Publishers Weekly*

Praise for

MOMO ARASHIMA
BREAKS THE MIRROR OF THE SUN

"Shintō influences and Japanese folklore are blended in this action-packed fantasy that explores friendship, belonging, anger, anxiety, self-discovery, and embracing all parts of ourselves. **AN APPEALING ADVENTURE FILLED WITH BOTH ACTION AND HEART.**"
—*Kirkus Reviews*

MOMO ARASHIMA
DUELS THE QUEEN OF DEATH

Also by Misa Sugiura

Momo Arashima Steals the Sword of the Wind
Momo Arashima Breaks the Mirror of the Sun

MOMO ARASHIMA
DUELS THE QUEEN OF DEATH
Book 3

MISA SUGIURA

LR LABYRINTH ROAD | NEW YORK

This is a work of fiction. Names, characters, places, and incidents either are the product of the author's imagination or are used fictitiously. Any resemblance to actual persons, living or dead, events, or locales is entirely coincidental.

Text copyright © 2025 by Misa Sugiura
Jacket art copyright © 2025 by Vivienne To

All rights reserved. Published in the United States by Labyrinth Road, an imprint of Random House Children's Books, a division of Penguin Random House LLC, New York.

Labyrinth Road and the colophon are registered trademarks of Penguin Random House LLC.

Visit us on the Web! rhcbooks.com

Educators and librarians, for a variety of teaching tools, visit us at RHTeachersLibrarians.com

Library of Congress Cataloging-in-Publication Data is available upon request.
ISBN 978-0-593-56414-1 (trade) —ISBN 978-0-593-56415-8 (lib. bdg.)—
ISBN 978-0-593-56417-2 (ebook)

The text of this book is set in 11-point Horley Old Style MT Pro.

Editors: Liesa Abrams and Emily Shapiro
Cover Designer: Michelle Cunningham
Interior Designer: Megan Shortt
Production Editors: Barbara Bakowski and Clare Perret
Managing Editor: Rebecca Vitkus
Production Manager: Tim Terhune

Printed in the United States of America
10 9 8 7 6 5 4 3 2 1
First Edition

Random House Children's Books supports the First Amendment and celebrates the right to read.

Penguin Random House values and supports copyright. Copyright fuels creativity, encourages diverse voices, promotes free speech, and creates a vibrant culture. Thank you for buying an authorized edition of this book and for complying with copyright laws by not reproducing, scanning, or distributing any part of it in any form without permission. You are supporting writers and allowing Penguin Random House to continue to publish books for every reader. Please note that no part of this book may be used or reproduced in any manner for the purpose of training artificial intelligence technologies or systems.

For anyone out there who is feeling alone,
afraid, or misunderstood:

Hang in there. You've got this. I believe in you.

No One Likes an Angry Goddess

"**Why can't you just buy** me a cell phone and use the locator app like other parents?" I whined. "I'll look like a total weirdo!"

It was Monday morning, and after spending all day yesterday in bed feeling awful (I'll tell you why in a minute), I'd decided last night that I had to go to school no matter what. Mom had been difficult to convince, but I insisted that I was okay, that I was fine, that she didn't need to worry, and she had finally agreed to let me go—as long as I wore an extra-strength shimenawa around my waist. She'd woven the protective white rope herself last night, and it was as thick around as one of those corgi dogs. Then she'd enchanted it so that she would know where I was at all times.

According to Mom, a shimenawa was far superior to a cell phone because a cell phone would: (a) rot my brains, (b) make me obsessed with social media and ruin my self-esteem, and most importantly, (c) be useless against Izanami the Destroyer and any evil yōkai she might send after me.

"Oh, stop your sniveling," said Niko. The talking fox was one of my best friends, but he almost always took Mom's side over mine, probably since he'd known her for at least a hundred years. I gave him my best stink eye, but he pretended not to notice.

"If I had a phone, you could enchant it so that it shoots yōkai-killing magic laser beams," I suggested. "Danny's phone always points us in the right direction. And it keeps track of time on Earth even when we're in a time bubble."

Mom shook her head. "Just because Danny has something you want doesn't mean I have to give it to you. If Danny jumped off the Golden Gate Bridge, would you jump off as well?"

"Actually, I jumped first," I said, because it was true. Two times now, my best friend Danny and I had leaped through a portal that was located just off the top of the northern tower of the Golden Gate Bridge.

Niko started to laugh but turned it into a cough when he saw that Mom didn't think it was funny. "I'm giving you the shimenawa so you don't *have* to jump off any bridges," she said, and from her tone, I knew I'd just lost the argument. I let her put on the rope and enchant it so I couldn't take it off, and stomped out the door, muttering under my breath all the way to the bus stop. To be honest, it hadn't been an easy decision to go to school. And having to wear this big old ugly rope around my waist didn't make things easier.

The fact was, I *wasn't* okay, I *wouldn't* be fine, and Mom *did* have reason to worry—several reasons. But Mom only knew one of them, and I couldn't tell her about the rest. This made me even angrier at her, because I *should* have been able to tell her all of it. It was an awful feeling, being in trouble and not being able to ask anyone for help or advice.

I wished I could travel back in time to when everything felt safe. Like maybe six weeks ago to New Year's Eve, when I'd teamed up with Niko and my friends Danny, Ryleigh, and

Jin to secure the Mirror of the Sun and stop the nine-tailed fox demon Tamamo-no-mae from sucking the lives out of 888 kids. Or even just back to Friday night, when Jin had performed with his band, Straight 2 tha Topp, at Oracle Arena in Oakland, and Danny, Ryleigh, Niko, and I had had front-row seats and then had taken a limousine back to Jin's hotel.

But it turns out that things actually hadn't been safe at all; in fact, they were getting less safe every day. And unless I did something soon . . . my heart squeezed and I had to fight the urge to curl up into a little ball right there on the sidewalk. *Don't think about it. Breathe.* In three minutes, the bus would arrive, and I looked strange enough as it was with this giant white rope around my waist. I clenched my eyes shut and tried to breathe away my loneliness and fear.

After our New Year's Eve adventure, I'd given the Mirror of the Sun to Tsukiyomi, the kami of the moon, for safekeeping. He had promised to return it to its original owner, Amaterasu, the kami of the sun. But then he'd betrayed us all and taken it straight to Izanami the Destroyer, queen of Yomi, the land of the dead. That was the reason Mom was so worried that she wouldn't let me out of the house without magical protection. Everything else that had me in a state of nervous dread happened in a nightmare I had on Saturday night, the night after the concert.

I was in Yomi. Izanami had just informed me that Mom had been right all along: Ever since his boat had been lost at sea three years ago, Dad had been alive. He'd been transformed into a whale and spent years wandering the oceans, calling and calling for us until Izanami had taken him hostage.

Even though he was a whale, I recognized something in his

eyes—something kind and loving and brave. I'd seen it before, just off the coast of the Island of Mysteries, and in one of my lives in the Mirror of the Sun when Dad and I had been whales together. But my joy at seeing him alive was knotted up with fear and anxiety over his condition: His body was wrapped in razor-sharp metallic cords that gleamed in the murky water of the tank where he was being held prisoner. His skin was crisscrossed with scars. He looked defeated and worn out.

"Momo! Is that you?" he called out, as if he couldn't see me.

I'd nearly forgotten what he sounded like. And when I heard his voice, it was like three years of missing him burst out of a secret locked compartment somewhere deep inside my heart. It coursed through me, making my hands shake and my lungs gasp for air, as if my body thought breathing would bring him back to me and everything would go back to the way it used to be.

"I'm right here! In front of you!" I waved my arms, but he didn't seem to see them. "Are you okay?" I couldn't help asking, even though he was obviously not okay.

"Can't complain. I've tried but no one listens," he quipped weakly, and if I'd had any doubt about who I was looking at before, this was the moment when that doubt would have vanished. Even as a whale, even now that he was clearly suffering, he was the same old Dad with the same old dorky sense of humor, the same old urge to make me laugh so I wouldn't worry. My heart swelled with love until I thought it would burst.

Then with sudden urgency, he added, "Get out of here, Momo. It's not safe. Go home and take care of—" He gasped in pain as the cords tightened around him and his blood bloomed red in the water.

I screamed and lunged forward, reaching for him. But the murk closed around him, and he was gone. My arms met only air.

Izanami reached out a pale, bony hand, and I felt ice water slide across my scalp as she passed her fingers through my hair. I shuddered in revulsion but couldn't move to swat her hand away. When she spoke, her voice was as cold and sharp as a shard of broken glass.

"I'm sorry to cause you distress," she said, not looking at all sorry. "But I need you to know how serious I am. Fetch me the Jewel of the Heart—perhaps you've heard it called the Jewel of Kindness, but as with so much of what you think you know, you've been misinformed. Bring it to me, and I will let your father go. If you refuse, I can't predict how I will react. Most likely, I'll take my anger out on your father. I might even kill him. And then I might visit your mother and show her what you've done—how your reluctance to cooperate has caused your father to suffer and die. I wonder how she'd feel? It would break her, I imagine. She'd probably never recover." Izanami smiled and tapped her chin thoughtfully with a long black fingernail as she pretended to think.

"She *would* recover," I said automatically.

"Would she, though?" Izanami raised one delicately arched eyebrow, and that was enough to stir up a hornets' nest of my own doubts. Those years after Dad had died—I mean, disappeared—had been so hard. Mom had gotten lost in her grief and turned into a faded, empty version of herself. I'd been left to take care of both of us, to worry constantly not just about groceries and doctor appointments, but about whether she would get out of bed in the morning. If she found out that I could have saved

Dad's life and hadn't . . . An image of Mom, glassy-eyed and weeping, rose in front of me. She turned to me and whispered reproachfully, *How could you let him die?* Then she turned away and stared silently into space.

I shook my head hard. *Stop it. Mom wouldn't let herself go like that again. She loves me and she'll stay strong for me,* I told myself. But I wasn't sure I believed it.

"I expect you'd never forgive yourself. Killing your father and ruining your mother." Izanami shook her head and clucked her tongue. "You're a better daughter than *that,* certainly."

I opened my mouth to argue, but my throat closed up and my jaw clamped shut. I could barely even think. *I am a better daughter than that,* I wanted to say. *I would never let my father die if I had a way to save him.* But if I saved Dad's life and brought Izanami the jewel . . .

"Why do you want it?"

"The Jewel of the Heart?" Izanami sighed deeply and rolled her eyes, as if it should be obvious. "Well, for starters, it belongs to me."

Even in my fear I must have looked skeptical, because she said, "No, I mean it. It's mine. I had it at the very beginning. But it was stolen by my rat-clown of an ex-husband. And I think it's high time I got it back."

"But—"

"As you may know, Izanagi cast a spell that has trapped me here for eternity. He told everyone it was because I was so evil, but the real reason is that he ran away and took my jewel with him. If I can get it back, I will return to my full power. I will use Kusanagi—that is, *we* will use Kusanagi"—here, she paused and nodded at me—"to break down the gate between Yomi and the Middle Lands. Then I will cross over and, well. You know." She smiled and drew her finger across her throat.

"Kill everyone," I whispered.

"Ding, ding, ding! Give this girl a prize!" Izanami sang out. "That's right, my darling. At one time, I thought merely opening the gates and storming through with an army of demons would be enough. But meeting you last fall inspired me. I thought, why not use you to fetch *all three* Sacred Treasures? Then I could do things right! That sword of yours is an incredibly efficient killing machine, and with the jewel in my possession, at my full power, I can do a thousand times the damage at a tenth of the cost."

The Queen of Death times ten thousand. I felt like a sheet of aluminum foil that someone had crumpled into a tiny little ball and that would never be its smooth shiny self again.

"It's only fair. Izanagi took away everything I cared about when he locked me in here—for no good reason, I might add—and now it's my turn to do the same to him."

"But—"

"But that's not *nice*! But it's been so *long*! No one likes an angry goddess! It's not *becoming*! It's *ugly*! That's why no one *likes* you!" Izanami rattled off in a whiny voice, and then snorted. "Is that what you were going to say?"

"I . . ." Not exactly. But it wasn't *not* what I had been going to say.

"Izanagi ruined my entire life for all eternity and told everyone that it was *my* fault. He *deserves* my wrath. He *deserves* what's coming to him." Her eyes burned red, and her voice grew deep and menacing. I shrank away from her.

"So, my dear. Do we have an understanding? Will you fetch the Jewel of the Heart for me?"

My stomach twisted, and my thoughts ricocheted around my brain like bumper cars. I could fetch the jewel, rescue Dad, and allow Izanami to revenge-kill everyone on Earth. Or I could refuse, let Dad suffer and die, and watch Mom turn into an empty shell of herself once again. Were these my only options? How could I get out of this? What else would Izanami do if I refused?

"Speak when you're spoken to, Momo." Izanami's voice sliced its way into my thoughts. "Do you understand and accept the terms of my offer?" I felt one frosty fingertip under my chin, and my face tilted up so I was forced to look into her black, black eyes.

I knew what I *ought* to do: sacrifice Mom and Dad to protect the rest of the world. I wished I had the strength of will to shout, "No! I reject your terms and your offer! I refuse to fetch the jewel for you!" But I couldn't. I couldn't let Dad die. I couldn't face a lifetime with a mother who wasn't really there. The best I could manage was "I don't know."

Izanami nodded as if she'd expected this. "I shouldn't have given you a choice—too much pressure, I suppose. So, all right. I'll give you until the day the first peach blossoms bloom at the base of Mount Fuji. With any luck, that day will coincide with Hinamatsuri. That seems like the perfect time for Princess Peach to join the Queen of Death on an attack against Izanagi the Creator, don't you think?"

My first thought was *They have Super Mario Bros. in Yomi?* But then I realized she was referring to my name, Momo, which means "peach." Then it hit me what she'd said about the deadline—Hinamatsuri was Girls' Day, when families celebrated their daughters with elaborately dressed princess dolls. But Girls' Day was March 3. And tomorrow was Valentine's Day. Which left me . . .

"Just remember: the longer you wait, the less time you have, and the more your dear old daddy suffers. And you can trust me on that, Momo. I am a woman of my word." She smiled at me, just enough to show her blackened teeth.

"What if I don't—what if I can't—"

"You don't want to know the answer to that question."

Izanami took each of my hands in hers and turned them over and pressed her thumbs into my palms. She bent her head and blew a stream of ice and gritty black ash that coiled itself around our hands and then enveloped the rest of me, stinging my skin and making me cough until I woke up wheezing and gasping for air.

"Momo!" Mom had appeared in the doorway, silhouetted against a rectangle of light that streamed in from the hall. Instantly she was at my side, stroking my hair and feeling my forehead. "Are you all right?"

"I had a d-d-dream," I'd said through chattering teeth. "Izanami . . ." But when I felt Mom's hand stop moving at the mention of Izanami's name, I hesitated.

"What? What about her?" Mom asked. She was clutching my arms now, and I could feel her terror in the strength of her grip. Her face was a mask of fear, and her voice was strained. She gave me a little shake. "Tell me, Momo. What did she say? What did she do?"

Another fit of coughing saved me from having to answer right away. After it passed, I wheezed slowly and carefully, buying time to think. Mom had promised never to leave me alone again after the Mirror of the Sun adventure, when she'd rushed off after hearing a rumor that Dad was out there somewhere. But given the way she gazed at the photo of the three of us on her island when she thought I wasn't looking, I knew that she was always on the verge of breaking that promise. The more I thought about it, the clearer it became to me that she *would* try to rescue Dad if she knew where he was, with or without the jewel. What would I do if she ventured into Yomi and never came back?

"I d-d-don't remember all of it," I'd said finally. "I think it was just a d-d-dream."

Mom had looked unconvinced. But she'd stroked my hair and said only, "Close your eyes. Don't talk any more. I'll be right back with something to make you feel better." She'd disappeared, then reappeared with a mug of something hot and savory that eased me into a long, blissfully dreamless sleep.

I woke up the next day hoping it had been a nightmare and nothing more. But I discovered that someone—or something—had drawn a bare branch dotted with . . . I counted seventeen buds and one blossom on each of my palms. I dashed to the bathroom and scrubbed and scrubbed, but the drawings would not come off.

I was stuck. Dad was alive and would die without my help. But if I helped him, I might bring about the end of life as we knew it. The end of life, period, even. Despair and fear and indecision braided themselves into a thick, heavy rope that settled around my shoulders and weighed me down so that I didn't mind when Mom announced that I was not to get out of bed, that she would call the school on Monday and tell them I had a terrible illness and would stay home for the foreseeable future.

But it wasn't just the weight of my decision that kept me in bed on Sunday. It was also the fact that I couldn't bear to face Danny and Ryleigh, who were sure to see that something was wrong and badger me into confessing. I was already exhausted by Niko, what with his constant trotting in and out and fretting that I looked peaked and pale, and worrying that whatever had gotten me might get him.

If I told my friends I was in trouble, they would insist on helping. Danny would raise his fist and shout "Team RyJin DaMoNik to the rescue!" or some nonsense, and off we'd go on a rescue mission, or a quest, or whatever wild idea he came up with. That is, if Ryleigh or Jin didn't make me feel ashamed for selfishly putting Dad's life ahead of the fate of the world. No, I decided, I couldn't ask anyone to risk their lives to help me.

But I also wouldn't be able to forgive myself if I didn't try to rescue Dad. And that's what had made me insist on going to school today. Dad was in danger, and I was in trouble, and I couldn't tell Mom, and I couldn't tell my friends, and I felt all alone and scared out of my wits—but I couldn't sit at home and let Dad suffer and die. I'd have to get out there and figure it out on my own. I'd done it before—I'd been doing it since Dad disappeared. I really didn't want to do it again. But I had to. So I would.

Add It to the List

Usually when I saw Danny and Ryleigh sitting halfway back on the bus and saving a seat for me, my mood improved. Something loosened in my chest and lightened in my shoulders. But not today. Today, despair solidified inside me like a block of ice.

Ryleigh waved and called out, "Momo! Over here!" She and Danny were sitting one behind the other. Ryleigh grabbed her backpack and scooted over to make room for me to sit next to her.

Come on, Momo. Pull it together. I put on a smile and went up the aisle toward them.

But as I sat down, someone yelled from the back, "Hey, why're you wearing that giant rope around your waist? What are you, a hitching post?"

Brad Bowman brayed with laughter and pointed at his head and twirled his finger in a circle. His horrible bros cackled. Two rows back, Kiki Weldon smirked.

That jerk. My rage monster prodded me, and I stood back up. I'd had just about enough of him and his—

"Get a life, Bowman!" Danny said. He stood at my shoulder,

facing down his former pack of bro-bot buddies. To me, he whispered, "I've got you, Momo."

From the front, the bus driver shouted, "Sit down right now, you two, or I'll kick you off the bus!"

"Get a sense of humor, Haragan!" Brad called to Danny. "It was just a joke!"

"Psh. I'll laugh at your jokes when they're funny," said Danny with a grin, still standing.

There was a loud "Ooohhh!" from the back of the bus, and the mean comments stopped. Even though Danny was no longer captain of the bro-bots, he was still captain of the basketball team and that got him some respect.

"You think I'm not serious?" the bus driver said. "One more second on your feet and you can use them to walk to school!"

Danny sat down. "Sorry, sir!" he said cheerfully, and he reached back and put his fist over the seat for Ryleigh to bump, which she did. And then he held his fist out to me.

A few months ago, I would have been grateful that Danny had stood up for me. I still was. But also, I didn't need him to be my hero anymore. What had I learned to use my anger for, if not to defend myself? As soon as I had this thought, my rage monster flared up at him as well. "You didn't have to rescue me," I groused, and pushed his fist away.

Danny looked taken aback. "Okay. But—"

"I could've handled it myself." I was going to have to get used to handling things myself, especially since I wouldn't be able to take him—or Ryleigh or Niko or Jin, for that matter—when I went after that jewel.

"Could you, though?" said Ryleigh. For a moment I thought

she'd read my mind and was asking whether I could save Dad on my own, not whether I could handle Brad Bowman on my own. I stared at her, and she stared back and said, "What?"

I came to my senses and shook my head. "Nothing," I mumbled.

"Even if you can handle it, that doesn't make it okay for them to pick on you. Someone still has to call them out," Danny said. "And, like, honestly? It has to be someone they think is one of them, or they won't take it seriously."

The truth of that stopped me. "You're right. I'm sorry," I said.

"I mean, you could just ignore them or, like, you know, do this." He made a rude hand gesture. "Do that without even looking at them, like it's barely worth the effort, you know?"

"Easy for you to say," I scoffed. "If *you* did that to Brad, he'd laugh and move on. If *I* did it, he'd be all in my face, like, 'Why are you being rude to me, weirdo?'" I made my voice low and brutish, just like Brad's. "It's like you said. You have to be one of the cool kids for them to think it's cool."

"Oh." Danny looked thoughtful. "Yeah, huh. That stinks."

"Cool-kid privilege," Ryleigh quipped.

Which was when Kiki Weldon said just loudly enough to be heard from her seat two rows back, "Seriously, though. That... *thing* she has around her waist? I mean, can you even? Like, does her mom not like her or something? And don't even get me started on her new best friend." She and her minions giggled. Ryleigh stuck her hand up in the air and did just what Danny had described.

Kiki and her minions kept giggling, and I felt my face get

hot. When Ryleigh had started hanging out with me, she'd given up her cool-kid privilege, just like Danny. But she didn't have a sports team to make up for it.

I spun around in my seat and said, "For your information, my mom thinks this rope will keep me safe. That's why she made me wear it, even though I didn't want to. Because she likes me. But you wouldn't understand, because your mom probably lets you do whatever you want, because she doesn't like you enough to care."

If I'd had a mic, I would have dropped it. It wasn't fair of me, because Ryleigh had told me once that Kiki was afraid of this very thing. But I was angry, and I wanted to do more than stand up for myself. I wanted to hurt Kiki as much as she was trying to hurt me and Ryleigh.

Kiki just laughed and said, "Whatever. Come back when you have something normal to say."

But I saw the flash of pain in her eyes, and I knew that what I'd said had hit home. And I'm ashamed to say this, but it felt great. I felt powerful. I, lowly little Momo Arashima, seventy-first most popular kid in seventh grade, had hurt Queen Kiki. She'd hurt so many kids, so many times, and she deserved to be on the other end for once. Thank goodness Ryleigh wasn't friends with her anymore.

"SIT DOWN!" roared the bus driver, and Ryleigh yanked me down next to her before I could say anything else.

"So, is Angry Girl gonna be your whole personality now, or what?" Ryleigh said.

I shrugged. "Maybe."

"Fine. But you might want to take it down a notch," said Ryleigh. "You're kinda scary when you're really mad."

"Good," I said. "It's better than being scared."

"What's the deal with that thing, anyway?" Danny nodded at my shimenawa, clearly trying to change the subject. "Did something happen? Are there more demons we need to take care of?"

A chill swept through me, and my palms began to itch. I closed my fists and dug my nails into my palms. I couldn't let Danny and Ryleigh know. I couldn't drag them into my problems.

"No, it's nothing. My mom's just being overprotective." It was partly true, I figured.

"Are you sure that's it?" Danny said.

"Uh-huh." I couldn't look at him. "My mom's the worst."

Danny frowned. "I think there's something else. Ry, what do you think?"

"Huh?" Ordinarily, Ryleigh would have seen right through my lie, but she was distracted by something Kiki was doing behind us. And ordinarily this would have annoyed me, but today I was just grateful that she wasn't paying attention.

Still, Ryleigh was Ryleigh, so she'd heard everything, even if she hadn't caught the lie. "Your mom's not so bad," she said. That was because Mom had been helping Ryleigh hone her ninja skills by teaching her to tap into the energies of the spirit realm—but without putting any pressure on her to become a top-tier ninja, which was key. Ryleigh actually loved ninjutsu, but her own mom sucked the joy out of it by insisting that she had to do it to make up for the fact that her wildly talented big brother had walked away from the family tradition.

For example, Ryleigh had a hat that made her invisible, but with Mom's help, she had learned to cast a sort of shadow on other people, so that *they* could go unnoticed for short periods of time. Not only that, but she'd learned a cool new trick called root-kata, where she connected things to the earth like roots, so they wouldn't move.

"Okay, fine," I conceded. And then I came up with the perfect diversion to steer the conversation away from nightmare territory. "It's just that she doesn't get what it's like to be a human kid in twenty-first-century America. She was like, 'It looks fine! All of my siblings and friends wore shimenawa as children!'"

Ryleigh nodded sympathetically, as I'd known she would. "Asian moms are the worst. My mom is always going on about 'when I was a kid in Japan, this' and 'when I was a kid in Japan, that.'"

I snorted. "Omigosh, same! I mean, how long has it been since she was a kid—three thousand years? Four thousand years? And on a whole other continent! Like, hello, Mom, things are different here. Times have changed!"

"Right? My parents are like that, too," said Danny.

Ryleigh and I exchanged amused glances, and Ryleigh rolled her eyes. "Nah, your parents are white. Asian moms are in their own category."

Danny's face took on a strange expression. "Yeah," he said. "I guess I wouldn't know."

"Oh." Ryleigh looked mortified. "Wait, I didn't mean it like—"

"It's okay," said Danny.

"It's just . . . it's different, that's all," said Ryleigh, her cheeks growing rosy. "Having—I mean, being raised by Asian parents versus white parents."

"Yeah, no, I get it, it's cool," Danny said. He smiled, but it didn't look quite real to me. He had an Asian mom, too, somewhere out there. And an Asian dad. And I knew that even though he loved his white (adoptive) parents, he felt weird when they seemed to try to pretend he wasn't Asian. I wished I could say something to make him feel better, but I didn't know what that could be. I hated feeling like there was an issue dividing us that I didn't know how to talk about.

Add it to the list, I thought, and my palms stung so hard, I had to turn away so no one would see me wince.

"Anyway, I can't wait till Friday, can you?" This time it was Ryleigh who changed the subject.

"Bro, this weekend's gonna be amazing!" Danny said. Maybe he was eager to talk about something else, too.

Friday was when the fifth member of Team RyJin DaMoNik was finally going to join us. Now that the Straight 2 tha Topp tour was over, Jin was doing one last charity appearance at the San Francisco Public Library before officially retiring from public life. Ryleigh, Danny, and I were going to skip school and ride with Niko in a limousine to the city to see Jin, and afterward all five of us would take a private jet to Anaheim, where we'd spend the rest of the weekend at Disneyland.

"Wanna come over on Thursday night and watch a movie, since we don't have to go to school on Friday?" Danny asked.

I hesitated. Would I still be here on Thursday?

"Momo, can you make it?" Danny prodded. He didn't even

bother to ask if I *wanted* to, because of course the answer would have been yes.

So I said, "Duh. Of course." I thought longingly of Jin and Disneyland. My palms itched and my heart ached. I wished I could tell the truth. I wished my friends could help me figure out what to do.

"Ryleigh, you're coming, right?"

"Uh, yeah. I think so. I mean, I should be able to." Ryleigh had been watching Kiki again.

"What's that supposed to mean?" asked Danny.

"What do you mean, 'what's that supposed to mean?'" Ryleigh demanded. "I said I should be able to. What's wrong with that?" She glanced at me, but she looked away when we made eye contact. That was unusual. She was a very look-you-right-in-the-eye kind of person.

Danny seemed taken aback. "It's just, I dunno. Kinda weird?"

Ryleigh rolled her eyes. *"You're* being weird." Then she pulled out her phone and said, "Anyway. Have you seen Straight 2 tha Topp's latest behind-the-scenes video from the tour? It's from when they were in New York two weeks ago. Jin, Tai, Mal, Lex, and Bax each ate ten bags of French fries in ten minutes!" She found the video and held up the phone, and I found that if I concentrated very hard, I was able to forget about Izanami the Destroyer, my dad being held hostage, and the fate of the world being on my shoulders. And for the rest of the bus ride, I was just a regular kid laughing over a silly tour video with her friends, and everything was okay.

Protect the Chillldrennn!

I didn't leave that day. Or the next day, or the next. Izanami didn't send me any more visions of Dad, but it didn't matter. Three blossoms bloomed on the branches, one for each day that had passed. My palms tingled constantly, and I felt like my brain was on fire. *I have to go,* I kept telling myself. *I have to find the Jewel of the Heart and rescue Dad.* But I was paralyzed with fear and self-doubt. Where would I go first? How would I find the jewel? Maybe I *shouldn't* go. The world would be safer if I didn't. Mom would be worried sick if I just disappeared. And if I failed, she would have lost both Dad and me. I wished more than ever that I could tell her everything, that I could trust her not to rush out the door and leave me behind. I was angry at her for being the kind of mom that I had to worry about, which maybe wasn't fair to her. On the other hand, it wasn't fair that I had to worry.

Thursday came and went without movie night at Danny's; I was too preoccupied with my burden, so I told him that Mom wanted me to stay home to rest up for the weekend. And Ryleigh canceled, too, saying she didn't feel well.

"But what about the concert tomorrow? And Disneyland?" Danny had asked.

"I'm sure I'll be fine by tomorrow," Ryleigh had replied. I was pretty certain she wasn't really sick, and I almost called to ask if she'd been having nightmares, too. But I didn't, because what if she asked me why? What would I say? So instead I agonized all night about whether I should say something; worried about how I was going to find that jewel all by myself; and wished I were more excited about seeing Jin, riding in a private jet, and going to Disneyland with my best friends.

But the next morning, I suddenly, desperately wanted to go to see Jin, ride in a private jet, and go to Disneyland with my best friends. Maybe because just as Niko and I were about to walk out the door to join Danny and Ryleigh, who were waiting in the limousine in the driveway, Mom stopped me and told me I had to stay home.

"I'm sorry, Momo," she said, blocking my path. "I've changed my mind. You know I didn't feel good about you going in the first place. And now—"

"But Mom! The limousine is literally *right there*."

"The event is in one hour," Niko observed. "The seconds are slipping away."

"Niko, you can still go."

What? I stared at him, and he gave me an apologetic smile.

Time to stand up for myself. Rage monster, activate! "But that's so unfair! You *promised!*"

"I just don't think it will be safe."

"We'll all be together, *and* I'll have my shimenawa on! Right, Niko? Tell her!"

Niko inclined his head and didn't say anything. Ugh! He was useless when it came to arguing with Mom.

"You could be kidnapped! Even if I knew where you were, your kidnappers could hurt you or kill you! Or take you somewhere that I couldn't follow!"

"I have Kusanagi! If I get kidnapped, I can take care of myself!" I was shouting now.

"You can't."

Before I even realized what I was saying, I'd said it. "I can, too! I've defeated Shuten-dōji and Tamamo-no-mae, haven't I? And I took care of myself for years before I even got Kusanagi! Remember? After Dad was lost at sea and you stopped doing, like, *everything*? I did it all by myself, even though it was your job. And it's too late to make up for it by treating me like a little kid, because like I said, I can take care of myself!"

I pushed past her and stormed to the limousine, my heart pounding and Niko whining at my heels about not being a disobedient daughter, half hoping Mom would come running after me and shove me back into the house. But she didn't. I pretended I hadn't seen the sad, stricken look on her face as she stood frozen on the doorstep.

Feeling mad was better than feeling terrible about hurting Mom the way I had, or feeling scared that she was right and that it *would* be better for me to stay home. Besides, I was standing up for myself to do what I wanted to do! I remembered that only a couple of weeks ago I'd really been looking forward to all of this: seeing Jin, riding in a private jet, and going to Disneyland with my best friends.

And you should *be excited,* said my rage monster.

Okay, I thought, drawing on my anger for courage. I would give myself a break. I'd have fun for a couple of days. I would prove that I was just fine on my own. And I could start worrying about everything again once the weekend was over. I closed my fists so I wouldn't see my palms, where five more peach blossoms had bloomed. Twelve buds—twelve days—left.

The children's section at the San Francisco Public Library was packed, and everyone was spellbound: little kids, tweens, teens, grown-ups, librarians, reporters. When Jin was in full sparkle mode, he cast a warm golden glow over everyone within hearing distance and enchanted his audience into hanging on every word that came out of his mouth. Even Danny, Ryleigh, Niko, and I had fallen under his spell. We leaned toward him, completely oblivious to anything but the story he was reading—until a high, screechy voice pierced the air from somewhere above us.

"Protect the chillldrennn!"

A swarm of winged creatures with tiny gray bodies and angry, red needle-nosed faces hovered near the ceiling like an army of evil fairies. They looked like a cross between wasps and mosquitos. Waspitos. They were clearly yōkai—monsters from the spirit world who interacted with the human world. And as small as they were, something larger, something dark and menacing and malicious, seemed to swirl slowly in and around them like a cloud of poisonous smoke. This swarm was much more dangerous than it looked.

My palms began to burn, and I understood that these guys were here because of me. *Mom was right,* I thought. *I shouldn't have come.* But it was too late. Everyone here was in danger, and it was my fault.

The swarm gathered itself and plunged downward, then

swooped up again. It began circling the room, zooming through the crowd and around the bookshelves.

"Killer bees!" someone shouted. "Run!"

There was a stampede toward the exit. A couple of kids whipped out their phones and started recording the pandemonium, but a grown-up shouted at them to "get off your devices and get to safety!" and began herding them out. "All you kids care about these days is going viral! No common sense, any of you!"

Meanwhile, Danny had taken out his bow and arrows. Ryleigh had her pouch of shuriken in one hand and her invisibility hat in the other. Jin had donned his feathered cloak. Niko dove under a table, and I gripped Kusanagi in my hands. If it was my fault these monsters were here, I would fight them to the death.

"How are we supposed to battle those things?" Jin asked. "And why do they keep saying they're here to protect us?"

"Maybe we're *not* supposed to battle them?" Danny wondered aloud—though he kept an arrow nocked and his eye trained on the swarm as it darted in and out among the stacks.

"I mean, they haven't actually attacked any—" Jin started to say, but he was cut off by a human scream.

"Let me go!" It was Ms. Gomez, the children's librarian who had introduced Jin at the beginning of his reading. She was so completely covered in demons that she looked like part of the swarm. They dragged her kicking and clawing to the middle of the room, where they dropped her in a heap and formed a circle in the air around her, like a giant living Hula-Hoop.

"Fire!" came an ear-piercing command, and thousands of

pinpricks of light streamed down to the floor. *Whoosh.* A ring of fire rose up around Ms. Gomez, who screamed again, not in fear but in outrage.

Now the swarm broke up into little squadrons and began pulling books off the shelves and hurling them into the fire. Ryleigh whipped her hundredfold shuriken at the waspitos, and soon the air was filled with the knife-edged iron stars. The demons sparked and crackled like bugs on a bug zapper, but there were thousands of them and Ryleigh couldn't keep up.

"Help me!" she called to the rest of us.

"I'm trying!" Niko yelped from under the table. "I'm just doing it from a protected position!" I did see books zooming through the air that seemed to be hitting the waspitos instead of flying into the fire, so that must have been Niko using his telekinetic powers.

"I can't help!" Danny shouted. "They're too close for my arrows to do any good."

"Filthy-dirty!" screeched the demons as book after book landed in the flames. "Thinky-stinky!" The protective plastic covers began to curl and melt, and the books smoldered as the fire ate away at the pages, burning up knowledge and turning kids' favorite stories to ash.

"Nooo!" Inside the ring of fire, Ms. Gomez was doing her best to save the books and put the flames out with her cardigan. "Kids!" she shouted when she saw us. "Get out of here! Get to safety!"

But what kind of person runs away while a swarm of book-burning demons tries to destroy a library, and the librarian herself is trapped in a ring of fire—and is still trying to rescue books? Not me. My school librarian, Ms. Nguyen, was my favorite grown-up at Oak Valley Middle School. She always knew exactly the right book to give me when I was feeling down and needed to escape somewhere that would let me forget my worries for a while. She told me once that books had superpowers: they could take you to new worlds, they could show you what it was like to be someone totally different from yourself, and they could even rescue people. In fact, Ms. Nguyen had become a librarian because *her* school librarian had given her a book about a queer Asian girl that had literally saved her life by showing her that she wasn't alone.

Let's go! said my rage demon. *Fight them now!*

Destroy the waspitos! growled Kusanagi. *Nobody gets away with attacking librarians!*

I took a few solid swings with Kusanagi but had to stop. "I keep slashing books instead of demons!" I was almost screaming in my frustration. "I need a bigger target!"

"Then try something else! Strike them with lightning or something!" Ryleigh barked.

"Are you kidding me? A lightning bolt inside a library?" I shouted. "The books are already on fire!" I could still feel something bigger in the swarm, though, a malevolent force that was controlling its actions. *Come out,* I willed it. *Come out and let me see you.*

Meanwhile, Ryleigh hadn't given up. "Sing to them, Jin!" she commanded, still hurling her shuriken at a furious rate. "Make them stop!"

Jin looked around in anguish. "I promised my mom I would

never use my voice to make someone do something they don't want to do."

"But they're evil! They're setting books on fire!" Ryleigh argued. Then she noticed me trying to mind-meld with the force behind the swarm, and Danny, who was now trying to smack individual waspitos out of the air with a book. "Danny, what are you *doing*? Momo, why are you just standing there? Help me!"

"It's just that mind control is kind of a slippery slope," said Jin.

"I'm *trying* to help!" shouted Danny. "This is the best I can do!"

"We're all doing our best, Ryleigh, so stop shouting at us," I snapped. Why did she have to be such a bossy-pants? Kusanagi and my rage monster had me buzzing with pent-up angry energy. I needed a target. Where was my target?

Ryleigh ignored me and refocused on Jin. "Okay, so sing about a book you love," she said. "That's not mind control, is it?"

"I can do that." Jin rose into the air and began soaring around the room, singing in his most enchanting voice, and finally, finally, the tide turned.

I never knew how high the sky was
till I saw the words you wrote
and then all of a sudden I was
surrounded by stars, no longer alone.

The horrible little demons slowed down and looked at each other, confused. A few even put the books down on tables and opened them, as if suddenly curious about what they were tossing into the fire. Between Ryleigh's and Jin's work, the book-burning frenzy slowed down considerably.

But then the inferno roared back to life—literally. The flames climbed higher, and thick black smoke poured out to form a creature with a mouth full of fire, eyes that glowed like burning coal, and so many arms I couldn't count them all. It lunged after Jin and enveloped him in a cloud of swirling black soot. Jin plummeted to the floor, coughing and choking and covered with ash.

And Now a Word from Our Sponsor

"I'm okay! I'm okay!" Jin gasped. But the little fire demons were already breaking out of their trances and slamming their books shut.

The smoke monster rose to the height of the ceiling, and a nasty red smirk broke across its face as it took us in. "Hello!" His voice was low and dark. "Just who I was hoping to see. I am Mokugon-bake, eraser of stories and destroyer of knowledge. Gatekeeper of learning and power."

Niko whined in fear under the table, but Kusanagi zinged a bolt of fresh energy through me. *Yes!* Finally, a target big enough to fight. Mokugon-bake thought he could get away with threatening a librarian and burning up a library? Wrong. I would *destroy* him. I would make him suffer for the harm he was doing.

Everything else faded away as I drew Kusanagi back and prepared to strike.

"I have a message for you from the kami who lives in darkness! From the one who ends *all* stories!" he bellowed.

I was already midswing. I couldn't stop. A bolt of lightning pierced the smoke monster, but all that did was swirl him around a bit. And blast a hole in the ceiling. And cause a huge chunk of plaster to fall and almost hit Ms. Gomez inside the ring of fire. I stepped back, horrified.

"Stab, stab, stab, as hard as you can! You can't kill me, I'm the Mokugon-man!" he jeered. "Helping to keep the world in ignorance and darkness through fear and hatred since the dawn of stories! And now a word from our sponsor." The smoke parted to reveal Izanami's pale face. I felt as if I'd been turned to ice. Even my rage monster felt sluggish and fog-brained.

"Hello, Momo," Izanami said. "Just popping in to make sure you haven't forgotten about me. Oh, are those your friends? It's so nice to finally meet you! I'm Momo's auntie Izanami." She smirked down at Danny, Ryleigh, Niko, and Jin, who gaped back at her in helpless silence. The smoke around her face gathered itself into ropes that snaked across the floor and coiled around us.

It's just smoke, I told myself. *It can't hurt us. She can't hurt us.*

"I must say, Momo, I thought you'd have started searching by now. It's been five whole days, after all." She sighed. "I'm beginning to get bored of waiting. And do you know what I do when I get bored?" She exhaled a stream of smoke that became a whale thrashing in pain. I swallowed a scream.

"He looks like he could use some help," she mused. "Remember, as soon as you bring me that jewel, I'll give him back to you. I know I told you that you had until Hinamatsuri, but you really should hurry, because the pain could scramble his mind before then. It would be a pity if you did all that work and he couldn't even recognize you anymore." She waggled her fingers at us. "Well, I must be off. Toodle-oo! Remember to make good choices!"

Her face faded, and I jolted out of my trance to see Mokugon-bake gathering himself into a column of smoke and fire. With one last, desperate surge of power, I plunged Kusanagi into the smoke monster, being careful to point toward one of the windows. A blast of wind smashed the glass and blew an astonished-looking Mokugon-bake and his fire demons into the sky, where he seemed to dissolve and drift away. One last waspito remained, and as Ryleigh took aim at it, it screeched, "You haven't seen the last of us! As long as ignorance and hatred exist in the world, Mokugon-bake and his army will be there to destroy new stories and spread old fears! Mua-ha-ha-ha-haaa! Mua-ha-ha-ha—"

Bzzzt-pop! Ryleigh's shuriken found its target.

"Woo-hoo!" Danny said. "That's how you defeat a demon!" He pumped his fist and put his hands up for high fives all around, but Ryleigh, Jin, and Niko were staring at me.

"Was that really . . . ?" Niko started.

I nodded. How could I lie to them, after what they'd heard and seen?

"Why did she follow you here?" Jin asked. "What was that about Hinamatsuri?"

Danny dropped his hands and joined in. "Yeah, and what's the deal with that whale? Why do you have to help him? What jewel is she talking about?"

And then Ryleigh, with arms folded and eyes narrowed, said, "What are you hiding from us?"

Before I could decide whether to lie or tell the truth, a crew of firefighters brandishing fire extinguishers burst into the room and rushed toward Ms. Gomez. Ryleigh popped her invisibility hat on and cast a shadow over me, Danny, Jin, and Niko. We snuck out the door, leaving behind Ms. Gomez, the firefighters, a lot of charred and soggy books, and the lingering smell of smoke.

"So?" Danny said. "What's going on and why haven't you told us?"

They had cornered me somewhere in the nonfiction section of the library. Four pairs of eyes stared me down. I tried to stare back, but my friends were ruthless. They waited silently until I cracked and told them the entire story.

"Why didn't you tell us?" Danny demanded again when I was finished. "Were you ever going to?"

"She didn't trust us," Ryleigh said, her eyes accusing and angry.

"Why not?" Jin asked.

"Not even me, your faithful fox friend," said Niko mournfully.

I looked down at my palms and fought off a wave of guilt. "It's not that I don't trust you," I said. "It's more like, it's my problem. It's my dad. I didn't want to drag you into it and make you risk your lives. It's not like last time, when there were all these kids' lives at stake."

"Yeah, this time it's the entire world," said Ryleigh dryly.

"Even if it was just your dad, you can't keep secrets like that! It's not what friends do. You have to let us help," said Danny.

"No, I don't." Why couldn't he see that I was only trying to protect him?

"Not if it's hazardous to our health," Niko agreed.

Jin shook his head. "We can talk about it, at least."

"No, it's okay, I really—" I started, but it was too late.

"*I* think you should do something," Danny said. As if I'd asked, which I hadn't. So I glared at him.

"Like what?"

"You have to get the Jewel of the Heart and save your dad."

"Uh-uh. She can't give the jewel to Izanami," said Ryleigh.

"Are you kidding me? Momo's dad is being *tortured*, Ry. And if she doesn't get the jewel, he could die. Are you saying that's okay?"

"Of course it's not okay," Ryleigh huffed. "But if Izanami gets the jewel, we all die. You. Me. Our families. Everyone in the entire world. *Everyone,* Danny. In the *entire world.* Are you saying *that's* okay?"

"And this is why I haven't told anyone," I said wearily. "I can't let my dad suffer and die, but I can't save him and let the rest of the world die. I don't think it's your decision to make, and I don't want you to risk your lives because of my dad. So can we just move on?"

"But the longer you wait, the more he suffers," Danny pointed out. "And it's February eighteenth. You only have, what, less than two weeks until—"

"I *know!*" I shouted at him. "Do you think I haven't thought about that?"

"What if we do both?" Jin suggested. "Like, rescue Momo's dad *and* save the world. Is there a way to do that?"

"Yes! Jin for the win! We can totally do both!" Danny shouted.

"No, we can't. We can't do either," I said.

"We can if we try. You need to stop listening to your anxiety, Momo. You need to believe in yourself," said Ryleigh.

"No, it's not that. The problem is you don't believe in *us*," Danny said. "You need to believe in Team RyJin DaMoNik."

"It's both. You need to believe in yourself and in us," said Jin.

Here, Niko finally jumped in. "I'm sorry, but have you forgotten that Izanami is the Queen of Death? *Death,* you dingdongs! And here you come telling poor Momo it will be easy! Find a jewel that has been lost for centuries, you say! Defeat the most evil, most powerful kami in the kami-verse, you say! Just believe in yourself! No problem! Well, I'm here to tell you that it *is* a problem, and I, for one, am *glad* that Momo is reluctant to risk our lives, and I won't hear any more discussion on it. New topic!"

I smiled at him gratefully. At least *he* understood.

"I still think you should do it," said Danny stubbornly.

I put my hands over my face. "Do you know something I don't?" I demanded. "Do you have a plan?"

"Nope," said Danny, looking completely unconcerned.

I groaned.

"Oh, did I say no? I meant not yet," Danny said. "But we'll come up with something. We always do, right?"

"Not this time!" I snapped. "It's my problem and my responsibility, and you can't just 'make things up as you go' with Izanami because she's too smart to beat that way. And if you make things up as you go and you *die,* it will be my fault. Why can't you see that?"

"Sometimes you just gotta seize the moment," Danny said. "Why can't you see *that*? Why do you always have to take everything so seriously?"

"BECAUSE EVERYTHING IS SERIOUS!" I screamed at him.

"Whoaaa," said Danny, stepping back. "You don't have to shout."

"You really don't think we can handle it, do you," said Ryleigh. "Well, we can."

"Yeah, you saw how Ryleigh took charge back there with Mokugon-bake," said Jin. "We can't go wrong with Ryleigh giving directions."

I remembered with only a teensy twinge of resentment the way Ryleigh had ordered us around in the library like she was the only one who knew what she was doing. *Who doesn't trust who, now?* I wanted to ask. But that's what Ryleigh did. She took charge. I expected her to say "That's right!" but instead, she glowered at Jin and said, "Are you making fun of me right now? Are you saying I screwed up?"

Jin blinked at her in surprise. "No. I was . . . complimenting you? I guess?"

In response, Ryleigh just side-eyed him. Strange.

But whatever. "It doesn't matter, because you're not going," I said.

"That's right. And I am making sure of it," said Niko. He had folded a square of white paper into an airplane, which he launched into the air. As it vanished into a portal, he said, "I have informed your mother of your ill-considered ideas, and any minute now she will come to collect you and stow you safely at home where you belong."

"What?" I shrieked.

"I am merely doing my duty as a guardian, which is to ensure your safety," he said. "Why else do you think I'm here?"

That changed everything. If Mom caught up to us, she'd lock me in the house and go looking for the Jewel of the Heart—or Dad—herself. I couldn't let that happen. I couldn't lose both of them.

"Fine. I'm doing it. I'm going," I said.

"Yes!" Danny jumped up immediately. "C'mon, you guys. We can do this. Team RyJin DaMoNik!"

"No, not you. *I'm* going. By myself."

I barely caught the look that passed between my friends before Ryleigh had tackled me at the knees, Jin was sitting on my back, and Danny was holding my shoulders down. "If you don't take us with you, we'll just stay here until your mom comes," Ryleigh said.

"You can't come!" I struggled for a full minute, but they didn't budge.

Use me. We can fight them off together, Kusanagi whispered.

That was ridiculous. I could never actually hurt my friends, no matter how much they might stand in my way. So with a sigh, I gave in.

"Fine. You can come."

"Yes!" Danny said, and they let me go.

"No," Niko insisted. "I say you may not go!"

"Okay, then, we'll go without you," Ryleigh said. "And you can take the blame for letting us."

Niko gasped. "You wouldn't!"

"Try us," Danny said.

Except how would we go? And where? And what about my

shimenawa? As long as I had it on, Mom would be able to track us down instantly.

"Try using Kusanagi to cut it off," said Ryleigh. "Isn't it supposed to be able to cut through, like, all kinds of spells and curses?"

Of course. Why hadn't I thought of that myself? Within seconds, the rope lay on the floor like a dead snake, while Niko paced and whined more fretfully than ever.

"I might have snuck a couple of pieces of magic origami out of your house," said Danny a little sheepishly. "We could fold them into cranes and fly to the portal to the Sea of Heaven."

"Do it," I said.

We found a stairwell, hurried up to the roof of the library, folded the cranes, and climbed on: me and Jin on one and Danny and Ryleigh on the other. "Last chance, Niko," I said.

"I did not sign up for this!" Niko howled. "This is blackmail, you dastardly ding-dongs!" But he leaped onto our crane just as it lurched to its feet, and a few seconds later, we were soaring toward the Golden Gate Bridge, on our way to the Sea of Heaven.

Dangerous and Foolhardy

"No," said Daikoku. She adjusted the cuffs of her pinstriped suit jacket and crossed her arms as we stood before her on the deck of the *Takarabune*. "Absolutely not. You're lucky that any of us are even here to ask."

"What do you mean, absolutely not?" Danny asked. "It's for a good cause."

"Shhh!" Niko hissed at him. "Mind your manners!"

"But—"

"She said no, rodent!" boomed Bishamon, the circle of fire behind his head flaring. "And she speaks for all of us." He nodded at Daikoku and swept his arm to take in Hotei and Ebisu, whose expressions made me think maybe she didn't speak for *them*. "Asking us to help you find the Jewel of the Heart is the same as asking us to break our sacred vow. *Our sacred vow!* I ought to throw you back home for your disrespect!" The kami of warriors directed his fiery gaze at the dragons who were lazily circling the *Takarabune*, the home away from home for the Seven Lucky Gods. "And you! Why did you bring this bunch here when you knew we were in a meeting? I thought we had you better trained."

The dragons responded by spraying water at him. Bishamon spluttered and shook his fist over the side of the ship as his circle of flame guttered out and relit itself. Watery squeaks and chirps that sounded suspiciously like dragon giggles bubbled up from below.

"You know as well as we do that if by some miracle you find the Jewel of the Heart and bring it to Izanami, she will regain her full power and use you and Kusanagi to attack the Middle Lands. And as Bishamon has just said, the Seven Lucky Gods are sworn to protect the Middle Lands," Daikoku explained. "We cannot break that vow. And therefore, we cannot help you find the jewel. Especially not when you only want it so that you can free your father."

"What if you fought Izanami?" Danny suggested. "You could get all your friends together and—"

"No," Daikoku said. "An all-out war in the kami-verse is not an option. I refuse to risk something so potentially catastrophic for the sake of one human life."

I knew it was the sensible choice, but how could they just abandon Dad like this? Now that I'd made my decision to rescue him, I couldn't believe I'd ever hesitated. Dad had always had my back and never let me down. He'd held me in his lap when I got shots at the doctor. He'd gobbled up my broccoli for me when Mom wasn't looking. He'd even convinced Mom to let me get a Poopsie Surprise Unicorn, which she thought was an abomination. I pictured him floating there in the darkness and my heart broke all over again.

"What if I took a guess where it is? Like, a *lucky* guess," Danny tried next, looking hopefully at Ebisu. When Danny was a baby who needed to be adopted, Ebisu had arranged for Danny's parents to find him and fall in love with him.

Niko groaned and covered his eyes with his paws, and even Ryleigh—usually Danny's number one fan—rolled her eyes.

Hotei roared with laughter. "Ooh, that's a good one, little dude! 'Cause Ebisu is the kami of luck, right?"

Danny shrugged and smiled. "I mean."

Ebisu looked at Bishamon. "What do you think?"

"No." Bishamon banged his staff on the deck. "General luck, okay. Luck specifically meant to help them find the key to the end of the world as we know it, not okay."

At this news, Ebisu's shoulders and cheery smile drooped. "I wish I could help you," he said to Danny.

"I don't think this is fair. I think you should take a vote with all seven of you here," said Ryleigh. "I bet Benzaiten would be on our side."

Jin winced a little when Ryleigh mentioned his mother's name. Benzaiten was the kami of music and words, which explained his incredible talent. But she'd disappeared from his life when he was just a baby, and even after they'd been reunited this past New Year's Eve, he still couldn't count on her to show up regularly. I knew it made him wonder just how much she cared.

Hotei heaved a tragic sigh and produced a bowl of shrimp chips from his giant sack. "Here, little buddies. Maybe these will make you feel better." He gave them to Ryleigh, who took a handful and passed them on.

"No, thanks. I don't eat seafood as a snack," said Danny, wrinkling his nose.

"What, seriously? But shrimp chips are the best! What kind

of Asian are you, anyway?" Jin joked. He popped a few chips in his mouth and crunched loudly.

Danny looked indignant. "I can't help it if my parents are white," he said.

"Oh!" Jin's eyes widened. "Sorry, bruh, I didn't mean—"

"Whatever. It's fine," said Danny. "Forget about it."

He didn't look like it was fine, just like with the Asian mom thing. It had to be hard, going through life knowing he stood out from his white friends because of his Asian face, but also being told by Asian kids that he didn't "get" Asian stuff because of his white parents. I just wished he wouldn't let it bother him so much. It wasn't up to other people to decide how Asian he was.

But I didn't have enough brain space or time to worry about that right now. I *had* to convince the Luckies to help us. But how?

"What if Momo promises to destroy the jewel as soon as she finds it? Would you help us then?" Ryleigh said.

I stared at her. What was she saying? How was that even possible?

Bishamon's bushy eyebrows went down. "Are you implying that Momo is willing to make such a promise?" he demanded.

"So it *can* be destroyed," said Ryleigh with a triumphant grin. She seemed to have gotten over whatever had been bothering her about the library battle.

Bishamon's eyes closed, and he let out a low groan. I could almost see a thought bubble that said "D'oh!" over his head.

Daikoku sighed. "Yes, theoretically, Kusanagi could destroy the Jewel of the Heart. It's the only weapon in the kami-verse strong enough to do it."

"Good guesswork, young ninja," Bishamon grumbled.

Ryleigh blushed, and Danny and Jin looked admiringly at her.

"Um, can you excuse us for a moment?" I said in my politest voice. Bishamon nodded his assent, and I grabbed Ryleigh's arm and pulled her farther down the deck, motioning to the others to join us.

We huddled up and I opened my mouth to whisper-scream at her, but she was too fast. "Look, Momo. They'll never help us if they think it'll *endanger* the Middle Lands. But if we say we're going to destroy the jewel, we'll be helping them *protect* the Middle Lands. They can't say no to that! We just have to make them believe us."

"So you're saying I should lie and say I want to destroy the jewel?" I asked. "You know I'm terrible at lying!"

"Honestly? I think you *should* destroy it, but whatever. I didn't say you actually *would*. I only asked if they would help us if you *promised* to destroy it." Ryleigh opened her eyes wide and blinked, all innocence. But there was a knowing glint that I recognized from her mean-girl days, when she'd say things like *I never said your shirt was ugly. I only asked if you got it at the ugly store!* This plan was peak Ryleigh and I respected it. Except for one thing.

"But if I actually *make* that promise, it *will* be a lie." Now that we knew I could destroy the jewel, that was obviously the right thing to do. It was bad enough that I didn't *want* to do the right thing. *Promising* to do the right thing and then purposely not doing it felt even worse.

"We can't lie to the Luckies!" Niko's voice was somewhere

between an irritated growl and a nervous whine. "What if they find out?"

"It doesn't have to be a lie," Danny said. "It can be part of the plan! Step one: find the jewel. Step two: rescue your dad. Step three: destroy the jewel! Boom!" He mimed having his mind blown by flicking his fingers at his temples. "Am I a genius, or what?"

"But Ryleigh said Momo would promise to destroy it *right away*," Jin reminded him. "If Momo changes the words, the Luckies are sure to notice."

"But 'right away' is relative. You know, like Hotei always says: time is a construct." Danny grinned.

"Except the 'rescue Momo's dad' part involves giving the jewel to Izanami, you overhyping orange smoothie," Niko pointed out.

"Don't worry about that part. We'll—"

"Wait, lemme guess," I said. "We'll figure it out?"

"Yeah, we will!" Danny grinned. "How'd you know I was gonna say that?"

"This is not a game, Danny. It's not just win or lose! People's lives are at stake!"

Danny rolled his eyes. "You think I don't know that? It's your *dad*, Momo. Do you want to save him or not?"

"Don't forget the whole entire word," Ryleigh said.

"Your dad *and* the whole world," Danny agreed. "That's why you have to stop overthinking every single tiny thing and just go for it."

"We've got you," said Jin.

"*You've* got you," said Ryleigh.

Niko only groaned and muttered, "We're doomed as donuts in a dragon's den."

"Dragons like donuts?" Jin asked.

Niko rolled his eyes. "Obviously. Who doesn't know that?"

"Come on, Momo. You can do it," said Danny.

Why did everyone want me to lie when they knew I couldn't? But I couldn't think of another way to get the Luckies to help, and no one else could lie for me: Kusanagi was mine, and the Luckies would want *my* promise. Danny was right. It all came down to me. If I didn't step up, it was as good as quitting on Dad. That image of him floated up in my head again: thin, exhausted, battered, bleeding. How could I allow him to suffer if I had the power to save him? He had never quit on me. I couldn't quit on him.

"Okay, fine," I said, even though it made my stomach turn. "I'll do it."

"So," said Bishamon. He and Daikoku looked stern; Hotei and Ebisu looked hopeful. "What do you have to say? Do you promise to destroy the Jewel of the Heart as soon as you find it?"

"Of course!" I said. I tried to make my voice sound honest, which apparently meant making it too high and fake-cheery. I glanced guiltily at the others, who looked like a series of emojis for the word "cringe."

"We mean it, Momo. You must promise that if you find the jewel, you will destroy it immediately." It was Daikoku who spoke this time.

I took my voice down a few notches and said as sincerely as I could, "If we find the Jewel of the Heart, I promise to destroy it so that Izanami can never use the power of the Three Sacred

Treasures to take over the kami-verse." I was careful not to say "immediately." I hoped no one would notice.

"Immediately. Promise to destroy it immediately," Daikoku said.

Darn it.

"Immediately."

It wasn't a full sentence, so it wasn't a real promise. And technically if it wasn't a promise, then it wasn't a lie.

Daikoku nodded grimly and said, "Look at me, Momo."

Her dark eyes had taken on a scary intensity. If I looked back at her, she would surely see the lie in my face. But if I looked away, she'd know I was afraid she'd see it. I closed my eyes and did a couple of rounds of deep breathing. *Time is a construct. Time is a construct. If I want to save Dad, I have to do this.*

"Momo?" Daikoku's voice broke through my thoughts.

"Yes?" I was stalling, and I knew she knew it.

"Your promise. Look into my eyes and promise."

I took another deep breath and tried to dislodge the lie from my throat, where it seemed to have decided to dig in its heels. But I couldn't get it out, so instead I begged silently, *Please help me find the jewel.* I didn't let myself think anything else.

Looking into Daikoku's eyes made me remember that long ago, before she had arrived in Japan and become Daikoku, she was a deity of time, destruction, and creation in India. I felt like I was floating in endless darkness pierced with tiny, brilliant lights that flickered and flashed like electrical impulses.

The lights swirled together like a flock of starlings, and I heard Daikoku's voice in my head. *I know what you plan to do,* she told me. *It is dangerous and foolhardy.*

My throat went so dry, I nearly choked. Did she mean the fake plan to destroy the jewel? Or had she seen the real plan (or lack thereof)?

You cannot do this without Kusanagi, and you have not learned to use its power to serve you.

Okay, this I could handle. *Yes, I have. I know how to—*

No. You haven't.

I blinked at her. *Yes, I have.*

You have accepted your anger, and Izanami has taught you to use Kusanagi to destroy your enemies. But that is not enough.

That made zero sense. Wasn't destroying enemies the whole *point* of a sword (no pun intended)? Wasn't I *supposed* to destroy the Jewel of the Heart? And how was I supposed to defeat Izanami if I didn't destroy her?

I don't understand, I said in my head.

You can't beat Izanami the Destroyer at her own game. You must find another way. You must embrace your true power and move beyond destruction.

Huh?

You and the sword are deeply connected. But mortals who wield Kusanagi are too weak to resist its violent tendencies. They fall in love with the power of their own anger and cannot see any way to use that power other than to destroy.

To guide Kusanagi beyond its desire for destruction, you must embrace your own source of power along with the power of the sword itself. If you succeed, it will transform everything. If you fail, your spirit will fall under the control of Kusanagi's most violent impulses.

What power is that? How am I supposed to find it? I said.

Only you can answer that question.

The swirling lights faded away, and I knew that Daikoku had left the building, so to speak. I had so many questions: What did it mean to guide a sword beyond destruction? The source of my power was my rage monster. Wouldn't embracing it make me *more* dangerous and destructive? Wouldn't it make me fall under Kusanagi's spell that much faster?

I blinked, and the darkness lifted. I was still on the deck of the *Takarabune*. Daikoku and the others were whispering urgently together. Hotei and Ebisu appeared to be pleading with her and Bishamon.

"What happened? She didn't catch on to you, did she?" Ryleigh asked me.

I shook my head. "I'm not sure." I thought about telling them what Daikoku had said about moving beyond destruction and embracing the source of my power. But what good would it do? It was an impossible riddle. Danny would probably say that "beyond destruction" meant going extreme supersonic ballistic so I could wipe out death altogether. And Ryleigh would just tell me I needed to be more confident.

The kami-huddle broke up, and Daikoku, Bishamon, Ebisu, and Hotei turned to face us. I could tell right away from Daikoku's face what she was going to say, and my heart sank.

"I am sorry, Momo," she said. "But—"

"I'm here!" Benzaiten burst through the doors of the cabin in the middle of the ship's deck. "I'm here! Sorry I'm late."

Jin's face took on an expression I couldn't read. "Mom!"

She looked at him with amazement, and her face broke into a warm smile as she opened her arms and cried, "My baby! What are you doing here?" As she folded him into a hug, I thought nervously of Mom, who was probably out there searching for me right now.

Daikoku took out her pocket watch and looked pointedly at it. "Nice of you to show up to the meeting, Benzi," she said with one eyebrow arched. "You're only an hour late."

"I know, I'm sorry. I got busy." She smiled. "So! What are we doing?"

The Luckies went into another huddle, and a few minutes later they faced us again. Daikoku spoke. "We took a vote, and foolish optimism prevailed."

"We will help you," said Benzaiten.

"Woo-hoo, yesss!" Danny pumped his fist. "Let's gooo!"

"This calls for a celebration!" Hotei opened his sack and tossed handfuls of candy into the air.

I nearly collapsed with relief.

"Enough!" Bishamon roared, and we all quieted down. "Being given permission to go and risk your necks—and all of the Middle Lands—is no cause for celebration! This is a huge responsibility, rodents, and if you fail, I will personally make sure that each one of you—"

"No threats, Bishamon." Daikoku interrupted him. "Anyway, we all know you would never harm these children."

"Especially not mine." Benzaiten looked uncharacteristically fierce. Jin looked uncomfortable.

"Bishamon is right, though," Daikoku said to us. "Your journey will be neither safe nor easy, so I suggest you temper your excitement with caution. Only a fool faces danger unafraid."

Fantastic. And completely unsurprising.

Daikoku went on. "But at least your journey will start with a stroke of luck: Benzaiten's brother-in-law is the last known keeper of the Jewel of the Heart."

"Who's that?" Ryleigh asked.

"Ryūjin."

Niko inhaled sharply. "Not the dragon king!" he wailed. "He'll serve us for snacks! He'll dice us up for dinner! He'll—"

"Stop your foolishness, fox. You know as well as anyone that he's harmless," Bishamon snapped.

"Everyone knows he has a taste for monkey livers. What if he also likes fox livers?" Niko shuddered.

"He needed that liver to heal a rash, is what my mom told me," I said.

"Ugh, that's gross," said Jin.

"Barf," agreed Danny.

"You will be safe," Benzaiten assured us.

"Ryūjin is the ruler of the undersea world," said Ebisu, getting us back on track. "Everything that falls into the sea belongs to him. He could even have laid claim to Kusanagi if he had chosen to. Though I doubt that Susano'o would have let him keep it without a fight."

That sounded about right.

Benzaiten added, "His palace, Ryūgū-jō, houses a collection of priceless jewels. The Jewel of the Heart is—or it was once— one of them. Ryūjin is more responsible and more powerful than the Taira clan, who hoarded the Sword of the Wind only so that they could one day rise up and rule the surface again. If

Ryūjin does not currently have the jewel in his possession, it is by his own choice, for a good reason. And he will know exactly where to find it."

"So all we have to do is ask him for it?" Jin said.

"Yes."

"But will he give it to us?" I asked. In my experience, the kami never gave up anything valuable without a fight.

"Good for you. You're anticipating problems. Asking the right questions," Bishamon said, nodding and scowling. "And the answer is no. He won't give it to you."

"Do you have any tips? Or maybe a map of secret passageways or something?" Danny asked.

Hotei spoke up now. "The interior of the palace shifts around, so a map won't be helpful. And you'll need to keep track of the time. As you know, it goes by fast down there."

"Speaking of time," said Daikoku, "that's quite enough of it spent talking. It's time for action. We have a meeting to finish up, and you have a jewel to find and destroy."

"So be it." Bishamon banged his staff and leaned over the edge of the ship to call the dragons. As we said our goodbyes, I noticed Benzaiten giving Jin an extra-long hug. Now, instead of hoping Mom wouldn't catch up to us, I thought about why she might be looking for us: she probably just wanted to make sure we were okay. Then I thought about how I'd shouted at her for not taking care of me before I'd basically run away from her. Why had I been so awful? What if I never got to see her again and those were the last words she ever heard me say? What if she thought that was how I really felt about her?

But I couldn't go down that road. I had to stay focused. I

would save Dad and destroy the jewel, and everything would be okay.

As long as I could figure out how to use Kusanagi before it took over my spirit.

"You okay, Momo?" Ryleigh asked.

"Mm-hmm," I said, and pasted what I hoped was a brave smile on my face. No more time for doubts or questions. I had no choice now but to go forward.

A moment later we were clambering into the rowboat and waving goodbye as the dragons spun us back to the Middle Lands, to Ryūjin's palace at the bottom of the sea.

One molecule-splitting portal passage later, I was lying on a broad stone plateau, with dark, jagged mountains rising sharply in the distance. In the middle of the plateau was a bonfire nearly as tall as a house, encircled by a stone wall low enough to sit on. The fire gave off quite a bit of light, but no heat or sound. Next to me, Jin and Ryleigh looked like they were about to pass out from holding their breath.

"It's okay. You can breathe," said Danny. "Because magic." He did sparkly jazz hands.

"Oh, thank goodness!" Jin let out a burst of air, and he and Ryleigh both began taking astonished, experimental little breaths. I'd forgotten that this was their first time being magically transported underwater.

"I don't see a palace anywhere," Niko said.

"Maybe it's through those mountains?" Jin suggested. He pointed at a narrow path that led into a ravine on the far side of the plateau.

"Or maybe we're already at the gates," said Danny. "That

fire thing looks like the fountain in front of the gates to the Palace of the Sun."

"Wherever we are, we're not alone." Ryleigh looked up into the darkness just as something snakelike and sinewy undulated past, close enough for the distant firelight to cast a glimmering reflection on its scales as it slid in and out of the shadows.

"What's that?" I whispered.

"Maybe it's a dragon," said Jin hopefully.

"Maybe we should get moving," said Niko. "Danny, if you please?"

Danny took the hint and pulled out his phone. The flashlight blinked on obligingly when he pointed it in the direction of the bonfire. "Yes!"

But halfway there, something swooped down from above and blocked our path, and I choked back a scream.

It was a mermaid.

Pretty, but Stabby

I know. You're probably thinking, *What's wrong with you? I would love to see a mermaid!*

But this mermaid was not the kind you see in Disney movies, with a seashell bikini top and sparkly Disney princess eyes and a tail with a cute little ruffle around the waist. She was not one of those mermaids that comb their hair with forks and dream of marrying a handsome prince who falls off his private yacht at his twentieth-birthday party. Nooo.

This mermaid—a ningyo—was (not to exaggerate or anything) absolutely freaking terrifying. I mean, okay, her body was legitimately beautiful, with its gleaming golden scales, shimmering silver fins, and rainbow-colored tail. But the *rest* of her was absolutely freaking terrifying. She was gigantic, first of all—easily as long as a minivan. And she didn't have a human torso at the end of her scaly fish tail. She was all fish, all the way to a scaly green neck that ended in a grotesque face with pale, smooth human skin; round, glassy, fishy eyes; two slits for a nose; thin green human lips around a monstrous fang-filled fish mouth; and a pair of gleaming white horns set in a head of tangled black hair. She had arms, but they were long, scaly arms that ended in long, scaly hands that ended in long, scaly fingers with long, daggerlike claws. They poked out of her fishy body like a pair of weird killer fins.

Ryleigh's shuriken clinked next to me, and Danny's arrows rattled on my other side. I reached for Kusanagi. Niko nodded at a rock, which rolled silently across the sand toward us. Jin began humming the opening bars to "Under the Sea."

"Seriously?" Ryleigh muttered. "Now?"

But Jin kept humming. Music was the only tool he could use to help keep us safe, so I didn't blame him. On the other hand, the prospect of fighting for our lives while he sang, "We got no troubles, life is de bubbles, under the sea!" was a bit unsettling.

With a hiss and a powerful flick of her tail, the ningyo bared her fangs and surged closer, but stopped abruptly when we raised our weapons. She swam back and forth, fixing us with a glassy-eyed glare, arms drawn back and claws extended, as if she was still considering attacking.

"Haghhhh," she snarled. "Landwalkers. Warmbloods. They are alive. How can this be?"

"Who's she talking to?" Danny murmured.

"It speaks," she said. "It asks silly questions." Then she cocked her head for a moment and actually bobbed along in time to "Under the Sea," which Jin was still singing. "Pretty," she said. "Bouncy."

She extended one skinny arm toward Jin, fingers and claws outstretched, but hastily withdrew it when we raised our weapons.

"Sharp, stabby. Fighty. Bitey. Must be careful." She hissed and showed her teeth again.

Jin bravely kept singing, but Niko whimpered. "Ohhh, no, no, no," he said. "Be careful. Oh, be careful."

"Uh, who are you talking to?" Danny asked. "Us or her?"

"You! Us!" Niko said, his voice strained. "We have to be careful!"

Suddenly I remembered. "It's bad luck to kill a mermaid," I said.

"Even in self-defense?" said Ryleigh incredulously.

"I don't know! I just know that it's bad luck! We could be cursed or something!" I snapped.

"Okay. So we talk her down. We make it so we don't have to fight her," said Ryleigh.

"I got this," said Danny immediately, which didn't surprise me one bit, because he saw himself as the world's best smooth talker. He cleared his throat, made a show of lowering his bow and arrow, and put on the smile I'd seen him use dozens of times to get himself out of trouble with teachers. "Uh, hello there, ma'am. Please don't eat us. We don't mean any harm!" Danny said.

The ningyo stopped swimming for a moment and stared extra hard, still nodding her head in time to Jin's music. "Pretty," she said again. "But stabby." She started swishing herself back and forth. "Friend or foe? Friend or foe?" she mused.

"Friends! Friends!" Niko yelped. "We're definitely friends!"

"We're looking for Ryūgū-jō," I said. "Can you help us?"

At the mention of Ryūgū-jō, the ningyo glanced over at the silent bonfire and frowned. Then she turned back to us and said, "Don't like Ryūgū-jō."

"We're not from there," Danny said cheerfully. "We just need to go there."

But even as he said it, I wasn't so sure I agreed. Because the shadowy figures of two more long, sinuous creatures with human heads were taking shape inside the flames.

Beside me, Niko moaned, "We're doomed. Done for. Pickled as pike. Flattened as flounder."

"Need to go to Ryūgū-jō . . . to fight and bite?" the ningyo said, looking as hopeful as a hideous fish monster can look. "To poke and stab?"

"Uh." Danny glanced at us. "Well."

The creatures in the fire were nearly solid now. They twisted and twined around each other, clearly impatient to get out. *Would* we have to fight and bite?

"I know!" The ningyo smiled—at least, she drew her lips back and showed all her sharp teeth. She pointed at Jin with one long, bony finger. "Give me the pretty-bouncy. Then go to Ryūgū-jō."

We looked at Jin, who stopped singing in his surprise. "The what?"

"The song," Ryleigh said. "She wants the song!"

But how did you give a song away? Or did she actually mean Jin himself?

"Pretty-bouncy!" the ningyo shrieked. "Give me the pretty-bouncy!" She reared up to her full height, her fish eyes flashing dangerously.

"Sing, Jin!" Niko urged him. "Sing for your life!"

But it was too late. The enraged ningyo was already diving at Jin, apparently intent on tearing the pretty-bouncy out of his throat.

I threw myself in front of him. I felt my rage monster's energy flowing into Kusanagi: *Get her!*

The ningyo reared back in surprise. Daikoku had said to embrace the source of my power, right? Okay. Fine. I brandished Kusanagi and allowed myself to soak up the storm of fury that surged through me.

What else had Daikoku said? The electric energy was making my memory staticky. Something about transforming everything.

The ningyo had recovered and was preparing to attack. She gathered herself.

Just let her make one move, one twitch of one fin. I'd transform her, all right. I would make her into ningyo sashimi. I would make a cape out of her tail. I would—

Someone grabbed my arm. I shook them off.

Someone cried out, "Momo, stop! The curse!"

"Shut up!" I shouted back. "I don't care!"

Someone was singing. Something nice. Something so pretty, I almost lost focus.

The ningyo noticed it, too, and she *did* lose focus. She relaxed a little, listening intently.

Big mistake.

I rushed and swung. I would have sliced her right in half, but two giant, golden-scaled creatures with antlers on their human heads shot forward and yanked the ningyo out of the way by her spindly arms. The three became a tangle of flashing fins and thrashing tails. The ningyo screamed—a sound like a pitchfork screaking across a giant sheet of metal—and I screamed, too.

"She's mine! Lemme at her!" I fought with Danny and Ryleigh, who had *me* by *my* arms.

"You . . . can't . . . kill her!" Ryleigh panted.

"But she wants to kill Jin!" I protested.

Let it go, let it go,
Just relax and let it flow.

Wait—that was Jin's voice. He was . . . okay? I twisted in Danny's and Ryleigh's arms to find him. He waved and smiled: *See? You can stop fighting now.*

So I did. But I wasn't ready to relax just yet. "Where's the ningyo?" I asked.

"Look over there," said Niko, pointing. "They've taken care of it."

The golden-scaled creatures had, in fact, wrestled the ningyo into submission. One of them tied her arms with kelp while the other took a pipe from under one of their scales and blew a bubble around the snarling, twisting prisoner.

These two ningyo were different from the first one, and not just because they had saved our lives. For starters, they had proper human faces, with actual noses, and eyes that looked like eyes instead of giant marbles. Their hands did not appear to be tipped with deadly claws, and their arms were attached to proper shoulders on top of burly torsos.

"Now, then, Miss Fishy-fins," the one with the pipe was saying. "Be a good citizen and leave these nice landwalkers alone."

That was promising. Okay. Maybe I *could* relax.

The ningyo bared her teeth and lunged at her captors. But

the bubble around her was impenetrable, and she bounced back harmlessly.

I must have tensed up, because Danny's and Ryleigh's hands tightened around my arms. I made myself take a long, slow breath. "It's okay," I said to them. "I'm okay. You can let go now."

"You sure?" said Ryleigh.

"Yeah." I put Kusanagi away. What had just happened to me? I wasn't sorry that I'd leaped to Jin's defense—like Izanami had once said to me, anger is the protector of the weak and defenseless. But if the golden merpeople hadn't arrived and rescued us, I would have killed her.

My thoughts were interrupted by the one with the pipe, who appeared to be male. He turned to us and smiled. "Hello, there, humans. Mai-no-umi, palace guard, at your service. And this is Koto-no-umi. My apologies for the scare you got from our cousin, here."

Cousin? A light flicked on in my brain. "You're hime-uo!" I said. Hime-uo were the sophisticated, beautiful relatives of ningyo, and they served as courtiers and palace guards in Ryūgū-jō.

Mai-no-umi looked amused. "Yes, little landwalker, that's correct. Headquarters received a message from Benzaiten that a group of you would be arriving, but the message didn't specify where. We came as quickly as we could."

"We would have arrived sooner, but we don't post a regular guard at this entrance, as the large population of ningyo in the area tends to keep most landwalking intruders away," said Koto-no-umi.

"Of course, that does become a problem when those land-walkers are legitimate visitors," said Mai-no-umi. "But all's well that ends well, right?"

Inside her bubble-prison, the ningyo clawed and lunged, and I could hear muffled cries of "Pretty-bouncy!"

"I think she wants the song I was singing," said Jin, his hands straying to his throat.

"They do love music," said Mai-no-umi.

"I kind of feel bad for her," said Jin.

Danny rolled his eyes. "She just tried to tear your throat out, bro. Don't feel bad for her."

"It's not her fault she doesn't understand how singing works," Jin protested.

"You must be Benzaiten's son! She told us you were part of the group," said Koto-no-umi. Instead of looking proud and happy, Jin grimaced. Odd. Had he and Benzaiten had a fight? "You're right not to blame the ningyo, my kindhearted young man. She was only doing what ningyo do."

"I wish there was a way for me to give her what she wants," Jin said.

"There is." Mai-no-umi waved his hand and produced a conch shell. "Sing into this."

Jin did as he was told. Mai-no-umi took the shell back and thrust it into the bubble, where the ningyo snatched it up and began gnawing on its pale pink lip. A few seconds later, her expression changed from wild frustration to confusion to delight. (I'm not gonna lie, though, it still looked like something out of a horror movie.) "Pretty-bouncy!" she shouted at us. She held the conch to her ear and twirled in a happy spiral.

"See? It never hurts to be nice," I said to Danny.

"Says the girl who was ready to stab the ningyo to death," he replied.

Which . . . fair. I swallowed down a pang of anxiety and guilt. It was true. I hadn't just been *defending* Jin. I'd been *attacking* the ningyo. Was the thing that Daikoku had warned me about starting to happen? Was Kusanagi's will taking over mine? I could control the energy that Kusanagi stirred up. I could channel it and stay on top of it. But once I was locked in, it was like I didn't *want* to shut it down. All I wanted to do was destroy my target.

You can't beat Izanami the Destroyer at her own game. You must find another way. My heart began to thud. What if I didn't find that other way in time?

Before I could think about it any more, Koto-no-umi spoke. "Now that the ningyo's all taken care of, we should get going," he said. "The bubble is only temporary, and once she emerges, she's bound to go and show off her new toy. And then her friends will want one for themselves, and you'll be stuck singing here forever."

Yikes.

"Yes, perhaps we should proceed to the palace," said Niko. "Pronto."

We followed the hime-uo to the giant firepit at the center of the plateau. "After you," said Mai-no-umi. He bowed and waved his arms gracefully at the flames.

"Uh." Jin cleared his throat and pointed. "You mean in there?"

Mai-no-umi nodded. "It's the fastest way."

"Or you could take the mountain pass," said Koto-no-umi, gesturing at the dark crags on the other side of the bonfire.

"How long will that take?" I asked. "Is it dangerous?"

"Hard to say. Possibly the rest of your natural lives," said Koto-no-umi. "Years, anyway, if we're talking human time. And I wouldn't say it's dangerous, but there are a few hundred ningyo nests along the way, so it's not ideal."

"I think the fire will be fine," said Niko.

"It's not even hot," said Ryleigh, stepping on the low stone wall of the firepit and stretching her hand out toward the flames.

I put out my hand experimentally. "You're right!"

Ryleigh side-eyed me. "Of course I'm right."

"We can all go at once," said Jin.

So we stood on the wall together, and Ryleigh counted us in. "Jump on three. One . . . two . . . three!"

We landed inside the firepit. The ocean wavered on the other side of the dancing flames, and a wild, hot wind blew up from underneath our feet. When I looked down to see where it was coming from, I grabbed the nearest arm in panic. We seemed to be standing on thin air. Or maybe it was water. Who knows how magical ocean portals work? Not me.

"Ow!" said Danny. "You're gonna cut off my circulation!"

"Sorry." I *was* sorry, but I also wasn't quite ready to let go. "Why aren't *you* scared? I thought you were afraid of heights."

"I dunno. This is different. This is—" He looked down, swayed a little, and squeezed his eyes shut. He reached out his free hand and grabbed Ryleigh's arm. "Thanks a lot. Now I'm scared."

"Sorry."

"I got you," said Ryleigh. "Relax. Breathe."

"We'll be fine," said Jin. "This is magic, remember?"

"Easy for you to say with your fancy flying cape," said Danny.

"I was talking to Niko," said Jin. I turned to see Niko quivering in his arms. But I didn't turn away quickly enough for Niko to miss my grin.

"I won't have you judging me! It is my job to protect you, and I can't protect you if I drop to my death, can I?" he said. And then he yipped, "Don't let go!" and scrambled up Jin's chest to his shoulder.

"I wasn't letting go," Jin reassured him. At the same time, I realized Danny's arm didn't feel as secure as it had a few seconds ago. I squeezed tighter, but my fingers suddenly felt weak; no matter how hard I tried, I couldn't get a good grip. In fact, all of me felt softer somehow, like I was melting away. I looked at the others, then at my hand on Danny's arm. Everything was slowly blurring at the edges like a video going out of focus. Colors were fading, too, growing fainter and more translucent.

"What's happening?" I tried to say, but it came out all slurred and far away: "Whashaffenn?" I would have felt afraid, but I couldn't seem to care, because even my thoughts and feelings felt fuzzy, and after a while, I gave up trying to do anything, and the world faded to a pleasant pastel blue.

A Glop of Chocolate-Covered Goo

Coming back felt the same way, but opposite. My eyes opened groggily to a blurry world of colorful blotches and muffled sounds that gradually sharpened and clarified until I was standing inside a dancing blue fire just like the one we'd left. I looked down to see my feet on a slab of very solid-looking rock. *Whew.*

"Whoaaa, that was sick!" said Danny. "I think I like undersea portals better than the regular kind."

Through the flames, I saw a brightly lit space filled with color and music. "If we're to believe the hime-uo, on the other side of this fire is the court of Ryūjin, the dragon king," said Niko. "So mind your manners and don't do anything too mortifying."

We stepped out of the fire and onto a dais on one side of an enormous pavilion. Unlike the Taira ghost clan's dark and gloomy undersea palace, which was dimly lit by bioluminescent plankton, this palace was strung with sparkling, festive lights of all colors. A crystal chandelier added to the party atmosphere. The pillars and roof looked like they'd been made of all different kinds of coral woven together: yellow, blue, purple, orange, and red; spikes, blossoms, fans, and wavy fronds. Schools of tiny fish chased each other in, out, and around, adding their own bright flashes of color.

Sea-kami laughed and chatted in small groups around the pavilion, dressed in shimmering ball gowns, rich silk kimonos, and elegant tuxedos. There were hime-uo as well, who had adorned their scales, fins, and tails with jewels. Plainly dressed octopuses carrying four or five trays each drifted from group to group, offering tiny plates of seaweed and sushi. In one corner, an orchestra played a lively tune that made me want to do a jig—that is, if I'd known how to do a jig.

Everyone was so busy having fun that no one even glanced in our direction until a gigantic lobster scuttled up to us. He wore an impressive suit of old-fashioned samurai armor, but the thing that made me stare was the mustachioed human head on top of his shoulders. "Ah, our honored guests have arrived!" he said. He turned to the crowd and clacked his enormous claws and boomed, "Attention, everyone!" A hush fell over the room, and suddenly all the party guests were staring at us. I wished I had a shell, so I could duck inside it. I felt like everyone was evaluating us to see if we measured up—to what, I couldn't have told you, but it didn't matter. It was the way I always felt in front of a lot of people, which is why I hated doing presentations at school. Also, the lobster-man seemed like a nice guy, what with his bowing and calling us "honored guests," but it's hard not to be nervous in front of a seven-foot-tall crustacean, even when he has a human head. Maybe especially when he has a human head.

"Welcome, granddaughter of the great Susano'o, Lord of the Sea and Master of Storms! Greetings, son of Benzaiten, benevolent kami of all that flows! Salutations, spirit child of Ebisu, the baby kami who was carried north to Ainu Moshiri! My compliments, young ninja, learning the ways of humans and nature! And my respect to you, honorable fox, for leading this intrepid band to our humble palace. Ise Ebizō the Fifteenth at your service."

Ise Ebizō the Fifteenth twirled his mustache and bowed deeply.

The room erupted in applause. I peeked at Niko for guidance, but he looked confused. I realized he couldn't decide whether to throw himself to the floor and grovel as usual, or to act dignified, like he and the lobster-samurai were equals. He compromised by slowly twirling his whiskers and lowering himself into a deep bow, just like Ise Ebizō had. "Greetings, Lord Ebizō. We are honored to be here." Under his breath, he muttered, "Bow, you bilious barnacles!" So we did.

Lord Ebizō motioned for the crowd to go back to their conversations. Then he spoke again in a lower voice. "I'm glad you arrived safely. Benzaiten told us that she was sending you on a diplomatic mission. I understand that you have important business to discuss with His Royal Majesty."

He drew Niko off the dais and nodded at the rest of us to follow him, twirling his mustache with one of his smaller skinny arms. Niko, clearly flattered to be seen as the leader, puffed out his chest and twirled *his* whiskers again as well. "Ah, yes, a diplomatic mission." He nodded sagely. "That is precisely our purpose."

As we crossed the pavilion, all the fancy ladies and gentlemen nodded and smiled and even bowed at us as we passed.

"Does anyone else feel super self-conscious?" I whispered.

"No way!" said Danny. "This is the best!" He waved to a group of kids, who collapsed into giggles and waved back.

Jin gave a wry smile. "My dad would love you."

"Huh? Why?"

"Because you like all that attention. I never have, and that's one reason why I'm retiring." He sighed. "My dad doesn't understand it. He says he wants me to be happy, but I know he's disappointed. I hate feeling like I'm letting him down."

Ryleigh nodded. "I know how *that* feels. It's like you have all this weight on your shoulders that you're so tired of carrying, but if you stop . . ."

"They'll fall apart," I finished.

"Who'll fall apart?" Danny asked. He waved at another group of kids.

"Our parents," said Jin.

"Why?"

"You wouldn't understand," said Ryleigh.

"What's that supposed to mean?"

"It means you don't have the responsibilities that we do," I said.

"I have plenty of responsibilities," Danny said, crossing his arms. "Trust me."

"It's not the same," Ryleigh said. "You're talking about chores, and we're talking about being responsible for family stuff."

"Yeah, you got really lucky with your parents," I said.

Danny stopped walking, and I realized my mistake. I'd meant that he was lucky because his parents didn't make him carry all their hopes and dreams and emotions like ours did. I hadn't meant to ignore the fact that they often left him on his own while they traveled. And I *definitely* hadn't meant to imply that he was lucky to have his adoptive white parents instead of his Asian birth parents. But it sure sounded like I had.

"Well, I'm sorry I'm not a literal *rock star*, or part of a super-rich *ninja dynasty*, or the granddaughter of the *storm god*. That must be so hard, having all that *responsibility* to your *families*."

"That's not what I said! I said you were . . ." But I didn't know how to say it in a way that didn't feel like a trap. I half hoped Niko would jump in and scold us for being argumentative adolescents, but he was deep in conversation with Lord Ebizō and seemed to have forgotten all about us.

"I'm sorry," I mumbled finally. "I didn't—"

"Whatever," Danny said.

"Anyway," Ryleigh said after a few awkward seconds of silence. "You better say hi to that hime-uo kid over there. They're totally making heart eyes at you."

"Where?" Danny looked around and spotted the young hime-uo that Ryleigh was talking about. His bad mood seemed to evaporate instantly. "Hey there!" He took a grand, sweeping bow. The hime-uo blushed and hid their face behind a fan. "Yep. Either you got it or you don't, amirite?" Danny said. He was smiling again, but I knew he was still upset, and I was the reason.

We passed a long table loaded down with bowls of caviar, sea urchin, and abalone. I made a face; I'd always thought sea urchin was disgusting. But then I saw a table of American junk food: a giant bowl of cinnamon-sugar pretzel bites, just like my favorites from Auntie Anne's. Another bowl of snack-sized bags of Takis. A plate heaped with Twix bars, another with hamburgers and hot dogs. A milkshake machine. And an extra-large pepperoni pizza.

"Help yourselves, children," said Lord Ebizō, producing five white porcelain plates.

We gratefully accepted our plates and had just loaded them up with snacks when one of the guests hobbled out of the crowd with a terrible shriek.

She was hunched and thin, with scraggly white hair. Her face was less a face than a mass of wrinkles with a nose, a gap-toothed mouth, and a pair of intense, beady little eyes.

"These aren't for you!" Her voice was like a dentist's drill. She slapped the plates out of our hands and trampled all over the food on the floor with savage glee.

Niko was the first to react. "How dare you purloin my pepperoni pizza, you creepy old crone!" he shouted, and he reached for another slice.

"No!" screeched the old woman. She limped along the table with surprising speed and began sweeping everything she could reach into a big pile. "Don't touch!" She tore open a Twix wrapper, crammed the entire candy bar in her mouth, and began chewing frantically. Bits of it fell out as she pushed a few pretzel bites inside, followed by a handful of Takis and a bite of hamburger. Her cheeks bulged, and a string of drool leaked down her chin.

"Gross." Ryleigh wrinkled her nose.

"Is she a shikome?" Danny wondered. He was referring to Izanami's death hags—one of whom had nearly dragged me into Yomi last October. They also love to eat.

But shikome were glamorous flying zombies who wore fancy ball gowns and too much makeup. This was a wrinkly old granny dressed in what looked like a fraying gray bathrobe. And the party guests were whispering and pointing and curling their lips as if the greedy old lady was a disgusting piece of garbage rather than a mortal threat from Yomi.

"She's nobody," said Lord Ebizō. Then he clacked his giant claws and called out, "Guards!"

The crowd parted and a feminine-looking hime-uo appeared, wearing the expression of someone who'd stepped in dog poop.

"All right, that's enough, Sen. Let's go," the hime-uo guard said. She poked the old lady's shoulders.

"Nooo!" Sen shrieked in her dentist-drill voice. She turned and spat the contents of her mouth at the hime-uo—a slimy, half-chewed hunk of hamburger, a glop of chocolate-covered goo, and little chunks of saliva-softened pretzel dough, all of it dotted with red Taki particles.

The crowd gasped and took a step back.

"Yes," said the hime-uo. This time, she grasped Sen's arms and started to steer her away from the table. Sen struggled and screamed, but she was no match for the giant mermaid.

Just before she was dragged out of reach, Sen screeched, "If I can't have it, no one can!" She grabbed two fistfuls of tablecloth and yanked. She wasn't very strong, but she was already surging away in the arms of the hime-uo, and the result was that everything on the table slipped off the edge and cascaded onto the floor.

"Haaahhh!" Sen screamed in triumph. As the hime-uo continued to drag her away from us, she swiveled her head, squinting and searching the crowd for a few seconds before locking eyes with me. Her tiny, blazing black eyes sparked as she thrashed and screamed at me, "Get out! Go! Go away now or you'll be sorry!"

The hime-uo picked her up under one arm as if she were a misbehaving toddler, but Sen kept kicking and shouting and flapping the tablecloth. The last I saw of her was the white fabric rippling and waving as she was hauled out the other side of the pavilion.

Once Sen had disappeared, a wave of whispers and nervous laughter eddied around the room. It seemed like everyone here was as freaked out and uncomfortable as we were.

"Whoa." Danny's eyes looked like they might fall right out of his head.

"I am sorry you had to see that," said Lord Ebizō.

"Who was that? What's wrong with her?" Jin whispered.

Niko opened his mouth as if to answer, but Lord Ebizō spoke first. "Long story. Not worth telling."

"I'd still like to hear it," I said.

"No, you wouldn't." Lord Ebizō clacked his claws. "It's dull and boring and completely unimportant." He twirled his mustache as he surveyed the mess, which was already being swept up by a crew of giant prawns. "I don't suppose you're still hungry."

We shook our heads. That whole incident had taken away my appetite.

"We will make it up to you," Lord Ebizō said with a bow of his head. "But now it is time to speak with the king." He turned and continued on the path we'd been taking. "Come along."

"That was really weird," Ryleigh whispered to me as we fell into step behind the others. "Did you get the feeling she was trying to tell us something?"

"Uh, like maybe get out? Go away?" I scoffed. "Do you think that was it?"

"No, I mean it," Ryleigh insisted. "She was looking right at you, like she was talking to you, specifically. I think we might be in danger." She scanned the room and patted her bag of shuriken.

"Benzaiten wouldn't have sent us here if it was dangerous," I said. But now I was nervous.

"Maybe Benzaiten didn't know whatever Sen knows," said Ryleigh.

"Maybe," I said, letting myself sound more skeptical than I felt, to give myself courage.

"Why don't you trust me?" It was a question, but it sounded like an accusation.

"I do," I said. "But—"

"Tsk. Whatever. Believe what you want, I guess." Ryleigh's voice was low, but she was clearly annoyed. "It's not like I'm a ninja or anything. It's not like I've spent my *entire life* training to detect threats in social situations." She sped up and walked ahead of me so I couldn't argue.

What was wrong with her? For that matter, what was wrong

with all of us? I thought we'd become friends after our adventure in the Sky Kingdom. I thought we'd become the great Team RyJin DaMoNik. But if that was true, why did we keep fighting with each other? My stomach twinged painfully. What if the Sky Kingdom success had been a fluke? What if we weren't a great team after all?

As we left the pavilion and entered the main palace, my worries mysteriously dissolved and were replaced by mild curiosity. Lord Ebizō led us down a long, narrow hallway with walls made of white coral. Eventually, a door appeared on the right, made of black-lacquered wood etched with golden waves.

Lord Ebizō knocked, and the door was answered by a woman wearing a pale green iridescent gown streaked with silver thread that caught the light in a way that made it look like the gown was made of water. The skirt, neckline, and sleeves were trimmed with pearls and pink coral beads. Her black hair was arranged in complicated loops and knots, and was held back from her forehead by a tiara made of pearls and shimmering emeralds. Her eyes were so dark, they were almost black, and deeply sad, even though she smiled when she saw us.

"Hello, Ebizō-sama," she said.

"Toyotama-hime," he answered with a deep bow. "The landwalkers have arrived."

Do You Get ESPN Down Here?

Toyotama-hime nodded. "I'll tell my father that you're here," she said, and disappeared.

Toyotama-hime . . . I recognized that name. "Wait, isn't she—"

"Ryūjin's daughter," Niko said. "She fell in love with Ho'ori the Hunter when he lost his brother's giant fishhook and came here looking for it. That was back when land creatures could breathe underwater." Lord Ebizō nodded approvingly, and Niko looked pleased with himself.

"I endlessly endeavor to educate my young charges," he informed the lobster-samurai.

"If she married a human, she probably likes humans. That's good, right?" said Danny.

"Didn't Ho'ori kinda betray her, though?" I asked. "She asked him not to watch her when she was giving birth to their baby, but he peeked and saw her in her dragon form. And she was so upset that she left him forever and closed the border between the sea and the land, and that's supposedly why humans can't breathe underwater."

"She's a dragon?" Danny whispered, his eyes widening. "I would not have known."

"Her *dad* is a dragon," Ryleigh pointed out. "What did you expect?"

"Why would she just leave her baby behind like that? And how could she leave her husband to raise their baby all by himself, and then *close the border*? She didn't even give her kid a chance to look for her." Jin looked more upset than I'd ever seen him. *Because that's what Benzaiten did,* I thought. She had never visited or contacted him or his dad until Jin had joined us in December and accidentally met her on the *Takarabune*.

At least Mom had stuck with her mortal husband—Dad—and me instead of running off and never coming back. But what about when Dad had been lost at sea and she'd stopped taking care of me? I took a deep breath. *It wasn't her fault,* I reminded myself sternly. I remembered my last words to her, and guilt and regret bored through me like ugly little worms.

"Maybe Toyotama-hime left because she told Ho'ori not to look, and he looked," Ryleigh said. "Why would you stay with someone you couldn't trust?"

Before anyone could reply, the door opened again, and Toyotama-hime appeared. We fell silent. I hoped she hadn't overheard us discussing her like she was some kind of movie character.

"My father is ready to see you," she said.

We followed her into a spacious room with walls made of mother-of-pearl, all silvery-pink and shimmering in the light cast by glowing white globes that hung from the ceiling. An enormous bench made of seashells, pearls, and coral dominated one side of the room. On it was a snakelike dragon with deep red scales trimmed in gold that matched his golden antlers. His golden eyes gleamed shrewdly at us under eyebrows that were so bushy, I would have laughed if I hadn't been so nervous. His mottled red-and-black snout ended in long white whiskers and a snub nose that needed nose-hair trimming. He smiled and picked something from a row of needle-sharp golden teeth with one of his glinting golden claws.

On each side of the throne were the hime-uo who'd protected us from the ningyo: Mai-no-umi and Koto-no-umi. Then there was Lord Ebizō and three other lobster-samurai, all dressed in armor and holding a couple of spears each in their claws. Toyotoma-hime nodded at them and they relaxed a little, but I could still feel their eyes on me, waiting for me to make a false move.

Then we were bowing to Ryūjin, and Niko was stroking his whiskers and rambling on about "delightful dragon" this and "sumptuous scales" that.

When Niko was finished, Ryūjin waved a lazy paw, an amused smile playing on his long snout of a mouth. "My, what pretty manners you have, little fox. You are an absolute delight!"

Niko usually hated being called little, but apparently he was willing to overlook it when the dragon king did it, because he practically glowed with pride. "Why, thank you, Your Scaliness!" he said. "And may I add that I have been admiring the artwork over there. So refined. So realistic." He gestured at a golden screen on one side of the room. It was painted with a scene of a fisherman riding a sea turtle—Urashima Tarō, who had saved the turtle from being tormented by a bunch of nasty kids. He'd been invited down to Ryūgū-jō as a reward and had fallen in love with another one of Ryūjin's daughters, Oto-hime. He'd spent three days down here, only to find when he went back up to the surface that three hundred years had . . .

Uh-oh.

An arrow of panic zinged through me. How could I have forgotten Hotei's warning about time in the dragon palace? How much time had we wasted? I checked my palms: five—no, six new buds had bloomed. Our time had been cut in half, and now instead of twelve days we only had seven.

I whispered the new number to Jin and Ryleigh. Then I stared at the back of Niko's head and willed him to take a break from spouting compliments about the artwork.

But no sooner had he stopped to take a breath than Ryūjin clapped his paws together and said, "What an absolute delight to meet a fellow art connoisseur! Tell me, how did you come to have such discerning taste? Where were you educated?"

"Ah, my education. Well, Your Divine Dragonity, as you no doubt know, I am the attendant of Takiri-bime, guardian of the Island of Mysteries. But I was educated on the island of Kabeshima, where . . ."

The rest of us exchanged anxious looks. I nudged Niko with my foot as discreetly as I could. But he ignored me. He'd never had an audience like Ryūjin, who was nodding politely and going, "Ah!" and "I say!" and "What an absolute delight!" He reminded me of a fancy, fussy old English nobleman. How was *this* guy in charge of all the creatures of the sea? Or was it an act? Was Ryūjin *trying* to waste our time here?

Danny did one of those coughs that's actually a low-key call-out. "Niko!"

Niko kept yammering on.

"Niko!" Danny fake-coughed again. This time, Niko turned and glared at him.

"*Do* you mind?" he huffed. "Of all the bad-mannered buffoonery!" He turned back to Ryūjin. "As I was saying . . ."

I rushed in before he could get going again. "Your Majesty, we're here because we need to know where the Jewel of the Heart is."

Ryūjin lifted a bushy eyebrow and frowned ever so slightly. "Oh? Why do you need it?"

"We need the Jewel of the Heart so we can, uh . . ." I couldn't help it: an image of Dad flashed in my mind, and I hesitated. Nervously, I cleared my throat to cover the hesitation, and started over. "What I mean to say is, Izanami the Destroyer is trying to collect all three Sacred Treasures so she can use their power to leave Yomi and destroy the Middle Lands. *That's* why we need the Jewel of the Heart. So we can, you know. Destroy it. That's what we want to do. Destroy it. So Izanami doesn't use it to destroy the world." *Ughhhh.* I could practically feel Ryleigh trying not to smack her forehead. "Um, anyway, Benzaiten said you would know where it is."

Ryūjin twirled his whiskers around a long, sharp claw and didn't say anything for a long time. (Side note: What was with all this whisker twirling in Ryūgū-jō? Was everyone just copying the king?) Finally, he murmured, "You intend to destroy it, you say?"

The polite, fussy demeanor was gone, and I saw the fierce dragon ruler behind what I now understood was a mask. I tried to smile like I had nothing to hide. "Uh-huh," I squeaked. *Don't think about Dad. Don't think about Dad.* Why, oh why, did I have to be so bad at lying?

"Hmm." He motioned for Lord Ebizō and Toyotama-hime to come closer, and then clapped his front paws and said, "Sphere of silence!" A giant bubble descended from the ceiling and engulfed the three of them. They had a very long, intense, and inaudible conversation while Niko, Danny, Jin, Ryleigh, and I squirmed under the baleful gaze of the samurai-lobsters.

Niko finally broke the silence with a complaint. "His Iridescence and I were having such a lovely conversation. A few more minutes and he would have been happy to reveal the whereabouts of the jewel, I'm sure of it." He sighed and twirled his whiskers again, à la Lord Ebizō and Ryūjin. "Kids these days just don't appreciate the arts."

"Okay, so, like, Niko? You're acting like a boring old professor and it's, like, super annoying. *And* you were wasting time," Ryleigh shot back in a voice that was very close to the mean-girl voice she used to use.

Jin's eyebrows rose, and Danny said softly, "Bro."

Niko drew himself up. "You of all people should understand the skills of statecraft! I am building a mutually beneficial bond!"

I cut in before things could escalate. "It's just that we've already been here for six days." If foxes could grow pale, that's what was happening to Niko under his fur.

"Jumping jitterbugs," he gasped. "Why didn't you say something? Oh, my claws and paws, we need to move things along!"

One more Middle Lands day slipped by while we waited for Ryūjin to conclude his little meeting, and by the time the Sphere of Silence finally popped, I was practically pulling my hair out with impatience. Toyotama-hime and Lord Ebizō stood on either side of Ryūjin, who combed his eyebrows, cleared his throat, and announced, "I have come to a decision."

I leaned forward. "Yes?"

"No."

"*What?!*" Danny blurted out.

Ryūjin lifted a caterpillar eyebrow and stared at Danny in apparent shock. A stream of bubbles rose up in twin columns from his nose. "My goodness. Did you just say 'What?' to me, young man?"

Niko groaned, and Danny took the hint. "Sorry, I meant 'Excuse me!' Your, um, Your Majesty? Could you please explain your decision?"

Niko howled, "Oh, regal Ryūjin, please forgive me! I have tried and tried—"

Ryūjin silenced Niko with a wave. "Not to worry. I've raised many a young dragon, and they all go through this phase. Now then." He cleared his throat and twirled his whiskers, and the mask of courtly refinement was replaced again by something stern and quietly powerful. "I have sent the Jewel of the Heart away from the Middle Lands, and I don't intend to let anyone find it. As you said, if it falls into the wrong hands, it could be the end of life as we know it."

"But—" I protested.

"Izanami will stop at nothing to get her hands on that jewel. I am prepared to die rather than reveal its location. In fact, I am prepared to let my family and my subjects die if it means I will protect the whole of the Middle Lands." He gazed at each of us in turn. "Are you?"

We looked at each other.

I knew the right answer. It was "Yes, absolutely."

But *was* I ready to sacrifice my family to save the entire world? What about my friends? Was I ready to sacrifice them? Would Danny sacrifice *his* family? Would Jin or Ryleigh? Guilt tugged at the base of my skull. I never should have let them join me on this quest. It wasn't fair to put them in this situation.

And I knew my *real* answer was no. Because if saving the Middle Lands really *was* more important to me than Dad's life, why was I taking the risk of saving Dad first?

It was easier not to think about it at all—to tell myself that we were going after the jewel because we wanted to save Dad *and* protect the Middle Lands, and we wouldn't have to sacrifice anything. Ha. It was what Danny and Jin had been saying all along. The difference was that they really believed it was possible.

As if he'd read my mind—and maybe all of our minds—Ryūjin nodded slowly, grimly. "Yes, that is the beauty and the tragedy of youth: You see only the path to success. You think you have considered all the obstacles and you believe you will prevail. But I, who have lived for millennia, can see what you cannot.

"Izanami will continue to wreak havoc and tragedy in the

Middle Kingdom through the yōkai who swear allegiance to her. But as long as the location of the Jewel of the Heart is kept secret, her power will be limited, and the Middle Kingdom will continue to exist. To reveal the jewel's hiding place to anyone is to risk total destruction and death."

"But Momo said she was going to destroy it!" Ryleigh protested.

"Your intentions may be noble, but your chances of success are practically zero. I will not allow it, and that is final." My spirits sank. What would we do now?

"I am truly sorry," Ryūjin said, not unkindly. His tone had changed again, I noticed with interest, from severe authority back to genteel politeness. It was smooth and polished, almost hypnotically soothing. "To make it up to you, I invite you to stay for a while and enjoy yourselves as my guests. You saw the food we prepared for you out in the pavilion, did you not? I apologize for Sen's rude interruption, by the way. When you return, you'll find that everything has been cleaned up and replaced. And we have planned a dance party later tonight. DRIFTY DRIFTY will be headlining—perhaps you've heard of them on the surface?"

We shook our heads.

"No matter. I know you'll love them. And while you're waiting, we've got a game room, a music room, a parkour course, a library, a gym, and a movie theater. You can watch *Finding Nemo, Raya and the Last Dragon, The Little Mermaid, Avatar: The Last Airbender*..."

I found myself overcome with a lazy, floating sensation. Maybe Ryūjin was right. Maybe we should just hang here for a while. If the jewel was hidden safely away from Izanami, there was no sense in going after it and potentially getting captured or injured or even killed. I wouldn't have to feel responsible for my friends' safety, or the safety of the Middle Lands, or anything, really, because Ryūjin clearly had things under control. I could relax, for once.

"I'd love to take some time to finish writing some poems," said Jin dreamily.

"I've been working on a new shuriken-throwing technique. Maybe I could use the gym," Ryleigh mused.

"Do you get ESPN down here?" Danny asked.

Ryūjin nodded. "You can watch as much basketball as you want."

Danny's eyes lit up and a smile spread across his face. "Sick!" he said.

"And perhaps Niko would like to tour the treasure gallery with me," said Ryūjin silkily. "We have a number of pieces that I am sure you would recognize. I would be delighted to hear what you think of them."

Niko's ears perked up. "Oh, dear me," he said, bowing his head modestly. "My humble opinions are hardly worth hearing." I would have laughed, but instead I found myself thinking about what Ryūjin had said about a movie theater. I loved *Raya and the Last Dragon*. I imagined myself sinking into a soft chair with a huge tub of popcorn as Raya did the battling on the screen instead of me.

Toyotama-hime led us out of the throne room and back down the white coral hallway toward the pavilion. But after a while it began to feel like the hallway was much longer than I remembered. And oddly, I thought I heard my rage monster shouting something from far away, but I couldn't quite make out what it was.

Ryleigh poked me, her forehead all wrinkled and her mouth set in a worried frown. "Which side of the hallway was the throne room on?" she asked. "Like, did we turn right or left when we went in?"

I tried to remember. "Right, I think."

"Right? That's what I thought. But that means we should have turned left coming out. But I'm pretty sure we turned right. Right?"

My brain felt all muddled and confused. Ryleigh was right. We should have turned left because we'd originally turned right. Right? Or had I remembered wrong? Maybe left was right? Or was it wrong, and right was right, after all? I wasn't great at directions, anyway, and now even the words were getting messed up. Meanwhile, I felt like my rage monster was desperately trying to tell me something, but I still couldn't quite catch what it was.

"Are we . . . going the wrong way?" I whispered.

Ryleigh shook her head in frustration. "I don't know. I don't understand. This should be easy for me." She stared at each of her hands, muttering, "Left, right. Right, left," over and over until finally she lifted her head and faced me with a look of deep concern.

"Something is very wrong."

Jellyfish Don't Have Ears

A door slammed behind us, and suddenly my mind was clear and my heart was racing. My rage monster's voice burst through, loud and clear. *Wake up! Wake up! They've fooled us!*

We weren't here to watch movies, write poetry, look at art, practice our ninja moves, or catch up on NBA basketball. We were here to search for the Jewel of the Heart. But in our lazy, hazy fog, we'd followed Toyotama-hime the wrong way down the hall, and now we were standing in a dark, damp, low-ceilinged chamber that was definitely not the party pavilion.

"What's going on?" I demanded. "Let us out, or we'll attack!" I reached for Kusanagi and felt it buzz to life in my hands.

Ryleigh cursed herself under her breath and whipped out her shuriken, and Danny fumbled for his bow and arrows.

See? I'm not so bad, my rage monster seemed to say, and I had to agree. All it really wanted was to protect me. I just wished it didn't also want to raze everything to the ground in the process.

"Put your weapons away." Toyotama-hime's voice was authoritative and confident. I guess being a dragon princess for thousands of years would make anyone confident. "You cannot hurt me. I am a kami." And maybe that, too.

"Kusanagi can," I said.

That's right. Let's go! She doesn't stand a chance against us.

Toyotama-hime raised a palm. "Don't be foolish. You were under my father's influence, and I led you far enough away so that it would fade. I am trying to help you, and the longer we stand here, the more time you waste."

Time?

Time. Oh, no. How many more days had gone by? This was what I got for letting someone else take care of things. I could never let this happen again.

"Why are you helping us?" Ryleigh asked. She didn't seem ready to trust Toyotama-hime, either.

The dragon princess gazed at each of us in turn, and I felt my heart soften. *Stay strong*, I reminded myself.

Toyotama-hime said, "We kami—my father, especially—tend to think we know better than humans what's good for the kami-verse, and sometimes we're wrong. My father does not think you can succeed. But I know that you have succeeded in all of your endeavors so far, and I think that you will succeed in this one. Simply put, I trust you."

Okay. Maybe we could trust her. But I couldn't look her in the eye, because if *she* trusted *me* to get rid of the Jewel of the Heart the moment I found it, she was trusting the wrong person.

"Do you know where the jewel is?" Danny asked, then added hastily, "Your Highness?"

Toyotama-hime shook her head. "It has never been a concern of mine. All I know is that it has been taken far away from the palace."

"Then how are you going to help us?" Ryleigh wanted to know.

"Whatever it is, we have to do it fast. It's already been thirteen days since we started," Danny said, checking his phone.

I looked at my palms. Only five buds were still closed. Five days left. I had to swallow hard so I wouldn't cry.

"Precisely," Toyotama-hime said. "And that is why you must do exactly as I say. Because I may not know where the jewel is, but I do know where my father keeps his memories."

Interesting.

"I don't suppose it's in an unlocked, unguarded room or anything?" Niko ventured.

Toyotama-hime shook her head. "I'm sorry to say that it is both guarded and locked. I have a key that opens any door in the palace, but I can't get you past the guards. No one except my father is allowed into the memory vault."

"So . . ." Jin cleared his throat. "How do we get in?"

"We ask Sen to help us."

My mouth dropped open. "Wait—you mean the same Sen who attacked us in the pavilion?"

Toyotama-hime nodded. "Yes. But she didn't attack you, did she? She only ate the food that was meant for you."

"You mean . . ." Niko gasped. "Of course!"

Another nod. "If not for Sen, you would have eaten the food and fallen completely under the spell of Ryūgū-jō. You would have forgotten your mission and spent decades—even centuries—enjoying yourselves here. You would have remembered yourselves eventually, just like Urashima Tarō did, but it would have been too late."

I saw Sen again in my mind—her fiery, desperate eyes and the way she'd made such a mess of the table. I remembered her screechy voice, and what she'd said: *Get out! Go away now or you'll be sorry!*

"So she *was* talking to me!" I said. "Ryleigh, you were right. She was trying to warn us!"

"I *know*," said Ryleigh. "That's what I *told* you. But you wouldn't listen, would you? It's like you don't trust me anymore. Why are you even friends with me if you don't trust me?"

I stared at her, flabbergasted. Hadn't we just been working together a second ago? I was used to her eye rolls and occasional smugness, but these weird accusations were something new.

"Relax, Ry. We trust you," said Danny.

"Right. Relax. Your solution to everything," Ryleigh muttered under her breath.

"What?"

"Nothing."

"So! Who is Sen, anyway?" Jin asked a little too loudly.

"Long ago, a human fisherman caught a ningyo," Toyotama-hime began. "As you may know, humans are forbidden to eat ningyo or hime-uo or any spirit-world creature they may happen to drag from the sea. But this fisherman cut up the ningyo and distributed pieces of the carcass to his friends. Those friends immediately threw the pieces back into the sea—except for one man, who took his piece home and secretly fed it to his daughter, because he had heard that eating mermaid flesh grants eternal life. The poor girl was doomed to walk the earth forever."

"But that's not so bad," said Danny. "You'd never have to worry about dying! And she probably lived in a time without cars or electricity, right? It must be so cool to see how much the world changes. I totally want to stick around long enough to see, like, flying cars and stuff."

"You may have noticed that she did not remain a young woman," Toyotama-hime said.

"Oh. Right." The light in Danny's eyes dimmed a little as he considered this.

"Imagine living so long that you see all your friends die. And then perhaps you make new friends and outlive them. This happens over and over until one day you throw yourself into the sea, hoping to beg the dragon king for a reprieve. But he refuses. And rather than return to the surface to continue to live while your loved ones continue to die, you lurk around the palace, where everyone is always young and strong, where they shun you for your age and your humanity, but at least they don't die and leave you behind to grieve yet another loss."

So *that* was a fun story. We all stood in silence thinking about how lonely Sen's life must be. No wonder Lord Ebizō hadn't told us her story. It wasn't a great look for Ryūjin. And it must have been much easier to think of Sen as a horrible nuisance rather than as a person who'd survived a long and difficult life.

"But it wasn't her fault she ate the ningyo!" Ryleigh said. "Why should she have to suffer for what her dad did? It's not fair!"

"Sometimes, children must suffer for their parents' mistakes," said Toyotama-hime sadly. "And the parents, in turn, must suffer knowing that they have caused their children pain. Sen's father probably wanders Yomi alone, constantly hearing of his daughter's misery. And this must make him miserable."

"He deserves it. He should have known better," said Ryleigh.

"Perhaps. But I'm sure he suffers deeply nonetheless," Toyotama-hime said.

I couldn't help wondering if she was talking about herself, too, and the way she regretted abandoning Ho'ori and her little baby boy. Did Mom suffer when she thought about not being there for me?

I decided that if I were Toyotama-hime's son I'd still be mad at her. And I got it if Sen was still mad at her father. Because it wasn't fair. Even if your parents felt bad, it didn't change the way things were. Was that mean of me? I didn't know.

Danny frowned. "Sometimes I wonder why everyone thinks the kami are so great."

"We are not perfect," Toyotama-hime agreed.

We followed Toyotama-hime through a maze of tunnels.

"So how can Sen help us?" I asked eventually.

"I have no doubt that you could overcome the giant eels who guard the vault," said Toyotama-hime. "And Kusanagi could easily sever the tentacles of the poisonous jellyfish who form a curtain around the shelves that contain my father's memories. But this would set off alarms that would bring the guards flying. I have heard about the mayhem you caused in Celestial City. I may not agree with my father that you should stay here for the next hundred years to preserve the safety of the Middle Lands, but I also do not intend to allow you to wreak havoc in the palace and destroy my home."

Fair enough. But I still wasn't sure where she was going with this.

"So..."

"Sen cannot die, which means that she can get past the eels

and the jellyfish to retrieve the memory box without having to fight them or cause an uproar. She's always getting into mischief, and no one will believe that it was us who directed her to sneak into the memory vault. By the time anyone figures out which memory was disturbed, you will be well on your way to the Jewel of the Heart."

Jin looked concerned. "Will she be okay, though? I mean, will the eels get out of the way, or is she going to have to get electrocuted and stuff?"

Toyotama-hime sighed and said only, "She will have to endure quite a lot."

"But that's awful!" I already felt sorry for Sen, having suffered all those years for something that wasn't even her fault. And now Toyotama-hime was suggesting we make her deal with poisonous jellyfish and electric eels for my sake. *And Dad's,* I reminded myself, but it didn't make me feel a whole lot better. "Isn't there another way? Ryleigh could use her invisibility hat to sneak past the eels."

"Could I? Do you trust me to do it right?" she deadpanned.

I was too stunned to answer, but Jin saved me by chiming in immediately, "Of course!"

Ryleigh sighed. "Yeah, I guess I could." She looked thoughtful. Maybe out of habit, she began planning out loud. "And I could throw a shadow over you all so that they don't see you. And there's got to be a way that we can get past the jellyfish and take the box without triggering the alarm." Now she was fully back in it, like her old self. "Like, what about rubber gloves? Or maybe you have some scuba gear lying around? That's supposed to protect human skin from jellyfish stings, right?"

Toyotama-hime shook her head. "I could ask the royal jellyfish handler for help, but she'd get suspicious. And we don't have that kind of time."

"What if I sang to them?" said Jin.

"Jellyfish don't have ears," said Toyotama-hime.

"No sense dithering and dawdling," Niko cut in. "We don't even know if Sen will agree to help us."

"I'm sure she will. But you're right. We need to hurry," said Toyotama-hime, and she glided off.

Finally, we came to an iron door at the end of a particularly narrow, dingy hall.

Toyotama-hime knocked three times on the door before opening it. I peeked around her into a space that looked more like a closet than a room. In the center was Sen, sucking forlornly on a pipe. "Go away," she said.

"I've brought the landwalkers," said Toyotama-hime.

At this, Sen stopped sucking and looked up.

"Show me."

Toyotama-hime stepped aside, and Sen stared at us. Now that she wasn't mashing treats into her face and screeching at us to get out, I could see the pain and loneliness in her eyes.

"What year is it up there?" she asked. She glared at Ryleigh's black cargo joggers and wrinkled her already wrinkly nose. "Those trousers are ridiculous."

I could feel Ryleigh bristling next to me. She'd just bought her pants and was kind of proud of them.

"Did you eat?" Sen asked before we could tell her what year it was, or that Ryleigh's pants were actually the height of fashion.

"No," I said.

"Good."

"Thank you for warning us," said Jin, ever the gentleman.

"You're welcome." Sen's wrinkles softened into something a little friendlier than a suspicious scowl. But then her expression hardened again. "Now scram!" she hissed. "Shoo! Leave this place and leave me in peace!"

"They will," said Toyotatama-hime. Her voice had taken on that soothing, hypnotic quality that her father's had back in the throne room. "But first, they need a favor."

Sen immediately clapped her hands over her ears and screamed, "No dragon magic! They can tell me themselves what they want!"

So we did.

Sen's eyes narrowed as she listened. When we finished, she said only, "It sounds like it will hurt."

I felt a little thud in my stomach and thought again that maybe this wasn't such a great idea. How could we ask her to do this scary, painful thing just so that we wouldn't have to risk getting hurt or causing some chaos in the palace?

"Is there anything we can give you as a reward?" Ryleigh asked.

Sen scoffed and turned her back on us. "Ha. I wish."

"What is it?" Ryleigh pressed her. "You obviously want something. How do you know we can't give it to you?"

"No one can give me what I want," Sen said bitterly. "Trust me, I've asked people with more power than you."

Here, Toyotama-hime floated forward and bent down to whisper in Sen's ear. She sat bolt upright, as if electrified, then glared at the dragon princess, who nodded her head. Sen turned slowly to face us again. She focused directly on me, and I could tell that if she'd had eyebrows, they'd have been drawn down in a fierce scowl. "Toyotama-hime says you carry Kusanagi, the Sword of the Wind."

I nodded, suddenly nervous. Surely, she didn't think I would trade my sword for the memory box! If so, she was wrong. I would never give it to her. Kusanagi might be hugely problematic, but it was my power—I mean, my problem. Besides, I needed it to defeat Izanami. And without it, I was nobody—just an anxious girl with a connection to the spirit dimension and nowhere to put her anger. A girl who'd have to rely on her friends to carry her burdens. I couldn't be that girl. I *needed* that sword or everything would fall apart.

"You can't have it." It was Danny. He took a step closer to me. "It's Momo's, and she earned it fair and square. And we need it to complete our mission. And it wouldn't work for you, anyway. It chooses who gets to use it." Jin and Ryleigh stepped closer to me, too. I felt a little whoosh of gratitude and relief. Maybe we weren't a complete disaster of a team.

Sen rolled her eyes and snorted. "I don't *want* it. I want you to use it."

Oh. That was more reasonable. Maybe.

"For what?" I asked.

She gestured for me to lean down so she could whisper in my ear.

"But . . . but . . ." was all I could say when she finished. "Are you serious?"

"Deadly serious."

Who Was That Guy?

She said it with a grin, but her eyes were hard.

I stared at her for a moment, and then shook my head. "I can't do it. I'm sorry. We'll figure out some other way to find the jewel."

"No, you won't," she said. "You'll fail for sure."

"What do you want?" Danny asked.

"That's between Momo and me," she said. And when I tried to tell the others what she'd asked for, I found that the words got stuck halfway between my brain and my tongue. There must have been something magic about that secret.

"We can do it without you. We're Team RyJin DaMoNik," Danny said stoutly. "We'll go with our first plan. Ryleigh uses her shadow-casting to get us past the eels. Or maybe we can find the ningyo who wanted Jin's song to help us. Can she get around the jellyfish?"

"Ningyo are terrified of jellyfish," Sen jeered.

"Okay, okay," said Danny. "So . . . one of us goes in and just, you know. Takes the box."

"And dies within minutes? Not on my watch!" Niko sprang forward. "I won't allow it."

"Knowingly sending a friend to die would be the same as killing them," Sen said. Her mouth curled into a smug little smile. "It would be murder."

We looked at each other. It *would* be murder. Or it would feel like murder, anyway. Sen's proposal was starting to look like our only option. But I still couldn't bring myself to agree to her price, which in the end also boiled down to murder.

Sen seemed to sense my hesitation. "Child of Takiri-bime. Granddaughter of Susano'o. Do you know my story?" she said quietly.

I nodded.

"Then you know that I've wandered the earth for centuries without a single friend. My body is old and tired and it aches all the time, and I've lost everything and everyone I've ever loved. And did I ever do anything to deserve any of it? No! But when I begged Ryūjin to lift the curse, he said my story was a warning to the landwalkers to respect the creatures of the sea. So now I stay here to remind everyone how they've made me suffer, but they don't even care. Just do this one thing for me, and I can be happy again."

Her eyes glittered in the dark. No one said anything. She did seem miserable. Maybe it would be a good thing to give her what she wanted.

And yet.

Niko cleared his throat. "The minutes are marching onward," he said gently. "We must make up our minds."

I still wasn't sure I'd be able to do what Sen had asked me to do. But I could promise to do it order to get what I wanted. I had to. For Dad.

"All right," I said. "I'll do it."

Another false promise. How many of these was I going to have to make? How long could I continue to put Dad's life ahead of the lives and desires of others?

More memories flashed in my head. Dad serving me chocolate chip pancakes in bed on my birthday. Dad carrying me home on Halloween night after I fell and hurt my knee and ruined my costume (a can of Pringles that we'd made together out of poster board) and buying me bags and bags of candy at the store the next day to make up for my reduced trick-or-treating time. And finally, again, Dad suffering in that dirty seawater. Izanami smiling.

If I did what Sen asked, she'd be free. And if I did what Izanami asked, Dad would be free. Maybe when Daikoku had talked about moving beyond destruction, she'd meant understanding that sometimes you had to destroy things in order to achieve something good, like freeing innocent people.

Could that really be it, though? It didn't feel quite right.

On the other hand, I didn't have much of a choice if I wanted that box of memories.

"Swear on your sword," said Sen.

Reluctantly, I pulled Kusanagi out of the backpack and laid my hand next to hers on the blade. "I promise that if you bring us Ryūjin's memory of where the Jewel of the Heart is hidden, I will . . ." I gulped.

"You will . . . ?" she prompted me.

"I will do what you've asked."

"And if you don't, may Kusanagi never work for you again," she added.

"And if I don't, may Kusanagi never work for me again," I repeated miserably.

"Good." She nodded. "Now follow me."

We convinced Sen to wear Ryleigh's invisibility hat so that she could at least make it past the eels and into the memory vault without getting electrocuted. Then we waited in the shadows of the hall around the corner from the vault for so long that I began to wonder if Sen had just run away with the hat. Finally, she appeared in front of us, pale and panting.

She sank to her knees and put down a red lacquered box covered with intricate, swirling brushwork. I couldn't bear to look at her; her face and neck were bleeding and spiked with little red needles, as were her hands and wrists. But Toyotama-hime knelt and took a little glass bottle out of her sleeve. She pulled out the stopper and dabbed a drop of shining green liquid on each of Sen's palms. The liquid stretched and curled like vines until it had wrapped itself all around Sen's fingers and wrists, and then slipped under her raggedy sleeves. More green tendrils soon spread around Sen's neck and face. She sighed, and her head sagged to her chest as the jagged red spikes twisted out of her skin and dissolved.

"Whoa. Are you healing her?" Danny asked.

"Her body is healing itself," said Toyotama-hime. "The medicine speeds the process and relieves her of her pain."

I knelt down next to Sen and took her wrinkled little hand in mine. "Thank you, Sen," I said. I didn't know what else to say. It didn't feel like enough.

But she sighed and gave my hand the slightest squeeze, like she understood.

"Let's open the box," said Ryleigh. She reached for it. "I hope it's the right one."

"Of course it's the right one. Can't you read?" Sen mumbled.

On closer inspection, I saw that what I had originally assumed was just artwork was, in fact, script in a language I couldn't understand.

"It says, 'The jewel leaves Ryūgū-jō,'" said Toyotama-hime.

We gathered around the box while Ryleigh lifted the lid. A cloud of black smoke wafted up and separated into gray threads that separated into more threads of paler gray, and all the curls of smoke twisted and twined around each other until they'd formed a hazy picture. I recognized the throne room. Ryūjin sat on his throne, facing a tall figure in a plain brown robe with the hood pulled so far forward that I couldn't see a face.

The dragon king handed over a silk-wrapped package and bowed. The robed figure accepted the package, bowed, and left the room, and the image dissolved back into smoke.

"That's it? Who was that guy?" Danny asked. But Toyotama-hime only shook her head.

"I wasn't there," she said apologetically. "It looks like a private meeting."

I sank to the floor and put my head in my hands. What were we going to do now?

"It's probably someone trustworthy, right?" said Jin doubtfully. "Ryūjin wouldn't give the jewel to just anyone."

"It doesn't matter. We don't even know where he went."

"But we can't give up now," Danny argued. "We still have to save your dad."

"And destroy the jewel," Ryleigh said. "Just because Ryūjin trusted that guy with it doesn't mean we should."

Sen cackled. "That's the spirit, ninja girl! Trust no one. And keep your wits and weapons about you, because you'll need them once you've entered the land of the Spider People."

We all turned to stare at her. "The land of the who?" Danny asked. "What are you talking about?"

"I saw where Mr. Brown Robe went after he left the throne room. I followed him! No one cares what ugly old Sen sees or hears, so she sees and hears everything," she said.

"Why didn't you say something right away?" Ryleigh demanded.

Sen only cackled again.

Toyotama-hime said, "Sen can take you to the portal that will bring you there. Of course, you'll need to come up with a plan to gain passage through the territory."

Of course.

"Surely there's another alternative," said Niko. "I would really rather not—"

"No other way," said Sen decisively, and she tugged on Toyotama-hime's sleeve. "Come on, already!"

Toyotama-hime nodded at us and floated down the corridor with Sen hobbling after her.

We emerged onto a big balcony on the inside of a huge circular tower. The balcony was ringed with a row of tiny little arches about eight inches high—totally useless as far as protective barriers went.

"Please don't tell me we have to jump," Danny moaned.

"Why do we always have to be climbing rope ladders up cliffs and jumping off platforms? Why can't someone just build, like, a flat, one-story mansion? Or a decent set of stairs with railings?"

"We're in the water, remember?" Jin said. "Look." He pointed at a herd of giant seahorses bobbing just below us.

Toyotama-hime clapped her hands, and the seahorses rose up, turned their backs, and hooked their curly tails around the arches.

"Hop on!" cried Sen. She clambered onto the back of the seahorse closest to her and laughed at our clumsiness as we did the same.

"Wait," Toyotama-hime said. "A word of advice before you go." Her gaze lingered on each of us in turn for so long that I began to get nervous about how many days we were wasting. Finally, she spoke. "The biggest mistake I ever made was believing that I had to make myself smaller to be loved and accepted. I ran away rather than stay in my true form, and as a result I lost the two people I treasured most in the kami-verse. We all deserve to live in our full beauty and power, no matter how ugly or worthless we have been made to believe we are. And if you are to prevail, you must allow others to do the same." She paused and looked so sad, I thought she might start to cry. But instead, she smiled at us and said, "Farewell. Good luck."

No one said a word as we floated up and away from the platform. I thought about what Toyotama-hime had said. It seemed encouraging at first: your standard hero pep talk, where the wizard or the wise queen tells the hero that they can win if only they can embrace their true selves. And it sounded a lot like what Daikoku had said about embracing my own source of power. But the more I thought about it, the more discouraged I got. Because I knew I was at my most powerful when my rage monster connected with Kusanagi.

There's nothing wrong with being angry, my rage monster protested. *It makes you act instead of being afraid or sad! It gives you the power to protect and defend! The power to make wrong things right!*

True. But then why couldn't I just want to make things right? Why did I want to hurt the people who made things wrong, like that poor ningyo? Or even Kiki on the bus. I *liked* the thrum of power I felt when I was angry. Did that mean I was falling under Kusanagi's influence? How was I supposed to fight the very thing that made me strong?

Hundreds of doorways, each with its own platform, opened into the tower. Above each doorway was a sign with the name of a famous place, like the Empire State Building and the South Pole, or a place I'd never heard of, like Shoup Park and Nuuk. I caught glimpses of a silver skyscraper, a howling blizzard, a burbling creek under sunlit redwood trees, and a cluster of brightly colored wooden buildings on a grassy coastline.

We stopped at a sign that had a painting of a spider with eight bloodshot eyes, long, hairy legs, and a smile full of vicious-looking fangs. This doorway showed a narrow, overgrown dirt path through a forest in the middle of the night. My stomach clenched, and I heard Niko groan.

"Are we sure this is the one we want?" he said in a very small voice.

It was.

We clustered at the doorway and peeked through. The forest on the other side reminded me of every evil forest in every fairy tale I'd ever read. Tree branches loomed over a narrow path, draped with lichen that hung down like hair. An owl hooted. Something scurried across the path and scrabbled up a tree. A short distance ahead, moonlight ventured feebly through the canopy, casting just enough light to reveal a huge spiderweb that trembled as we watched. Was it the wind? Or was it something else?

Yeah, totally not creepy at all. Totally not the kind of place where murderous spiders might be lying in wait to pounce on you, wrap you up in horrible sticky thread, and suck down your blood the way Danny sucked down milkshakes.

"It's haunted by evil ghosts," Sen said cheerfully.

Great.

"Come on, guys. We've never lost a battle with yōkai," Danny said. "We've totally got this." I watched as he shot a careful glance at Ryleigh, who looked grim and didn't say anything.

"Wait, wait!" Sen screeched. "I've got something for you!" She dug into her pockets and held out two items on her wrinkly palms. One was a silk pouch. The other was a gold coin.

"Here," she said, and thrust the pouch at Jin. "You look like the one to trust with this. And you can take this." She pressed the coin into Ryleigh's palm.

"What am I supposed to do with this?" Ryleigh asked.

Sen rolled her eyes. "You figure it out!"

Jin loosened the strings that kept the pouch closed and pulled out a little glass bottle that looked suspiciously like the one that had held Toyotama-hime's healing serum.

"It's Toyotama-hime's healing serum!" Sen crowed. "One dose will heal anything but death."

Jin gave her a sideways look. "Did you by any chance—"

"Never mind where I got it," Sen said. "Now go, before you waste any more time!"

We stepped up to the doorway and clustered together in a group. This new challenge seemed to be pulling us back together, so even though I was scared, I was also a little grateful. Sen fixed her glittering black scowl on me and said, "Remember—you owe me!" I nodded and hoped that doing dark things to achieve good things was the secret to unlocking Kusanagi's power.

"Ready?" Danny said. We nodded. "On three. One, two, three!"

Just Keep Walking

"This isn't so bad," Danny said.

I knew he was lying because let me tell you—being in the forest was much worse than looking at it. From the outside, there had been nothing to fear except what lay ahead. On the inside, it felt like there was plenty to fear, not just ahead, but also behind, above, and to the left and right. My skin prickled and my hair stood on end, as if my body had turned itself into a danger antenna. The air felt heavy and damp and thick with ill will.

Kusanagi called to me from my backpack: *Hey! Lemme out! You need me for protection!* I drew it out of the backpack and immediately felt a little bit safer.

"This place feels alive," Jin muttered.

"It's a forest with trees and animals and stuff. Of course it feels alive," Danny said, his voice clipped and short.

"That's not what I mean, and you know it," said Jin calmly, as if he knew Danny was only being rude because he was scared, too. "It feels, like, *alive*-alive. Like it's watching us. Like it's aware, like it has feelings. Like it's . . . what's the word?"

"Sentient," said Niko, because of course.

"Yeah, that. Sentient."

"Sentient forests are never good. We've made a massive mistake," Niko whined softly.

As if to confirm our fears, the leaves above us began to rustle and sigh, even though there was no wind. We froze, instinctively standing back to back, weapons out.

At first, it was just indistinct murmuring, but the more I listened, the more I thought I could make out actual words.

Go away. You are not wanted here.

"Did you hear that?" I whispered.

"Sounds like someone doesn't want us here," Danny joked.

"Look, if someone's gonna attack, they're gonna attack whether we're standing around doing nothing or whether we're walking. Let's just go," Ryleigh said.

We followed Ryleigh in single file: first Jin, holding Danny's phone flashlight up high and humming something low and soothing under his breath. Then came Danny with his bow and arrow drawn. Niko and I brought up the rear. Niko whined softly to himself about surprise attacks always coming from behind and what had he done to deserve this, it wasn't his idea to go on this wild-goose chase, what would Mom say when she found out where we were and what he'd let us do, et cetera, et cetera. . . .

"Shh!" I shushed him, even though his complaining was kind of comforting in its own way. It made things feel normal, somehow. When he stopped, the space he'd been filling with his words felt enormous. Thank goodness for Jin and his humming.

I did my best to walk like a ninja, the way Ryleigh had taught me: rolling my weight slowly from heel to toe, every nerve aware of every divot and pebble under my foot. But inevitably I stepped on a twig, which caused Danny to whirl around, nearly knocking me over and making me squawk in alarm.

"Shhh!" Ryleigh hissed from the front. "Can't you people do anything right? All you have to do is walk!"

"Sorry," I mumbled. In my head I added, *We can't all be perfect, you jerk.*

Should we get her? Let's get her! Or Danny—he's the one who scared you!

"No!" I snapped at my rage monster, horrified. "What is wrong with you?"

"Shh!" Ryleigh said again.

"Who are you talking to?" Danny whispered.

"Uh . . ." Had I just said that out loud? "No one. Sorry."

Get a grip, I told myself. *We're a team.* Ryleigh might once have been my worst enemy—or more accurately, my biggest bully—but now we were friends. Real friends. I knew that Ryleigh was probably nervous, too. She demanded a lot of herself, and she expected everyone around her to push themselves as hard as she did. And when people fell short of her high expectations, she tended to be pretty hard on them—though not nearly as hard as she was on herself when she fell short. Was that why she was being so snippy? Could she actually be mad at *herself*?

Now that I was wondering if Ryleigh might be upset at herself, I felt less angry at her. But now that I wasn't really angry, I started feeling scared again. Fear sat on my shoulder as we walked. It made me flinch when something scrambled up a tree trunk and shook the branches above us. It made me want to cry when the trees whispered to each other: *Four human children and a fox. A bow and arrow. A sword. Danger.*

"It can still see all of us," I whispered. I didn't like being scared. I needed to get angry again. I needed to want to fight whatever was out there.

"Yeah, but you know what? I think *it's* afraid of *us*," whispered Danny.

Ooh. Good point. I felt my fear grow a little lighter.

"That doesn't make it any less dangerous for us," Niko countered. "A frightened enemy is a deadly enemy."

Also a good point. Fantastic. The fear settled back down, wrapped its strong, skinny arms around my neck, and dug its dirty nails into my skin.

"Remember why we're here," said Jin. "That always helps me."

So I thought about Dad. The last time I'd seen him was when he'd taken me to the mall and bought me a bag of Auntie Anne's cinnamon-sugar pretzel bites. I wished I'd brought some with me so he could have one the moment I rescued him. I thought about how good it would feel to see him and hug him, and maybe even bring him back home and show Mom once again that I could take care of myself. Ha.

Aaaand there was that wave of guilt again. Okay, fine. I would succeed so that I could tell Mom that I loved her and that I was sorry for saying those mean things to her.

Of course, if we failed to find the jewel, none of that would happen because we'd all be dead. *Sigh.* At least I wasn't scared anymore. Now I was just suffocating with guilt and anxiety.

Thankfully, Jin had begun to sing:

Just keep walking,
Just keep walking,
Just keep walking, walking, walking . . .

"You know, I think I like it better when you sing your own songs," Danny grumbled.

"Oh, really? You once told me my songs were too mushy," said Jin.

"I never said that," Danny protested. "I just said they were too mushy for *me*."

"Okay, how about this?" Jin cleared his throat and sang,

Fear is walking with us but we won't let it stop us
We'll keep walking in the dark and holding on to light
As long as I've got you, as long as you've got me
Even when it's dark and cold, we will be all right.

"Better," said Danny. "You're good at that stuff."

"You gotta admit that 'just keep walking' is pretty catchy, though," said Jin.

Hoping to keep the good vibes going, I decided to get Niko on board as well. "What about you, Niko?" I asked. "Do you like Jin's original songs better, or his covers?"

Niko said, "YAAAAAA!"

Then his voice came from above: "It's an ambush! It's a trap! Run for your lives!"

We ran. There was a *crack* and a *whoosh* and I was falling—but only for a little bit, because I was stopped by a net.

Whew.

Then the net dropped. I screamed and flailed pointlessly until—*snap*—I jerked to a stop again. At least one, maybe two of the others were trapped with me.

We swung for a moment in the darkness. Then Ryleigh's voice called down from somewhere above us. "You guys okay?"

"Ungh. Not exactly," Danny grunted next to me. "But at least I'm not a pile of broken bones at the bottom of a deep, dark pit."

We swung for another moment while that sank in. "On the other hand, we're smushed together in a giant net and we're dangling above who knows what," I said. I didn't want to think about what could be down there in the dark. Snakes? Alligators?

"What happened?" asked Jin from right behind me. "Why are we down here and you're up there?"

"You panicked," said Ryleigh's voice. "You listened to Niko and ran. You should never run when someone's been trapped like that—there's going to be other traps lying around and you'll run right into one. Which is what you did."

"Thanks. I'll try to remember that thirty seconds ago," Danny said, a little bitterly.

"Sorry," Ryleigh said.

"Also, can whoever's got their foot in my face get their foot out of my face?"

"Sorry, I think that's me," Jin said.

"Can you get us out of here?" I called up to Ryleigh.

"I can try. But I don't want to get caught by whoever set this trap."

Old, angry-at-Ryleigh me thought, *She's going to abandon us. Typical.*

But then she said, "I'm gonna try to set Niko free first. And then we can both help you." Oops. Why had I assumed the worst of her? Why hadn't I just admired her skill and believed she was going to help? I became aware of Niko howling in the background, and I felt bad about underestimating Ryleigh. And then I heard her go, "Unh." Then came a noise that sounded suspiciously like the body of a twelve-year-old ninja falling to the ground.

"Ryleigh?" Danny's voice cracked with panic.

"Ryleigh!" Now Jin and I were shouting, too. No point in being quiet anymore if we were trapped anyway.

No answer. Now I felt *really* bad.

"Can anyone see her? What happened?" I asked the others.

But the only answer I got was silence. And just as I began to wonder why, I found myself staring into eight beady black eyes and a pair of black fangs. The eyes loomed closer and I opened my mouth to scream, but before I could, there was a sudden sharp pain in my leg, and the world went dark.

I woke to the sound of a high, reedy voice singing to itself.

Spin, spin, silk and steel
Spin like a top, spin like a wheel
We've trapped you good, we've wrapped you tight
You'll never get away, try as hard as you might!

My head ached and my body felt numb and heavy, except for the places where it felt prickly and on fire, like when your foot falls asleep.

Spin, spin, silk and steel, the voice sang.

Who was spinning? Was it me? It sure felt like it.

Spin like a top, spin like a wheel.

I waded my way through brain fog as thick as cotton. Where was I and why did I feel so awful?

We've trapped you good, we've wrapped you tight—

I was trapped—we were trapped. And wrapped. Images flashed through my mind: Niko being swept into the trees . . . falling . . . the net . . . those eyes . . .

You'll never get away, try as hard as you might!

The realization struck me, sharp and bright and sudden as one of Ryleigh's shuriken. My heart lurched and I opened my eyes to find myself on the floor of a large, candlelit room—a cave, by the looks of it, with rock walls that curved into a rock ceiling. Nearby were three person-sized bundles and one fox-sized bundle. And just as I'd feared, a little farther off was a gigantic, hairy, horrible spider as big as a couch, clicking its feet and rocking to and fro in time to the music.

But it wasn't the spider who was singing. It was a girl about my age.

Good Boy, Jojo!

She was pale and thin, dressed in what looked like a brown sack. She wore a crown of daisies, and strands of her brown hair fell out of a messy ponytail tied with a bit of string. She was sitting on a rock in the middle of the room and sharpening an evil-looking knife as she sang that awful song. She paused for a moment to reach into a sack by her side and pulled out a wad of shiny string about the size of a soccer ball. She tossed it to the spider, which sank its fangs into the ball and tore away a patch of string to reveal a giant insect head, its big buggy eyes staring blankly out at nothing. I swallowed a scream and watched the spider attack the exposed bit of dead fly and gulp down its liquefied insides. Green goo dripped to the floor as the spider slurped and gurgled. I had to close my eyes.

When I opened them again, the girl was leaning over me and grinning.

"Gross, huh?" She glanced over her shoulder at the spider, then back at me. "Don't worry. He won't eat you. He'll be as happy as a kitten as soon as he's done with his fly."

That would have been more comforting if my entire body

from my ankles to my neck hadn't been bound with the same shiny string that was wrapped around the fly.

"Who are you?" I asked. My tongue felt thick and doughy. "Where am I?"

"I'm Yasome," said the girl. "And you're in the dungeon."

"Whose dungeon?" came Jin's voice.

"The Tsuchigumo," Yasome replied.

Tsuchigumo. The Spider People.

"Are you also a prisoner, perhaps?" Niko asked. "And now you must earn your keep by caring for other captives? Ah-choo!" He sniffled. "Forgive me. I'm allergic to daisies."

Yasome snorted. "I am the princess of the Tsuchigumo clan, you nincompoop."

"But—but—" Niko stammered.

"Yeah, yeah, yeah." Yasome sighed heavily. "You learned that the Tsuchigumo were these horrible, people-eating spiders who live in holes in the dirt. Am I right?"

"Err...," said Niko. "Umm..."

"That's wrong?" I asked timidly.

"Yes, it's wrong!" Yasome nearly shouted. "It's one hundred percent, totally, completely wrong. It's just a mean, dirty lie that the Yamato clan spread about us when they came up into these mountains with the evil sword Kusanagi and wiped out our village. They literally drove us underground."

I gasped and hurriedly turned it into a cough. Kusanagi had destroyed *an entire clan of people?*

Maybe she was lying. It would make me feel a whole lot better if the Tsuchigumo had been an evil, murderous clan who attacked the surrounding villages with their giant poisonous spiders, and the Yamato had only wiped them out to protect innocent citizens.

"Who are the Yamato clan?" Danny asked from a few feet away.

Yasome sighed again. "They're the big bullies who came stomping into our mountains like they owned us, and they treated us like we were—well, like we were horrible dirty spiders."

The spider abruptly dropped his fly carcass and made a sound that was halfway between a groan and a burp. (In case you're wondering, spider burps smell like week-old garbage.)

"I know, Jojo, I know," Yasome crooned at him. She put down her knife so she could reach out and scratch the spot just above its eight eyes. "Spiders aren't horrible or dirty, are they? Spiders are good. You're a good boy, aren't you, Jojo?" The spider purred in response.

"But wasn't that, like, a thousand years ago?" Ryleigh asked.

"Yeah. A thousand years of living underground," said Yasome. "Because we refused to pay tribute to that awful Prince Takeru. He killed our queen and swore that if he ever saw signs of us again, he wouldn't stop until he'd killed off every last one of us."

"Ah-choo!" Niko sneezed. "I wish I had a tissue," he said plaintively, but Yasome ignored him.

I thought about my theory of moving beyond destruction, about how sometimes you have to destroy things to achieve something good. Maybe there had been a noble purpose to Prince Takeru's invasion and his threat. But what? What could possibly justify massacring Yasome's people?

"Oh, dear! What a terrible tale," Niko said. "Only—ahem. In all my hundred years, I've never even heard a hint of it."

Yes! Niko had a point. How could Yasome's story be true if even Niko had never heard of it? Maybe she *was* making it all up.

"Yeah, well. It's hard to get your story out when you've been driven underground," said Yasome.

"That sounds like what my tutor says," Jin put in. "History is written by the powerful. You hardly ever read about what happened from the point of view of the oppressed. So if the Yamato clan used Kusanagi to defeat you, it makes sense that they would portray you as monsters because they saw themselves as the good guys. And your story's been, like, erased from history. It's like the way Mokugon-bake burns up books to spread fear and ignorance."

I wanted to tell Jin not to encourage her. But what if he was right? What if the story that Niko and I knew had survived because Mokugon-bake had somehow burned up Yasome's story centuries ago to keep it from spreading? Even worse, if Yasome's version was true, what did that say about Kusanagi? Was Prince Takeru one of those mortals who Daikoku had warned me about, who eventually fell under Kusanagi's control? Was that my destiny? Just the thought made my stomach hurt.

"I'm, um. I'm sorry that happened to you," I said to Yasome. *Please let her not have found Kusanagi,* I prayed silently. But I'd dropped it when we'd fallen into the trap.

"*Are* you sorry, though?" Yasome asked, her voice prickly with suspicion.

"Well, yeah! I . . . I . . ."

"Because I saw you carrying a sword earlier. Yeah, that's right. I saw it all." She was glaring at me with unmistakable hostility now. "I was out walking Jojo, here, and the five of you appeared out of nowhere, armed with deadly weapons. Which I've confiscated, by the way."

Oh, no.

"Where are they?" Danny asked.

"In a safe place," said Yasome, and I wanted to weep—and also to scream, "GIVE ME BACK MY SWORD!"

I realized with sudden dismay that I wanted it back even if it *had* taken over Prince Takeru's spirit and wiped out Yasome's village.

No, I told myself. *Takeru was a prince. I'm just a girl.* Conquering was what princes did back then. *I* wasn't planning to colonize innocent people. In fact, it was the opposite—I wanted to keep Izanami from colonizing the Middle Lands. Theoretically. Once I'd rescued Dad.

"You're the only one who wasn't armed." Yasome looked over her shoulder to where Jin's voice had come from. "But that doesn't mean you're not dangerous."

She walked over to Niko next and nudged him with her toe. He sniffled pitifully. "And then there's you. You're clearly magic. I can see it in your aura."

As scared as I was, I couldn't help thinking, *Niko will like that.* Sure enough, the Niko-shaped bundle stopped sniffling and gave a self-satisfied little wriggle before sneezing twice.

"But those weapons were for self-defense!" Danny protested. "We're not here to start a fight or hurt anyone. We're on a quest! We're just passing through!"

"You entered Tsuchigumo territory without permission, and you had weapons. And weapons are for hurting people. That's literally their only purpose."

"Uh. If you don't mind my asking," Ryleigh said, "what are you going to do with us?"

"Oh! Jojo and I are going to bring you to my mom—Itsuma-hime to you. Aren't we, Jojo?" She turned to Jojo again, and he waggled his behind obligingly. "And then everyone will see that I'm just as important to the clan as my siblings. Right, Jojo?" Jojo panted like a dog, only it was less of a pant and more of a sickening raspy gurgle that made my skin crawl. "Mama's going to be so impressed, isn't she? And who's the good boy who helped me? Was it you? Was it you, Jojo?"

More horrible gurgle-panting. Jojo clicked his pincers and tapped his feet.

"That's right, good boy. It *was* you!" Yasome reached into her sack and pulled out another bundle, which she tossed down a corridor that led out of the cave. "Fetch!" The spider scuttled off after the bundle, and in a couple of seconds, I heard it tear into the dead insect and start slurping it down.

"We're on a quest," Danny tried again. "Our whole mission is to save the Middle Lands from attack. We're your allies. Believe me, you want to let us go."

"Save it for my mom. As far as I know, you're an intruder. Even though you *are* kind of cute." Yasome whistled, and Jojo came galloping back. "Jojo, bodies up!" she said. Jojo trotted over to the nearest bundle—Danny—and closed his jaws on Danny's shoulder.

"Danny!" I screamed.

Danny yelled and thrashed as Jojo dragged him across the floor toward a waiting cart that I hadn't noticed before. But Danny could have been a fuzzy little caterpillar as far as Jojo was concerned.

I struggled helplessly inside my cocoon. "Put him down!"

"Call off your spider!" Ryleigh shouted.

"Please, please stop!" Jin begged.

We watched in anguish as Jojo lifted Danny off the floor and deposited him in the cart with no effort at all. Danny rolled across the boards like a pencil until he came to rest with a gentle bump at the end of the cart.

"Good boy, Jojo!" said Yasome. "Now do the rest. Bodies up!"

One by one, we were dragged to the cart and tossed in. A few minutes later, Jojo had been harnessed to the front of the cart and Yasome was driving it down a long, dark corridor, whistling happily to herself.

"Her mom will understand, right?" I whispered. "Her mom's the queen. The queen has to do what's best for her people, and what's best for her people will be to let us go, right?"

"Or she may decide to ingratiate herself with Izanami," said Niko gloomily. "Despite what Yasome says, this is a forest of dark creatures with dark cravings. The Tsuchigumo are like onryō—ghosts whose desire for vengeance is so strong that it allows them to stay in the Middle Lands so they can get back at the people who hurt them. And if they find out about *you-know-what*, we're dead as dodo birds. Ah-choo!"

"What's *you-know-what*?" Danny asked.

"You know! A certain sword once belonging to a certain girl's grandfather? The reason the Tsuchigumo's spirits have stayed in the forest instead of going to Yomi?"

"Ohhh, right."

"The Tsuchigumo clearly hate and fear Kusanagi and all it represents with a depth that defies definition," Niko said. "We cannot under any circumstances allow them to discover it."

"Niko, shhhh!" I whisper-screamed. "Follow your own advice!"

"Too late," Yasome sang out from the driver's seat. "You guys really need to learn how to talk more quietly. I know everything now. So you can just relax and prepare to face your doom."

Not Comfortable

It turns out that relaxing and preparing to face your doom are two mutually exclusive activities.

And Niko was no help, of course. "We're cooked as cabbage! We're finished as French fries!" he wailed. "We're crushed as croutons! Ah-choo!"

"Be quiet and let us think!" Ryleigh hissed. "I think Momo's right. If the queen is a good queen—"

Niko stopped wailing long enough to whisper, "How can she be good? Yasome could be making things up. I'm telling you, every story I've ever heard about the Tsuchigumo says they're evil monsters!"

"Just because you've never heard their side of the story before doesn't mean it's wrong and you're right," said Jin. "I believe Yasome."

"Me too," said Danny and Ryleigh.

As for me, I didn't want to believe Yasome's story. I didn't want Kusanagi to be a bloodthirsty, culture-destroying weapon. I'd feel a lot better if the Tsuchigumo were evil, and Prince Takeru and Kusanagi had been forced to wipe them out for the greater good.

"Giant spiders. That's all I'll say," said Niko, sniffling.

"Anyway," Ryleigh said in her Ryleigh-est voice, "If we tell Itsuma-hime that we're trying to save the Middle Lands, she'll see that we're on the same side. We just have to convince her that we're telling the truth."

I winced. *Truth.* The word felt like an accusation.

The cart came to an abrupt halt, and Yasome's voice said, "Hey, I gotta run and get something. Don't go anywhere while I'm gone!" She chuckled to herself, and I wished I could make a face at her.

"Maybe Jin's voice will work on them," said Ryleigh.

"You know I don't use my voice to lie," Jin warned her.

"Tell her we're on a quest," said Ryleigh. "That's true, right? A quest to find the Jewel of the Heart so we can save the Middle Lands. That's what we told Ryūjin."

"But you know that's not the whole truth."

"This is to *save Momo's dad,* Jin," said Danny. "Just break the rules, for once."

"It's to save the Middle Lands. So it's not breaking the rules," said Ryleigh firmly, almost like she was arguing with Danny, and suddenly I was sure she was actually going to try to make me destroy the jewel as soon as we found it. That had been her original argument, after all. I hoped I wouldn't have to fight her on it.

"If you don't do it when we meet the queen, we might not get another chance," Ryleigh added ominously.

"Don't do what?" Yasome's face appeared over the side of the cart.

"Ah-choo!" said Niko.

"None of your business," said Ryleigh.

"It *is* my business since I'm the one that captured you, but whatever." Yasome heaved a big sack onto the driver's seat and clambered up next to it. "Giddyap, Jojo!"

"It's not a lie," Ryleigh whispered to Jin once we were rolling again.

Jin sighed. "Yeah, yeah. I'm still not comfortable with it."

Speaking of not feeling comfortable, something else kept digging its sharp little knife point into my thoughts: I couldn't stop thinking about Kusanagi. Where was it? How could I get it back? I felt like my body was full of bees and it wouldn't be able to settle down until I had Kusanagi in my hands again. I really hoped Yasome's story wasn't true.

After riding in bumpy silence for a while, I heard a man say, "Whatcha got in there, Your Highness?"

"Spider food," Yasome said cheerfully.

Niko groaned.

We passed through a tall archway, where the thick iron spikes of a portcullis hung over us like huge black teeth. Then the ceiling opened up and now, instead of just our cart rattling along the stone floor, there was a chorus of sounds: human and spider feet hurrying up and down the hall, conversations, arguments, and the haunting sound of a shakuhachi—a bamboo flute.

The cart came to a stop. Rough hands reached in, yanked me out, and set me on my feet, in line with the others. Yasome approached Ryleigh, who was standing on the end, with her evil-looking knife and an even more evil-looking grin. My mouth went dry. Ryleigh's eyes widened with fear, but she didn't say anything. I could see her jaw clenched tight around whatever words she might have been thinking, but I wasn't too proud to beg for her life. "Please don't—" I croaked.

With one swift motion, Yasome sliced her blade through the thick white cords that wrapped Ryleigh from head to toe, and they fell in a heap at Ryleigh's feet. She sagged with relief before being jerked upright by the guy who was holding her in place.

"You don't need to help me," Ryleigh snapped. "I can stand on my own just fine." He just sneered and spun her around to face him while Yasome wrapped a new cord around her wrists to hold them behind her back.

The rest of us received the same treatment before being marched into the second throne room we'd been inside that day—no, that week. My palms began to itch again. How quickly did time pass here? I wished we could hurry up and get this over with.

The vibe here could not have been more different than at Ryūgū-jō. While the dragon king's throne room had been a riot of color and light, glittering with jewels and glowing with mother-of-pearl, the Tsuchigumo throne room was more like a fortress. The walls were a mass of twisted, gnarled roots, dripping with gray cobwebs and lichen and pockmarked with dark nooks and cubbyholes. The only bright colors were the eyes that gleamed from the shadows: red, yellow, green. I tried not to look at the spiders that scuttled back and forth around us, or the ones that dropped from roots above on their gleaming silk threads to hang nearby and examine us with their cruel, beady eyes.

At the front of the room was a throne made of the same thick, twisting roots all wound around each other. And on the throne was the queen. She was short, like Yasome, and stocky. She gave off the impression of great strength, like an Olympic gymnast. I was surprised to see that she was decked out in a fancy silver robe that shimmered in the light from the torches that ringed the throne room—I had expected something dark and grubby, or at least dirt-colored. Her hair was braided with more silvery silk thread, and her skin was so pale that it seemed to glow as well. She was engrossed in a conversation with some kind of official to her right.

Two teenagers stood on the left side of the throne—Yasome's siblings, I guessed. One was short and sturdy-looking, with the beginnings of a wispy black beard, and was clad in a dark blue robe; the other was tall and thin, with more feminine features, and wore a white robe. They both shared Yasome's and Itsuma-hime's thick black eyebrows. They frowned at us as we shuffled in.

"Where have you been?" the taller one in the light robe said, scowling. "You're filthy!"

"You're in so much trouble!" said the bearded, blue-robed sibling with a grin.

Yasome called out, "Mama! Mama, you won't believe it! Look what Jojo and I trapped!"

"Shhh!" the older two hissed, but the queen's face broke into an indulgent smile as she ended her conversation with the official.

"Goodness gracious! Four children and a fox! That *is* unusual." Then her expression grew concerned. "But you know the rule about children, my dear. You have to let them go. We're not barbarians, after all." The courtiers murmured in agreement.

"And next time you come to court, please do me the courtesy of taking a bath and wearing clean clothes." The crowd sighed and shook their heads, and the two teenagers smirked. I almost felt sorry for Yasome. Almost.

"And the fox, O majestic monarch? Will you let the fox go as well?" Niko quavered. "Ah-choo! Oh, dear, please excuse me. I'm allergic to your delightful daughter's daisy crown."

Before the queen could answer, Yasome stamped her foot and said, "But these aren't just any children, Mama. This isn't just any fox. Look at what they were carrying!"

She lugged her sack off the cart and slashed it open with her knife. The contents spilled out with a clatter. Our weapons! Instinctively, I tried to dash forward, but the arms that held me back were too strong.

"See?" Yasome said, rummaging through our stuff. "I confiscated this from that girl there." She pointed at Ryleigh and fished a shuriken out of Ryleigh's black bag. Then she hurled it at the wall. The crowd gasped as a hundred shuriken lodged themselves in the roots. Yasome smiled. *Now* people were taking her seriously.

"So you found one ninja kid with a magic shuriken," the teenager in the white robe drawled. "Did you forget that the ninja are our allies?"

"Seriously," said the teenager in the blue robe. "First you come in here looking like something the tarantula dragged in, and then you dump this pile of junk—"

"Shiro. Ao. Be kind to your sister," Itsuma-hime admonished them.

"There's more!" Yasome continued. "There's this bow and

these arrows, and these backpacks seem like some kind of portal . . ." She chucked each item into the middle of the room as she spoke. "And . . ." She picked up Kusanagi, which had assumed its guitar form. "Well, this used to be a sword. It used to be Kusanagi."

At the word "Kusanagi," another gasp rippled through the room.

"Yasome." Her mother's voice was stern. "Don't joke about these things."

"I'm not joking! I even heard them say it! Here. You look at it and tell me what you think." She picked up Kusanagi and brought it over to her mother, who took it into her hands and examined it carefully. She spent a long time looking at the moving image of the waving grass that had been painted onto the front. Meanwhile, seeing Kusanagi in someone else's hands seemed to have woken up my rage monster. It was spinning itself into a frenzy, screaming *She can't take it! Don't let her have it! You're powerless without it! It's ours! Ours! Ours!* My body strained toward Kusanagi of its own accord. I felt the grip of my guard tighten on my arms.

"Give that back!" I heard myself shout. The entire room turned to stare at me in shock, except for Yasome, who grinned triumphantly. I stared back, equally shocked. Had I really just commanded the queen of the Tsuchigumo to give me back my sword-slash-guitar?

"Did you really just command the queen of the Tsuchigumo to give you back your guitar?" said Shiro, the tall one in white.

"I—I didn't mean to," I stammered. "I'm sorry. I don't know what came over me."

"Please forgive her, O Excellent Empress of the Earth-dwellers!" Niko begged. "Ah-choo! She has impulse control issues. And delusions of grandeur. We're working on it! It's been a process." He shook his head and let out a long-suffering sigh.

"I do not have delusions of grandeur! That's my sword that I earned from Susano'o, fair and square. Bring it to me and I'll prove it!" Once again, the entire room gasped. Niko, Danny, Ryleigh, and Jin stared at me in horror. If my hands hadn't been tied behind my back, they would have been smashed over my mouth. What was happening to me?

"Susano'o, you say?" Itsuma-hime looked first at me and then at Kusanagi, and back at me again, her gaze sharp and probing.

"I didn't mean that! I—Niko's right. I have impulse control issues," I babbled. "I—I thought it would be a funny joke, but it wasn't. I'm sorry! I'm not the master of Kusanagi, I'm not the master of anything! I'm just a girl, standing in front of a queen, asking her to—"

"Enough." The authority in Itsuma-hime's voice shut me right up. She motioned to Yasome to bring Kusanagi to me. As Yasome approached, holding the guitar out in front of her like some kind of ancient relic—which I guess it was—a strange mix of feelings coursed through me: a rush of relief, an overpowering desire to reach out and grab my sword, and a deep sense of dread that this was going to be our undoing.

Whether they were innocent victims or treacherous liars, once the Tsuchigumo knew for sure that this was Kusanagi, there was no way they'd see us as allies. They'd throw us right in jail, or maybe feed us to the spiders.

Yasome stepped hesitantly closer and closer, still holding Kusanagi out. She'd stopped looking so smug and was now pale and shaking. *It serves you right, you stinker,* I thought. I was shaking, too, but out of excitement and anticipation. Kusanagi was coming back to me. I could feel it quivering in response, and as we watched, it began to glitch and spark, flickering back and forth between its guitar form and its true form—the Sword of the Wind. I could feel the electric current that passed between us now, and my rage monster began muttering ominously about the injustice of being trapped here, about how rude Yasome had been, how these dirty, lowly Tsuchigumo had no right to stop us on our divine quest to conquer the Middle Lands . . . and that was the last thought I had before something stung me in the neck and the world began to spin.

Cat's Cradle

A grand throne room *with elaborately carved wooden pillars and a ceiling crisscrossed with gilded wooden beams. A messenger stands before the queen on the throne, reading from a scroll. The scroll is handed to the queen, who rips it up and hurls it into the fire. Faintly I hear her say, "If the Yamato wish to have our wood, they may trade with us. But it is not theirs to take as they please, and we are not their subjects."*

A field at the base of a long, low line of heavily forested mountains. The sounds of battle all around—the clash of steel blades, the smack of wooden staffs, the hiss and thunk of arrows. The shouts of fighting men, the groans of the wounded and dying. The coppery smell of blood.

The soldiers defending the mountains seem to have the advantage—they are riding giant armored spiders, and they are slowly beating back the attacking army. A tall man—a prince, from the looks of the elaborate golden crest on his helmet—glares at the mountain defenders and raises his sword. I recognize Kusanagi instantly—I can practically feel it in my own hands, and my energy rises to meet its bloodthirsty fury as the prince swings it with a roar, his face twisted with rage. The wind howls at our back, and lightning splits the sky. The mountain soldiers fall as one, like a thousand tiny dolls knocked over by an invisible hand. Like blades of grass bowing to the wind. I feel a wild rush of triumph.

A city at the edge of the wooded mountain has been struck by lightning, and the fire is eating it up house by house. The citizens are fleeing into the trees, scrambling up the steep slope and scurrying into the many caves that dot the stony mountainside. The giant spiders weave a protective web across the trees; another bolt of lightning sets the web ablaze. The prince and his troops thunder into the forest, slashing at anything that moves. The queen steps out to meet them. But she is a mere human, no match for Kusanagi. She falls immediately. In one of the caves, a girl screams.

Prince Takeru bellows at the hiding families, "You have seen what happens to those who reject the divine rule of the Yamato clan! These forests now belong to us, and if you dare to come out of those caves, you will be squashed like the disgusting ground-dwelling pests that you are!"

Dawn. The girl in the cave creeps to the entrance with a spider at her side. The spider spins a silk thread for her, and she weaves it into a cat's cradle. She murmurs something at the net in her hands and releases it to the wind before retreating underground. The wind carries the net in and out of the trees, all the way out to the battlefield. The silk unfurls, and an endless trail of silvery, almost invisible thread loops itself around the fallen Tsuchigumo soldiers and then back through the trees. The dead soldiers rise and drift back to the forest, where they melt into nothingness. The trees spread their branches and the canopy closes, shutting out the sun.

I'm Coming, Momo

My head hurt. Someone was shouting, far away. What were they saying?

Clear out! Give her some space! Make way for the queen!

I opened my eyes a crack to see a swirl of activity around me—familiar and unfamiliar human faces, a horrible monster with fangs and multiple beady eyes. I tried to twist away, and the world spun wildly. I sank back into unconsciousness.

Darkness. Nothing but me and my pounding head. And voices:

Mom was shouting at someone. *Tell me where she is!*

No, replied Sen's voice.

She's my daughter!

Then you should have watched her more carefully, shouldn't you?

A tall figure wearing a hooded brown cloak, striding through the forest. A beach. A bridge. A door.

The darkness again. And then Izanami's face.

Goodness gracious, what have you gotten yourself into?

I've been captured, I said.

Her porcelain brow furrowed. *Why is that a problem? Call your sword and fight your way out, silly girl!*

I shook my head, and for a moment, I was confused. Why was I saying no? Why *wouldn't* I call Kusanagi?

Izanami's face faded out and was replaced by Mom's. She was walking in a crowd of people on a narrow path through a dull gray landscape dotted with weak, smoky fires. Meido. The space between the Middle Lands and Yomi.

I'm coming, Momo, she whispered. *I don't know what you're doing, but I've figured out where you're going, and I'm coming to help you.*

No, I thought. She couldn't. Did Izanami know she was coming? What if she got hurt? Or worse, captured? I couldn't let that happen. I couldn't be the reason Mom died as well.

Then Dad's voice, low and urgent: *Momo, listen to me. Don't come for me. It's too dangerous. My life is not worth trading for—*

That's quite enough, thank you. Izanami's voice crawled with snakes and scorpions.

The sound of something large thrashing in the water, and then a thick, dark silence broken only by Dad's ragged breathing.

Not a Plan

When I finally woke up, I was lying on a pallet in a small, candlelit room. Next to me was a ceramic cup of water. I was gulping it down when Itsuma-hime entered, accompanied by a silver spider the size of a labradoodle. It was less scary than Yasome's companion, Jojo the pony-sized spider, but it was still pretty darn scary, and when it put two of its spidery claw-feet on my lap, I choked midgulp and had to be patted firmly on the back for a minute or two before I recovered.

"I'm glad to see you're feeling better," said the queen.

"What happened?" I asked.

"What do you remember?"

I closed my eyes and concentrated. Memories floated past me like leaves spinning down a stream: the forest . . . the throne room . . . the battlefield . . . the magic spiderweb—no, wait, those last two weren't real. I looked at Itsuma-hime, who was watching me with curiosity. I concentrated again. I'd been in the throne room, restrained by a guard. Yasome had been walking toward me, carrying—

Kusanagi.

It hit me like a bucket of cold water. "Where is . . ." The words died in my mouth when I saw the wary watchfulness in Itsuma-hime's eyes.

"Your sword is in a safe place," she said. "We had to knock you out before you got your hands on it."

I remembered the needlelike sting in my neck, and my hand went to the spot. Itsuma-hime nodded. "I am sorry we had to resort to such measures, but . . . How can I put this? You changed when the sword was brought to you. I'm sure you understand, given our history."

I remembered Yasome's face as she'd approached, and how much I'd wanted to reach out and snatch Kusanagi away from her, how it had felt like nothing else mattered.

"Uh." I swallowed nervously. "Changed how?"

"I think Kusanagi remembers this place. I think it wants to finish what it started. And you seemed to be of the same mind."

These dirty, lowly Tsuchigumo had no right to stop us on our divine quest to conquer the Middle Lands. The last thought I'd had before I'd been stung.

My tongue turned to sandpaper in my mouth. Had I said those words out loud?

"Your friends all swear that nothing like this has ever happened before. They tell me you have learned to control the sword instead of letting it control you. But there is no denying that you were possessed by its spirit. We were barely able to contain you."

The dream came back to me in full detail now: The queen's refusal to pay tribute. All those Tsuchigumo soldiers mowed down with one sweep of Kusanagi's blade. The fire, the queen's death, Takeru's cruel promise to stamp out the Tsuchigumo if they tried to rise again. The exhilarating sense of invincibility.

So it was true, then. Kusanagi was—or it could be—as bad as both Yasome and Daikoku had said it was. Forget about moving beyond destruction. Forget about destroying things for the sake of a higher purpose. Destruction had been the *entire* purpose. My heart fell into my stomach and I had to blink fast to stop the tears that suddenly welled up. "Oh."

"You saw what happened."

I wanted to protest, to shout, "Yes, but it wasn't me!" But that seemed beside the point. So instead I said, "I'm sorry."

She nodded sadly. "As keeper of the story, I have been granted visions of it myself. It was a massacre. And for what? For power. For glory. For greed. If not for Princess Yasome, my daughter's namesake, we would have been wiped off the planet."

I remembered the girl in the cave, with her spider-silk net. "What did she do?"

"She cast a spell that drew the spirits of our dead into the trees of the forest. It scares outsiders away so that we can live in peace, undisturbed. The wood crumbles and rots when it's cut down. The Yamato may have defeated us in battle, but they and their descendants have never been able to take our trees for themselves."

We sat for a while in silence. Finally, I apologized again. "I'm sorry. I didn't know about any of that."

"But now that you do, you can understand why I cannot let you have the sword."

Instantly, panic shot through my veins. "But you have to!" I blurted out. "I need it!"

She raised her eyebrows. "For what?"

"I need it to fight demons. I'm not like Prince Takeru. I'm not trying to conquer anyone."

"No, I don't believe you are," Itsuma-hime said, and I breathed a sigh of relief.

"So..."

Itsuma-hime exhaled slowly. "Your friend Ryleigh told me about your quest. She told me that Izanami is preparing to storm the gates of the Middle Lands, and that the only way to stop her for good is to find and destroy the Jewel of the Heart, which seems to be in the possession of a man in a brown cloak who passed through here some time ago. And she told me that you need Kusanagi to do it. So you see, I face quite a dilemma.

"No matter how I look at it, I risk the destruction of my people. If I return the sword to you, you could wipe us out the way the Yamato wiped out my ancestors. If I refuse to return it to you, not only will you be unable to complete your mission, but we will almost certainly face an attack from demons serving Izanami as they seek to take the Sword of the Wind for themselves."

Itsuma-hime paused to gaze intently at me. "Can we trust you with the Sword of the Wind?" she asked.

What could I tell the queen that would convince her to give it to me? *You can trust me*, I wanted to say. *I am not the spirit of my sword. I won't become addicted to its power like Prince Takeru.* But I had a feeling she wouldn't believe me.

I felt a gentle hand on my arm. "I see that you, too, are conflicted," Itsuma-hime said. "I am glad to see that you understand what's at stake for me and my people. And you should know that I intend to consider the situation carefully before I make my decision." Then she smiled and added, "In the meantime, your friends have been eager to see you." The silver spider had gone to sleep at her feet, and she leaned down to pat it on the head. "Wake up, Steve!"

Steve?

Steve sprang to his feet, panting and slobbering. His breath was just as bad as Jojo's.

"That's a good spider." She offered him a handful of beetles, which he gobbled up eagerly. "Go fetch Momo's friends," she said. She gave him a pat on his waggling butt and he scampered off, his feet clicking and clacking on the stone floor.

"I will go now. Enjoy your time with your friends." She got up and left the room.

A moment later, Danny burst through the door, followed by Ryleigh, Jin, and Niko. In a second, we were wrapped in a four-person, one-fox hug. It felt good to know that they still wanted to be friends with me after what had happened.

"We were worried you might be gone for good," Danny said. "You were scary, bro."

"What happened to you, anyway?" Jin asked. "You looked like you were possessed or something!"

"Uh..."

I wanted to tell them about the visions I'd seen—Kusanagi's memories of the slaughter of the Tsuchigumo army; how the Tsuchigumo people had taken refuge in the caves; the death of their queen; and the spell that the first Yasome had cast over the forest all those years ago. But if they knew that I was at risk of falling under Kusanagi's influence, they'd get all worried and scared. And we had enough to worry about, thanks to me.

"I dunno. The last thing I remember is seeing Kusanagi. Then I passed out," I said. I caught a glimpse of their faces and got the sense that they knew I was lying. I closed my eyes so I wouldn't have to look at them and tried to ignore my itching palms.

Wait. My heart jumped and my eyes flew open. "How long was I out?"

Danny looked uncomfortable. "Two days."

Sure enough, all but three buds had bloomed on my palms.

"Don't worry. I have a plan."

No, it wasn't Ryleigh. It was Danny.

"Oh, my voles and vixens, we've *talked* about this," Niko said.

"Whatever. Okay, Momo, are you ready?" Danny started pacing the room as he spoke. "First of all, Yasome has a crush on me."

"Danny! This is not a plan!" Ryleigh burst out. "And how do you even know Yasome has a crush on you?"

"She told me. Why do you think she keeps coming to visit?" Danny shrugged like it was no big deal, like kids got crushes on him all the time. Which, to be fair, they did. "And if certain people will let me talk"—he looked pointedly at the others—"I'll finish explaining the plan." He resumed pacing. "So I've been thinking. I'll turn on the ol' Danny Haragan charm and convince Yasome to tell us about a secret passageway—there have to be some secret passageways around here somewhere, right? And then I'll get her to leave us a key and distract the guards while we sneak out. And voilà!" He spread his arms wide. "We're free!"

I stared at him. "Please tell me you're not serious."

"That. Is not. A plan," said Ryleigh again, through her teeth. "That is a fantasy."

"It's the most preposterous plot I've ever heard," Niko agreed.

"Fine." But Danny wasn't about to give up. "Then let Jin do it. He can use his magic to make her like *him*. Then *he* can get her to set us free."

"I'm not lying to make a girl like me," said Jin firmly. "That's not okay."

"Omigosh, Jin! There are lives at stake here! Can't you stop being a goody-goody for, like, one single second?"

"Look. My mom lies to me all the time. After we rescued those kids on New Year's Eve and I told her I wanted to see her more often, she's been sending messages about how she's going to spend time with me, and how she wants to work on my poetry with me, and all this stuff, but she hasn't shown up once. Not once! And I'm not ever doing anything like that to anyone if I can help it. And also, I'm sorry, Danny, but your plan is missing kind of a lot of steps."

I couldn't help staring. I'd never seen Jin this fired up about anything.

"Sorry," he said. "Did I just make things weird? I didn't mean to lose my temper."

"No, you *should* be mad," Ryleigh said.

"Yeah, bro. You should tell your mom how you feel next time you see her," said Danny.

"Yeah," said Jin glumly.

"And I still think we should do my plan."

"No," said Ryleigh. "We are not doing your plan. Because it's *not a plan*."

"Fine. You make a plan, then," said Danny a little grumpily. "You're the master strategist, aren't you?"

"Right. I'm sure that's *exactly* what you think," said Ryleigh, and glowered so hard at the rest of us that no one dared to ask her what she meant.

I tried to ignore my growing anxiety stomachache while we sat in awkward, angry silence for a million years, until finally a guard appeared and announced, "The queen requires your presence." My stomachache got even worse.

The guard took us back to the throne room, where we were lined up in front of Itsuma-hime.

"Welcome," she said. "After a great deal of thought and soul-searching, I have made up my mind." She took a deep breath. "You will be executed in the morning."

Not Dead Yet

My chest went cold and my ears filled with a roaring, rushing sound. I couldn't possibly have heard her correctly. "What?" My voice sounded thin and far away.

"I am sorry."

"But—but you can't!" Danny spluttered.

"I can. And I must."

"Why?" Ryleigh demanded. "It doesn't make any sense!"

Itsuma-hime sighed. "I don't like this solution any more than you do. But my highest priority is to keep my people safe. And the two highest priorities for Izanami and her demons are to acquire the Jewel of the Heart and the Sword of the Wind. To allow you to leave with Kusanagi would be to risk Momo attacking us. I know you don't intend to, child, but the risk is still real," she said when I opened my mouth to protest. She kept going. "To allow you to leave *without* Kusanagi would be safer for us at first, but it would not protect us from any demons who want the sword. And to keep you here alive would be to invite the demons to attack *and* risk you getting your hands on the sword again.

"But if you die, the Sword of the Wind will go back to its

original owner, Susano'o. There will be no reason for Izanami's demons to come here. The jewel will remain hidden, Izanami will remain in Yomi, and we will remain safe from Kusanagi's mission to destroy us."

It was hard to argue with her logic. It really was the safest alternative for the Tsuchigumo.

"But that's still murder!" Jin said. I heard a layer of magic in his voice. He was finally coming through. "Momo's innocent. In fact, she's trying to keep the world safe! Can't we all try to be kind to each other? Can't we trust each other and work together against the forces of evil?"

I could see the queen wavering. I crossed my fingers. I crossed my toes. But . . . that was strange. Why wasn't I furious about this? Why wasn't I wishing I had Kusanagi so that we could fight our way out of this?

I heard Jin's voice laying the magic on a little thicker. "We're just kids. Like Yasome. I know you don't really want to kill us."

Itsuma-hime's gaze flicked into the crowd, where Yasome stood. Yasome's face was pale and serious, and her own gaze rested on Danny.

"I don't want to," said Itsuma-hime thickly. A tear trickled down her cheek. "But I must."

"You don't have to," Jin said gently.

The queen shut her eyes and waved her hand. A strip of silk cloth flew out of nowhere and wrapped itself over Jin's mouth. "I do," she said.

"No, you don't." I stepped forward. A solution had hit me with sudden clarity. "You just have to kill me."

The entire room gasped all at once. Itsuma-hime's eyes flew open and she stared at me.

"You sentenced us all to death, but I'm the one who's dangerous. I'm the one who's a threat. So I'm the one you should execute."

"No!" Danny shouted. "She shouldn't execute any of us! None of us has done anything wrong! If you try to kill her, you're going to have to get through *mmff*!" A guard stepped forward and put an arm around Danny's chest and a hand over Danny's mouth. Yasome let out a muffled squeak.

Itsuma-hime nodded slowly. "I never would have thought a wielder of Kusanagi could speak with such wisdom and selfless courage. And if it were any other sword, I might consider sparing your life for your bravery. Unfortunately, the only reward I can give you is to grant your request."

"Nooooo," Niko howled, and he was silenced as well.

"I am sorry," Itsuma-hime said to me, her eyes glistening with tears. "If I take pity on you and let you go, and we are wiped off the face of the earth as a result, I will have failed my people. I could never forgive myself in a thousand lifetimes."

With a nod of her head, she ordered a squad of guards forward. "I do not wish for you to suffer. I will grant you the dignity of a comfortable bed, a good meal, and a night in the company of your friends. Your death in the morning will be quick and painless, and we will give you a proper burial. You have my word as queen."

So that was comforting. Not.

We were marched out of the throne room, down a long corridor, and around a corner into another corridor that curved in a long, gentle arc. It was punctuated with doors every few feet; prison cells, I guessed.

"Momo, why would you do that? Why would you say they should execute just you?" Danny said as we walked.

"You're here because of my problems. It's my fault they don't trust us. And you shouldn't have to pay for it," I said.

"Ugh. Stop making this all about you," Ryleigh said with a vehemence that surprised me. "Did it ever occur to you that maybe we're here to save our own parents? Or our friends, or the rest of the Middle Lands?"

I was stunned into silence. Ryleigh was right. But that made me feel even worse. And it confirmed my feeling that I needed to shoulder the blame for our situation.

"Anyway, you shouldn't have done it," Danny insisted. "You can't keep doing things on your own without telling us. We could have gotten separated. You should have trusted us to come up with a plan."

"We're together now, aren't we? And I don't see a plan in motion. So it's fine," I said. As fine as being one night away from execution could be, anyway.

Once again, I had the odd sensation of not feeling what I should be feeling. Where was that hunger for Kusanagi?

"Listen to them with all their talk about plans," said one of our guards. "Isn't it cute?"

Another guard guffawed as he jingled a ring of keys. "Save yourself the trouble, kids," he said. "No one escapes the Tsuchigumo."

We stopped in front of a dark wooden door and were shoved into a surprisingly cozy room with thick carpets and a low table in the center, laden with fruit and cakes. At the far end of the room was another door. Four comfy-looking beds and one big floor cushion for Niko were arranged around the edges of the room. As if any of us were going to be able to sleep.

"Someone will be back tomorrow morning to lead you to your death," the first guard said.

The door went *thunk* and the lock went *click* and the guard added from the other side, "And don't bother trying to sneak out the back door. It leads to the execution ring. Hundreds of hungry spiders waiting for a meal to wander out."

The guards' boots echoed on the stone walls of the corridor and faded into a long, heavy silence. I sank onto one of the beds, covered my face with my hands, and tried not to cry. I'd failed. I was going to die. The man in the brown robe would disappear with the jewel forever, and Dad would suffer until Izanami figured out what had happened and killed him in a fit of rage. Mom would either get caught in Yomi or give up and sink into another depression, and there would be no one to help her out of it. And all because I hadn't been able to resist the pull of Kusanagi's power back in the throne room. Daikoku had been right to doubt my ability to carry this off.

I closed my eyes and focused on breathing in, out, in, out. I heard Ryleigh pacing around the room. I wondered what it would be like not to breathe anymore, not to feel anything or hear anything.

"Hey, don't give up," said Danny. He sat down next to me and put a hand on my back. "We're not dead yet, right?"

"We might as well be," said Niko gloomily. "We're ruined as rotten rutabagas."

"No, we're not! We can go out that way." Danny pointed to the door to the execution ring.

"Are you *kidding* me?" Ryleigh said.

"Why not?" Danny asked.

"Uh." I looked at the others. "How about hungry killer spiders?"

"Look. Would you rather sit here and do nothing and die for sure tomorrow, or try to escape and—"

"Get bitten by a giant black widow spider and die in agony today?" Niko finished. "I would prefer twelve more hours of peace before I perish, thank you very much."

"You're not going to perish," I reminded him. "You're going to be fine."

"Not if I go out that door," he said.

"On the other hand . . . ," Ryleigh said slowly. She eyed the door.

"Yes! Don't overthink it. Sometimes you just have to take a risk and *do* something," Danny said. "Come on, Momo. You think you got us into this mess, right? Fine. Let's get out of it!"

"All right. I'm in," said Ryleigh.

"Me too," said Jin.

"Fine," I said.

The three of us went and stood next to Danny by the back door of the cell and looked at Niko.

"I don't suppose you've ever heard the expression 'out of the frying pan, into the fire,'" Niko grumbled. But he padded over to join us anyway.

"See, that's what I'm talking about! Team RyJin DaMoNik!" Danny sounded triumphant.

He grasped the handle and slowly, carefully, began swinging the door open. I found myself feeling grateful for his boundless optimism and his ability to see a terrifying situation as a thrilling adventure. I was even beginning to feel a little hopeful myself. Maybe we could escape. Maybe the guards had been exaggerating to scare us. Maybe this one time, acting without a plan was better than sitting around and thinking about a plan.

But then we opened the door and I saw what lay on the other side.

Here, Pretty Babies!

Our doorway opened into a vast, circular space. And by "space" I mean "yawning expanse of darkness" both above and—*ulp*—below us. The, ahem, "space" was ringed with doorways like ours. Except ours was the only true doorway, in that ours was the only one with a door. All the other doorways were more what you might call cave entrances. Each of those cave entrances had a gleaming cable running out of it, and those cables crisscrossed each other to form a network that connected all of the caves. And by "network," of course, I mean "enormous spiderweb that swung gently over the yawning expanse of darkness below."

And judging from the scrabbly sounds that rose out of the yawning expanse of darkness below, there was a bottom somewhere, and it was full of creepy-crawly monsters. And was that a giant spider leg poking out of one of the doorways (that is, cave entrances) in the wall?

"Uh, Ry? Do you wanna lead?" Danny's voice shook just a little.

Ryleigh let out an irritated sigh, but as she peered into the darkness her irritability seemed to vanish. Maybe the challenge of crossing that spiderweb had activated her ninja brain. When she spoke, she sounded calm, cool, and collected. "Okay, I think we can do this if we're careful. I only see a couple of spiders active on the edges—maybe they've all just eaten or something. I'll go first, and you all put your feet exactly where I put mine. *Exactly.* Or you'll set off a vibration that will bring those spiders running. Got it?"

Okay. Sure. No pressure. Just one tiny misstep between escape and gruesome, painful death by giant spider bite. Every cell in my body was screaming, *No, thank you. I'd like to live another day, if you don't mind.*

But I thought about Dad wrapped in razor-edged cords, and our mystery guy who held the key to his release. Every step we took across that pit was a step closer to finding the jewel and rescuing Dad. And destroying the jewel. Obviously. Toward a time when we'd never have to worry about Izanami escaping Yomi ever again.

I took a deep breath. *Okay. Let's go.*

Ryleigh walked slowly, placing her feet with care and precision. Danny went next, then me, then Jin, and finally Niko, on his hind legs. I kept my eyes fixed on the cable, and focused on putting my feet exactly where Danny's had been. Step. Step. Step. As long as I thought only about the next step, I could block out all the creepy-crawly threats, as well as the impossible distance between us and wherever we were headed.

It reminded me of something our school counselor told us at a mental health assembly one time. If you're freaking out about the enormous scary thing you have to do, sometimes it's easier to adjust your focus and just do the next small thing, then the next, and the next. And before you know it, you'll be on your way to doing the big scary thing.

Until someone in your group says, "Hey, Ry, where are we going, anyway?"

Ryleigh stopped walking so abruptly that Danny nearly crashed into her, and the web swayed dangerously. I squeezed my eyes shut and waited for a stampede of spiders, but thankfully, none came.

"Why did you stop?" Danny asked. "What's wrong?"

"What's *wrong*?" Ryleigh echoed. "Nothing! Nothing at all. Why would anything be wrong? I'm in charge, aren't I?"

I stood there, still frozen, in confused silence. I'd always assumed Ryleigh *liked* being in charge.

Danny must not have been paying close attention or he would have caught the sarcasm in her voice. "I know," he said. "That's why I asked you where we were going."

"Okay," said Ryleigh. "Got it. Let *me* handle it. *I'll* come up with a plan. You all just relax and let me handle *everything* because I've never let you down." Her voice was hard and flat and thick, as if she was on the verge of tears. "You know, it wouldn't hurt if one of *you* took charge every once in a while."

"Uh, hello! Who's been coming up with escape plans this whole time? But you guys keep shooting me down because apparently my plans are, let's see, what did you say? Oh. Right. You said they were 'preposterous,' and 'not a plan' and 'a fantasy,'" Danny shot back.

"They're *not* plans," Ryleigh said. "Making it up as we go is not a plan! 'Step one, step two, step three, boom!' is not a plan!" She let go of the guide cable and mimicked the mind-blown sign that he'd done on the *Takarabune,* and I thought I would throw up from fear that she'd tumble into the abyss below. (She didn't, of course. Because ninja.)

"Um, can we get moving, please?" I asked. Standing still like this was making me jittery.

Ryleigh, thank goodness, took a few steps forward. But then she stopped again and turned around to face Danny, and I wanted to cry. "The problem is that you've never had any responsibility, like I said before," she said. "You've had this cushy life—"

"Says the girl whose parents hired Jin freakin' Takayama to sing at her birthday party," Danny cut in.

I tried to intervene so we could drop the subject and move on, literally. "Ryleigh's just saying you've never had to act like a grown-up. You've never had to make the kind of decisions the rest of us have."

"Not making it better, Momo," said Danny.

But it was true. Jin had been responsible for earning money to support himself and his dad. I'd had to take care of myself and Mom. And Ryleigh had been training to take over the family trade since she was little—and ever since her big brother, Tommy, had bailed, she'd been under even more pressure to succeed. Whereas Danny just got to be a kid. Even with all the weird things his parents told him about the importance of doing all the right activities and having the right friends and it not mattering about being Asian, at least he didn't have to feel like his family depended on him.

"Speaking of hard decisions, have you determined a direction?" Niko asked from the back.

Ryleigh went perfectly still, and I felt sure that she was

contemplating doing a backflip and kicking Niko off the spider-web. *Then* I felt sure that I saw a cross-cable twitch, and my heart jumped right into my mouth.

Finally, without another word, Ryleigh started walking again. Thank goodness.

But Danny wasn't finished. "I don't know why you're so upset. All I said was you were a great strategist. I was just trying to be nice, okay? Just trying to be supportive. Because we're supposed to be a *team,* remember? But I guess you don't need me," he said bitterly. "I wouldn't want to slow you down with my *irresponsibility.*"

"Can we please stop fighting?" Jin implored.

I knew we should apologize to Danny, but something inside me resisted. Everything we'd said was true. He had been luckier than the rest of us, that was all—at least in terms of the role he had to play in his family. If he felt a certain way about it, that was on him.

On the other hand, he seemed genuinely hurt. And I'd always told myself that I would never let anyone feel left out or like they weren't good enough. *Sigh.*

"I'm sorry, Danny," I said, but he said only, "Whatever," and I didn't know what else to do.

Why couldn't we get along? What was wrong with us? Another long silence followed, during which those terrifying scrabbly sounds continued. Were they growing louder? *Please let them not be growing louder.* We inched forward with agonizing slowness. Step. Step. Step.

"Stop right there. Go any farther and you're dead meat."

A shadowy figure dropped out of nowhere and landed

lightly in front of us in a crouch. The figure straightened up, and Yasome said, "I'm serious. You're doing a good job and everything, but what you don't know is there's a trip wire in the next section. But if you follow me, I'll get you out of here."

Ryleigh said the thing I'm sure we were all thinking. "Why should we trust you? You're the one who got us into this mess in the first place!"

"I know. I'm sorry. But I'm here to help you, I promise."

"Why?" Ryleigh demanded again.

Yasome sighed. "It's just . . . I'm so bad at court protocol, and I'm even worse at lessons. I can't sit still, I can't pay attention, I can't remember things. And Shiro and Ao are always laughing at me, and I just wanted to show everyone that I wasn't useless. I wanted to prove that I could be a great hunter. I didn't mean for any of you to die!" She looked pitifully at us, and I began to feel sorry for her. I mean, talk about unintended consequences. "You didn't do anything wrong, and if you were executed, that would make me a murderer. And my mother, too. I don't want either of us to be a murderer."

"You could have spoken up at court," I said.

"I tried! But I think Shiro cast a spell so I couldn't say anything. And then Ao tackled me. No one would have listened to me anyway." Her voice trembled. "No one ever listens to me."

She looked away and wiped her eyes with a grubby hand, then took a deep breath. "So, yeah. I want to help you escape and find that jewel so you can destroy it. To make up for capturing you."

"That'll make people pay attention to you, for sure," said Danny with a laugh.

"It would, wouldn't it." Yasome grinned at him. And batted her eyelashes. Then she flipped easily up to the guide cable, tiptoed over us, and dropped down behind Niko. "Come on."

I let out a long, slow breath. We were going to escape after all. Carefully, I turned around on the cable and followed behind Niko and Yasome, step by cautious step, and everything went perfectly until Niko sneezed.

"What-*CHOO!*"

Maybe it was the acoustics of the yawning empty space, or maybe it was just terrible luck, but that sneeze was bigger and louder than any dad-sneeze you've ever heard.

The chamber echoed with it, and the cables shook, and for three long bloodcurdling seconds, everything stopped. We froze in place. The scratchy sounds below dropped away. Even my heart might have stopped beating.

Then everything happened all at once. "Run!" Yasome shouted. "Forget about vibrations, just go! Go! Go!" She skipped down the cable, and we did our best to follow. From all around the web, giant spiders crawled out of their holes and began charging toward us.

"Here, pretty babies! Have some yummy flies!" Yasome hucked silk-wrapped packages in every direction, which slowed some of the spiders down.

"If only I had my shuriken!" Ryleigh shouted. "Too bad our weapons have been *taken* from us!"

"You mean too bad your fox friend couldn't hold in a sneeze!" Yasome shot back.

"I can't help it if I have ALLERGIES!" Niko yowled. "What-*CHOO!*"

Finally, we reached a small platform in front of one of the cave entrances. "Go, go, go!" Yasome urged us inside. Ryleigh crawled in, and while her feet were still hanging out, Yasome gave them a big shove. "Hurry!"

"HEYyyyyyyy!" Ryleigh's voice started loud and faded quickly, as if she were going down a long tube. Which wasn't comforting.

"Oh, forgot to tell you. Feet first!" Yasome said. She was stomping on spider feet that hooked themselves on the platform, and kicking them into the pit. "Go!"

Niko needed no more encouragement but leaped right in. Then Danny slid in, then Jin, then me. I looked back to see Yasome shove one last fly directly into the mouth of a spider just in time to avoid getting munched on the shoulder. Then gravity took over and both she and the spider disappeared from view.

Oof.

"Ow!"

My fall was broken by Danny, Jin, and Niko.

"Sorry," I said to the groaning pile beneath me.

Then it was my turn to go "Ow!" as Yasome landed on top of me. Of course, Ryleigh had apparently executed some kind of perfect somersault landing; she was standing off to the side with her hands on her hips.

Yasome rolled off the top of our pile. "What are you still doing on the floor? Hurry!" I noticed that she took the time to help Danny to his feet and smile at him before she rushed off.

We followed Yasome around a corner and into a long row of stalls. She jogged down the row, throwing doors open as she went. "Everyone's all saddled and packed. Choose a mount and follow me." Yasome put her fingers in her mouth and emitted a piercing whistle. "Meet Stripey, Daisy, Grogu, and Tom Hiddleston. And Jojo, of course."

Ryleigh let out a sound that was as close to a scream as I'd ever heard her make when the first hairy horse-sized spider lumbered out and gave her an inquisitive sniff.

"Well? Don't just stand there!" Yasome shouted. "Get on! We have to get out of here!"

There were now five spiders standing in the corridor, whuffing and stamping their feet as if to say, "Come on, kids! Let's go, already!"

Or maybe it was "Yum, yum! Let's eat, already!"

The sounds of slamming doors and shouting voices in the distance gave me the courage I needed. I picked a spider with pink and black stripes standing in front of a stall labeled STRIPEY and ran to it. When it saw me coming, it knelt down obligingly and I clambered on.

"Woo-hoo! Let's gooo!" Danny sat astride Jojo, behind Yasome. I have to admit, I was impressed. Never let it be said that Yasome didn't go after what she wanted.

"Hang on tight!" she shouted, and then we were galloping at breakneck speed down the row of stalls, through the wide-open double doors, up a narrow corridor, and then finally through a curtain of vines and into the gray gloom of dawn in the forest.

We're as Harmless as Hedgehogs

Have you ever galloped through a haunted forest on the back of a giant tarantula? No? Well, I am here to tell you that it is equal parts thrilling and terrifying. I don't know what all those legs were doing, but we practically flew through the trees. We were going so fast, I had to keep my head pressed to Stripey's back to avoid getting decapitated by low-hanging branches and vines. We blasted right through a curtain of cobwebs that left me spitting wads of sticky thread out of my mouth and wiping it out of my eyes. We sped across a field toward the edge of a cliff. And when we reached the cliff just seconds later, did we hesitate? No! Did we screech to a halt? No! Yasome shouted, "Yaaa!" and Jojo gathered himself and executed a magnificent leap, trailing a silky balloon behind him. The wind caught it and wafted Jojo, Yasome, and Danny into the air. Soon, Stripey and I were also sailing through the air, riding the wind down to the beach below.

We landed on a narrow strip of sand that sloped gently into a choppy sea, where the waves tumbled and broke over each other like they were wrestling. In the distance, a rim of mountainous gray coastline rose out of the water. The sun was shining, but a stiff, cold breeze made me glad I was wearing a jacket.

"This is where I leave you," said Yasome.

"Where are we?" Jin asked.

"The Bridge to the North," said Yasome. "Jojo says that's where the guy in the brown robe went." She patted the spider affectionately. "He's our best tracker."

"I don't see a bridge," I said. "Is it magic? Do we have to call it up somehow?"

"I don't know. All I know is that this is where it's supposed to be. And, um, fair warning? It might be better if someone besides you tries to call it. Because, you know. There's a reason why the Ainu people aren't in charge of their own island anymore." She made a sword-slashing motion with her arms.

Oh, no. "Really?"

"Yup."

The more I learned about Kusanagi, the worse I felt. Especially since the next thing I said was "Where's our stuff?" Meaning, of course, "Where's Kusanagi?" The familiar longing to have it in my hands was back, all of a sudden and stronger than ever.

Yasome patted a bundle strapped to Jojo's back. "Right here."

"Can we have it?" Ryleigh asked.

"Sure!"

She unwrapped the bundle and tossed over Ryleigh's shuriken and my backpack. Then she walked over and handed Danny's backpack to him, along with a ball of string. She pressed it into his hands and said, "Tsuchigumo spider silk. Light as air, strong as steel. And I enchanted it to follow orders from you."

Danny took it with a brilliant smile and said, "Thanks!" as Ryleigh rolled her eyes.

But I hardly noticed because I'd just checked my backpack and something was missing. "Where's my sword?"

Yasome tore her eyes off Danny and said, "Um, hello? I'm not about to risk you killing me with that thing. I'll toss it down from the top of the cliff."

Fair. But I still had a hard time smushing down the angry urge to knock her off her high spider and demand that she give Kusanagi to me right then and there. What if she intended to steal it?

"Thank you for enabling our escape, O dauntless daughter of Itsuma-hime!" Niko butted in before I could say anything rude. "We trust you. Right, Momo?" He glared at me.

"Right," I said, even though I didn't.

Yasome rounded up her spiders and scurried up and over the cliff. Moments later, a guitar attached to a silk parachute floated into my hands. Once my fingers closed around its neck, it was like my entire body sighed with relief. I felt like a big missing chunk of myself had been returned.

"How about you put that thing away for a second?" Jin said. "Since we're not fighting anyone right now?"

Erghhh. A little ashamed, I tucked Kusanagi into my backpack. Why hadn't I missed it this desperately when I'd been imprisoned without it just an hour ago? I hadn't even thought about it when we'd made our escape. What had triggered my longing for it to come back?

"And, uh, speaking of fighting, can we, like, not do it anymore?" Jin asked. "Can we try to get along and be a team?"

The rest of us looked at the sea, at the sand, at the cliffs—anywhere but at each other.

Danny broke the silence. "I guess so. But I got us out of there, so you have to admit my plan worked."

"No," Ryleigh said. "We got out because Yasome found her conscience and helped us."

"*And* because I charmed her with my charisma," said Danny.

"Totally beside the point," Ryleigh said.

"So you really *do* think you don't need me," Danny said accusingly. I wasn't sure if he was joking until he gave the sand a vicious kick.

"We totally need you," Jin said. "Someone has to be optimistic in the face of despair. Someone has to push us to take risks. That was you. You got us going when we were about to give up. Besides, it's no fun if everyone's too serious."

Danny stopped kicking and smiled gratefully at Jin. "Thanks, bro."

"Even though we practically perished in the process," Niko said.

"No, Jin's right," I said. I finally had the words I needed. "Danny, you drive me up the wall sometimes, but if it weren't for you, we might still be in that prison cell right now."

"Perhaps," Niko said grudgingly. "It's a thin line between bravery and buffoonery, but I suppose Danny is more often brave than buffoonish."

"That's right!" Danny joked, but then added with real feeling, "Thanks."

"And when we say we have real responsibilities, it doesn't mean we think you're irresponsible," I added. "It's just that you've never had to watch out for your parents. It's not just about pleasing them. Like, I feel like I'm responsible for my mom's actual happiness. And her health. And even her future. It's all upside down, but a lot of times it feels like there's nothing I can do about it because I'm her kid."

Danny dug his toe into the sand. "Oh," he said. "I guess I never thought about it that way."

"That's why I'm telling you."

He nodded. "Got it."

Jin smiled. "Good. Are we good?" he asked. "Ryleigh, you good?"

Ryleigh had barely looked at any of us during this whole exchange, but continued to stare at the gray water that stretched between us and the mountains on the other side. "I'm fine," she said.

"Okay." Jin let out a resigned sigh. "At least we understand each other now. Doesn't that feel better?"

I did feel a lot lighter and freer, like some of the strained, tangled, angry feelings that had been dragging us down had been loosened and unknotted. If only we could figure out what was bothering Ryleigh.

Meanwhile, Danny had bounced back (because of course he had) and waded into the water. He cupped his hands around his mouth and started shouting, "Hellooo! Hello out there! Can we come over the bridge?"

"What in the heavenly hash are you doing?" Niko barked.

"Calling the bridge," Danny said over his shoulder. "You got any better ideas?"

We did not. So we let Danny do his thing. Then we watched

with our mouths hanging open as the spray from the whitecaps rose and spun itself into a shimmering, swaying bridge across the strait.

Once the bridge was complete, a woman materialized on the span and glided toward us. She didn't look like any of the kami I'd ever seen. Her clothing wasn't modern, like Daikoku's suit or Susano'o's biker jacket, but it was nothing like the shiny silk kimono that Amaterasu and her attendants in the Palace of the Sun wore, either. This new goddess had a scarf around her head like a big, broad headband; it was embroidered with cool geometric patterns that reminded me of a maze, with thick lines that turned corners and doubled back on themselves. That same mazelike pattern ran along the bottom of her long jacket, as well as the sleeve edges and the collar.

She stopped where the bridge sloped into the sand and said, "Who calls Apasam-kamuy, the guardian of the Ainu border? Know that I will not let you pass if you pose a threat to our realm."

"Oh, no, ma'am. We're no threat. We're as harmless as hedgehogs," Niko assured her.

"We're here on a mission to save all of the Middle Lands from Izanami the Destroyer," Danny added.

Apasam-kamuy's expression darkened at the mention of Izanami's name. She frowned at us from her perch on the silvery bridge. "Izanami the Destroyer is a kami of the Yamato."

"Yes, but we're trying to stop—" Danny said, and then fell silent. We drew closer to each other as the whites of Apasam-kamuy's eyes disappeared and her dark pupils expanded. Her face began sprouting a beard, and her shoulders grew bigger and broader. Was she changing into a man? No. Yes. I couldn't tell. She was—*they* were—blurry around the edges, glitching back and forth between the woman and the bearded man.

"You may not cross," they said in two voices. "You have no place on the other side of this bridge."

"But—" Danny started to protest.

"*You're* fine. I sense a spiritual connection between you and this land," Apasam-kamuy said to a stunned Danny. "There's someone else." They extended their right arm and glared at each of us in turn.

I tried to shut out Kusanagi, who was calling me from inside the backpack. *The man with the jewel is somewhere across that bridge. Apasam-kamuy won't let you on without a fight. What are you waiting for? Let's fight!*

Apasam-kamuy pointed at me. "You!" they said, their expression equal parts shocked and furious.

"Me?" I looked around pointlessly—at Ryleigh, at Danny, at Jin, and then at Niko, who had thrown himself to the ground and was whimpering, "Mercy, please! They're just children! They're bumbling babies! Addlepated adolescents! And I'm just a harmless little fox—an unwilling chaperone—an innocent bystander, really!"

But there was no mistaking who Apasam-kamuy meant. "Your aura is vibrating at a frequency I have sensed only once before." Apasam-kamuy had fully transformed now and was looming over us: two kami in one, a man and a woman, both of them fearsome and glowering and ready to rumble.

NOW! NOW! Call me! Use me! Do it now! Kusanagi was

commanding me. My rage monster woke up and added its voice: *Yes! Fight!*

I was vibrating now, literally, partly because I wanted more than anything to call Kusanagi, and partly because I was struggling *not* to call Kusanagi. I folded my arms and closed my hands into my fists so they wouldn't fly out and summon the sword from my backpack, but it was hard work, and I was getting tired fast. My vision began to cloud.

Why was this happening? Kusanagi was supposed to respond to my rage monster, but I hadn't been angry. Apasamkamuy wasn't a threat. Did this mean Kusanagi was in control? Was this how Prince Takeru had become such a monster? I thought about the Tsuchigumo falling under Kusanagi's sharp blade, about the lightning that had destroyed their village. Had Prince Takeru understood what he'd done? Had he cared?

As if responding to the memory of battle, Kusanagi roared, *FIGHT!*

I don't understand . . . A tiny bell rang in the back of my mind. Jin's voice. What had he just said? Something about not fighting. About understanding each other.

Wait.

Maybe that was why I hadn't felt Takeru's towering rage at the Tsuchigumo after I'd woken up from the vision of their massacre. I'd finally understood their side. I'd even understood why Itsuma-hime had felt the need to execute me.

But Kusanagi was back on old territory now, wanting to relive the Yamato conquest of the Ainu, the way it had wanted to relive its conquest of the Tsuchigumo. I just had to—

FIGHT! Kusanagi and my rage monster had joined together now and were louder than ever.

I needed to remember the story of the Ainu. Who were they? What had happened?

But I couldn't remember. Because I didn't know.

Kusanagi snarled, *They are keeping you from the Jewel of the Heart. They are keeping you from your father.*

DAD. How could I have forgotten him? My vision cleared. Apasam-kamuy stood before me, blocking the bridge. Keeping me from rescuing Dad.

Several things happened at once. My rage monster and Kusanagi connected with an intensity that felt like lightning in my veins. The bridge flashed red and disappeared in a cloud of smoke. Someone shoved me forward and dunked me underwater. Then they let go of me—a fatal mistake. Who was it? Was it Apasam-kamuy? I came up spluttering. A figure stood above me, dark against the sun. Before they could get me, I charged and tackled them into the surf. We struggled, and I pinned them down in a bright white rage. I needed my sword. Where was my sword? I was just about to call for it again when I was distracted by someone shouting faintly, "Danny!" and then a little louder, "Momo! Momo, stop!"

Two pairs of strong arms hooked me under my shoulders and dragged me away from my enemy.

"Momo! Snap out of it! No one's here to fight you, you big, belligerent baby!"

No one was here to fight? Why not? I shook my head and blinked the water out of my eyes to see Danny staggering away from me, supported by Ryleigh. He was gasping and wheezing and spitting up water.

I pushed my hair out of my face. I was sitting in the shallows, still gripped by Jin on one side, and Niko in her human form—a red-haired girl with a fox's sharp nose and clever eyes—on the other. Both were breathing hard. Both looked pale and scared.

"What did I do?" I asked. My voice shook. I wasn't sure I wanted to know the answer.

"You tried to drown Danny," said Jin. His voice was low and serious.

"But why?"

"You called Kusanagi, and it appeared in your hand. You were going to fight Apasam-kamuy, I think. But Danny tackled you from behind and you dropped it. And then you grabbed him and..." Jin trailed off and looked toward the beach, where Danny was hunched over on his knees, his back heaving. Ryleigh sat next to him, talking softly.

"You nearly frightened the fur off me," said Niko. She shuddered dramatically.

I stole a glance at Danny, whose breathing seemed to have calmed. The water was freezing, but I didn't want to go ashore. How would I face him? How do you apologize to your best friend who you almost drowned in a fit of rage because he stopped you from trying to kill a kami from another realm?

Speaking of which... "What happened to Kusanagi? Where is it?" The question came out on its own, and I clapped my hand over my mouth in dismay. Jin and Niko looked at me warily.

"Why?" Niko asked. Her nose twitched.

"I don't know," I wailed. "I didn't mean to say that, I swear!"

"I guess you'll need it to destroy the jewel," Jin said slowly. "And it's probably not safe to leave it lying around."

"Maybe you should, though," Ryleigh called from the beach. "It only works if you prove yourself worthy, right? Are you still worthy?"

I didn't know how to answer that. Was she being sincere, or was she being snarky?

"Susano'o was the one who said she was worthy," said Niko.

I understood what she was saying. If Susano'o was the one who'd pronounced me worthy, what did "worthy" really mean? I'd always assumed that it meant I was good, somehow. That I was honorable, or courageous, or noble, or had "leadership potential," or something like that, because that was how people usually proved themselves worthy of legendary swords. But now that I thought about it, Kusanagi had first come to life in my hands when I was fighting that giant scorpion in Susano'o's fortress, and it had happened because I was angry at Danny for trying to take it from me. "Worthy" to Susano'o probably meant "has a tendency toward violence and destruction."

As if it had heard my thoughts, Kusanagi called out to me. *We are destined for each other. I'm here! Come and get me!*

Following the voice, I waded a few feet deeper into the sea. I reached down and felt my fingers close around its hilt. As I stood, I felt Jin's hand on my shoulder.

"Maybe you shouldn't touch it for a while," he said. "Why don't you let one of us put it away?"

"Careful, Jin!" Ryleigh called out, and I winced. I didn't blame her.

So I let go of it, and Jin picked it up and splashed back to shore. He handed it to Ryleigh, who shoved it into my backpack.

Niko and I followed Jin out of the water. Once we reached the sand, Niko shifted back into fox form and shook himself vigorously, spraying seawater everywhere. Danny lifted his head and smiled at Niko. He coughed once and looked at me. Ryleigh hovered protectively next to him. Jin knelt on Danny's other side.

"I'm sorry," I choked. "I didn't mean to hurt you. You know I'd never hurt any of you on purpose. You all know that, right?" Desperation made my voice shrill and tight.

"What happened?" Ryleigh asked. "To you, I mean."

I shook my head. I wasn't in the mood to discuss Kusanagi's growing influence on me, or whether my idea about understanding my opponent's story was the solution.

"You should tell us. Maybe we can help you," said Jin.

But it was too much. Too complicated. They would never understand my relationship to my rage monster and to Kusanagi. And anyway, I was exhausted. "Maybe later," I said.

"Well, whatever happened, I know you're good. I know you're not violent," Danny said. "I believe in you. You should, too."

Gratitude and relief swept through me so powerfully that I had to sit down and take huge, gulping breaths so that I wouldn't dissolve into a blubbering mess. After all that had happened, Danny still believed in me. He still wanted to be my friend.

I will make myself worthy of your trust, I promised him silently. *I will find a way.*

Orcas Aren't Whales

Unfortunately, Ryleigh wasn't quite as ready to forgive me. "I've noticed that you're basically fine until you and Kusanagi are in front of someone who Kusanagi thinks is an enemy. But if we go into the Ainu realm, that could be everyone," she said. "Especially now that Apasam-Kamuy's probably gone back there and told them what happened."

"And?" I said testily.

"Are you working on it, at least? Because that's a huge liability."

As if I didn't know that already.

"Do you have any ideas about what she can do to work on it?" Jin asked Ryleigh.

"I mean." She hesitated, which was odd. I'd never seen her think twice about telling people what to do and how to do it. "Ninja and samurai are trained to let our emotions flow through us when we fight. Like, just let them go. Then we can focus on what we have to do, instead of how we feel about it."

Interesting. Could I do that with my rage monster and Kusanagi? It would be a lot easier than reading up on the history of every single potential enemy I encountered.

Meanwhile, unable to resist a joke, Danny sang, "Let it go, let it *goooo*."

"Stop that discordant din," Niko begged him. "Anyway, enemies, friends, frenemies, flowing through, letting go—it's all moot! There's no point in picking apart the particulars as long as we're over *here* and our destination is over *there*." He pointed across the strait.

Which was when we heard someone in the water go, "Ahoyyyyy!"

"Did you hear that? Do you see anything out there?" Jin said.

"I don't see—no, wait! There's a waterspout! A whale!" My heart leaped. Had Izanami released Dad? Had he escaped on his own?

But when the whale leaped out of the water, I saw that it was jet black, with a white belly and white markings on the side. I couldn't help feeling a pang of disappointment.

"It's an orca!" Jin said.

"Ahoyyyy, Son of Ebisu!" There was no mistaking it. The orca was calling to us.

"Technically, orcas aren't whales," Niko said. "They're dolphins."

"Shhh." Danny flapped an impatient hand and stared out at the water. "Did it say, 'Son of Ebisu'?" He turned to us, his eyes shining. "Do you think that means me?"

"Son of Ebisu!" The whale—oops, I mean the orca—bobbed at the surface, only fifty feet away. "The Son of Ebisu called for help, and help has arrived! By which I mean *I* have arrived!" The orca popped his head out of the water and performed a little bow. "Which one of you is the Son of Ebisu?"

"Uh." Danny raised his hand timidly. "Me? I think? I'm Danny, and Ebisu is my spirit dad. Does that count?"

"Of course it counts! You don't have to be blood to be family, you know! Ebisu was not born of the orcas, but we made him a member of our family when we took him across the sea to the Ainu. If you are the spirit son of Ebisu, then *you* are a member of our family! And when family calls, family answers!"

As if to emphasize his point, he jumped out of the water again and did a full twist before splashing back down. "Welcome to the family, Danny!"

Danny's face split into a broad smile. "Thanks!"

"When did you call for help?" Jin asked.

"He was underwater!" said the orca. "That's how I heard him! 'Help!' he said. 'Help, help!'"

"It must have been when, ah . . . when Momo was, you know . . ." Danny cleared his throat and looked at me.

"Testing your lung capacity?" I offered. I tried a smile. *Please let him be ready to joke about this.*

"Yeah. That." He grinned, and I heaved a sigh of relief.

"But how did you call for help?" Ryleigh asked.

"I didn't. I was busy running out of breath."

"You did! You very clearly said, 'Help, help!'" the orca insisted cheerfully.

"Maybe I thought it. Maybe whales are telepathic," said Danny.

"Orcas aren't whales!" said the orca and Niko together.

"Right. Sorry," Danny apologized. "I'm so used to thinking of you as whales. But I know it's disrespectful, so I'll remember from now on, I promise."

"Thank you!" the orca said. "So! Do you still need help? Can I help you?"

"As a matter of fact . . . ," said Danny. He turned to us. "Should I ask for help crossing the water?"

"Yes! Yes, you should!" The orca performed yet another twisting leap out of the waves, as if the idea was too exciting to consider without a huge celebratory splash. "Go ahead! Ask for help crossing the water!"

"Okay, then! Mr. Orca? Ms. Orca? Mrs. Orca?"

"Call me Mako!" said the orca. "I'm a male! And this is my friend Cookie!"

"I'm a male, too! And I'm here to help the Son of Ebisu, too!" A second orca breached out of nowhere and crashed almost on top of Mako. "Hey, bro! Any family member of Ebisu is a family member of mine! Yeeeah, boyyyy!"

This was almost more enthusiasm than I could handle. In fact, it seemed to be more enthusiasm than Mako and Cookie could handle, because they were now breaching and crashing over and over again, as if they'd forgotten why they'd come to us in the first place. I nudged Danny, who was staring at his new orca brothers with shining eyes and seemed not to have noticed that they had completely lost the plot.

"Hey. Can you ask them for help?"

"Oh. Right." He cleared his throat. "Uh, guys?"

Mako and Cookie stopped midbreach and crashed enthusiastically back into the water before bobbing their heads up. "Yes!" they said in unison.

"Do you think you could help us get across the water?" Danny said.

"YES! Woo-hoo!" Mako and Cookie shouted together, and then did identical leap-and-twist things with a high five at the top, like this was the best news they'd heard all day.

"We can help you!" said Mako.

"We will help you!" said Cookie.

"Right now!" said Mako.

"Let's gooooo!" said Cookie.

They both nosed their way closer to shore.

"This is as far as we can go without getting beached!" Mako declared. "Come out here and hop on!"

"Don't worry, now! We'll stay right at the surface!" Cookie reassured us.

"We'll go nice and slow!" Mako added.

It wasn't exactly door-to-door service, but they weren't too far away. We pushed and bobbed our way through the chop toward our rides.

"Here you are! Now climb on!" said Cookie.

"That's the stuff!" Mako agreed. "One in front of the dorsal fin, one behind! And you, Mr. Fox, can sit wherever you like!"

We arranged ourselves on Mako's and Cookie's backs, and the orcas swam carefully into the strait. The sun had risen, and the water sparkled and rippled around us as we crossed to the other side. The wind tossed spray in my face and blew my hair every which way.

As we rode, Mako occasionally lifted his mouth out of the water so he could give us orca facts "to educate you about your family, Son of Ebisu!"

"Orcas can't smell!" he said one time.

"Different orca clans speak different languages!"

"Orca moms are *so* overprotective! Our mom will be furious when she hears that I took you across the water! 'Why would you risk his life like that?' she'll say!"

"Risk his life?" I quavered.

"I told you they're overprotective! Right, Danny?"

Danny sighed and smiled at me. "It's like they really want me to be one of them. I've never felt like that before."

"Like you wanted to be an orca?"

"No! Like people wanted me to be one of them. Like really, truly part of their group. Except my parents, obviously."

"You're one of us," I pointed out.

Danny just shrugged and said, "I guess." Before I could ask him what the heck that was supposed to mean, he leaned over and called to Mako. "Hey, tell me more about orcas!"

I could tell that he didn't want to say goodbye when we reached the other side, but Mako and Cookie didn't give us a choice—they rolled over and dumped us off their backs. The water was so cold, my lungs actually froze up for a second.

"Haha! Are you okay? That was a joke!" Mako said.

"W-w-we're ok-k-kay," I spluttered once I got my breath back.

"Gotta go, or Mom will be worried!" said Cookie.

"Orca moms, right, Danny?" Mako and Cookie squealed with laughter.

Danny looked uncertain. "I mean, I'm not *really* an orca."

"Yes, you are!" Mako insisted. "Just because you didn't grow up with us doesn't mean you're not one of us!"

"Orca bros for life!" said Cookie.

"Orca bros for life!" Mako chimed in. "Now your turn, Danny! It can be our thing!"

Danny beamed. He looked like he might cry. "Orca bros for life!"

Mako and Cookie breached and gave each other another midair high five. When they crashed back to the water, the wave sent us surging the rest of the way to shore.

"If you need us again, little brother, just wade in and give a shout!" said Mako. "Orca bros for liiiiife!" He and Cookie flipped their tails and disappeared under the surface. Danny stood at the water's edge and stared after them even when it became clear that they wouldn't surface again.

I thought about the way Mako and Cookie had welcomed Danny so easily. I knew he felt like he was fully his parents' child, but I also knew how hard it had been for him to leave the alternate life in the Mirror of the Sun where he was still with his birth family. I remembered how he'd yelled at me and Ryleigh and Jin about our having family histories, even if they were messed up. And how hurt he'd been about all the Asian stuff. He had such a sunny personality that I often forgot that there was heartache inside him, too. Big questions that might never get answered. And even if they were, there was no guarantee that those answers would ease his heartache.

The orcas wouldn't be able to replace a lost birth family, but they gave him another family to belong to unconditionally, and they clearly didn't give a fig about whether he was "really" an orca. No wonder he'd been so happy on Mako's back. If I were Danny, I wouldn't want to see my orca bros go, either.

"N-n-now what?" said Ryleigh through chattering teeth, and I realized I was shivering, too. "Why is it so much c-c-colder all of a sudden?"

"Because you're in Ainu Moshiri, the realm of the Ainu kamuy," said a voice.

The wind off the ocean gusted so hard that I stumbled and almost fell. It swirled around us, whipping sand into our eyes and tangling our hair before dying down as suddenly as it had sprung up. When I'd wiped the sand out of my eyes and shoved my hair out of my face, I saw a big, barrel-chested, broad-shouldered man with a bushy beard and shaggy black hair. He wore the skin and fur of a giant bear on his shoulders, with the bear's head and jaw over his own head like a hood.

"He must be a god. Be respectful," Niko warned us, as if we needed warning. "Keep it low-key."

The god frowned down at us. "Who are you, and what is your purpose here?"

Can't Stop, Addicted to the Shindig

I could feel Kusanagi's energy bristling in response to the challenge, and my hands began to itch. *Let it go. Let it gooo,* I thought. *Darn you, Danny!*

"We're here on a quest," said Jin.

"Ah," said the Ainu god. His expression remained stony.

Danny jumped in. "Ebisu's my spirit dad. I called these orcas—maybe you know them? Mako and Cookie? And they helped us cross over from the, uh, from over there." He pointed back to the other side of the strait.

"Ah," said the Ainu god again, and he smiled a little bit. "I remember when they brought baby Ebisu to our shores long ago. He was a good boy." The Ainu god nodded at Danny. "Any son of Ebisu's is a son of mine. Given your special relationship with him, I welcome you, young man. And your friends."

The wind returned and swooped us up over the bluff that overlooked the beach and tossed us onto a large wooden platform. We tumbled across the platform like dice and ended up in a tangled heap of arms and legs. Groaning, we untangled ourselves and rolled apart.

"Not cool," Danny muttered. "I thought he said we were friends."

"Just you," I reminded him. "Not us." I was starting to get that jittery feeling again. It didn't seem respectful to ask this new god to tell me right off the bat how his people had suffered so that I wouldn't attack him. Until I learned a little bit on my own, I'd have to try to find a different way to keep Kusanagi from convincing me that he was an enemy. *Let it go,* I told myself, seriously this time. *Let it go.*

When we stood up, we found the Ainu god waiting for us. "Allow me to introduce myself," he said. "My name is Kim-un-kamuy."

Danny gasped. "The Ainu bear god of the mountains? That's so cool!"

"Indeed," said Kim-un-kamuy, patting his bearskin cloak. "Good work, young cub."

"I'm trying to teach myself about the Ainu because of Ebisu," said Danny modestly.

"And what have you learned?" Kim-un-kamuy asked.

"The Ainu are the native people of Hokkaidō. And also some Russian islands," Danny recited dutifully. "They have their own language and culture, but Japan colonized Hokkaidō and gave all the land to Japanese officials, and they brought diseases that wiped out tons of people, and made everyone only speak Japanese and stop hunting and fishing and worshipping you and the other kamuy."

"That's a start," said Kim-un-kamuy. "Anything else?"

"Not a lot," Danny admitted. "But I know you're awesome."

Kim-un-kamuy looked pleased. "True! Keep learning, young cub. In the meantime, you may now tell me about your quest. Mind you, if you're here to plunder or pillage, I will kick you right into the sea." His voice turned into a deep and dangerous-sounding growl.

"No pillaging, Your Brawniness! No plundering! We promise!" Niko said.

This Ainu kamuy wants to kick us into the sea! He's slowing us down, hissed my rage monster.

Only because he's worried we'll treat his people like the Yamato did, I argued back. *He's not our enemy!* I dug my fingers into my palms, which were starting to sting.

Not yet, said Kusanagi.

"We're looking for someone who has something we need in order to save the Middle Lands from destruction," said Ryleigh.

"Which we will request from said someone with reverence and respect!" Niko added.

"I see. And who did you say this fellow was again?"

"We don't know," I said.

"He was wearing a brown robe," said Danny. "With a hood. Does that help?"

"A brown robe with a hood, eh?" Kim-un-kamuy gave each of us a long, appraising look before saying, "The one you seek did, in fact, pass through here not too long ago."

"What did he say? Where did he go?" I asked. *See? I told Kusanagi. He's helping us!*

Kim-un-kamuy shook his head. "I'm afraid I'm not at liberty to say."

Arghhh! My hands twitched, and I shoved them in my pockets.

He has no reason to trust us, I reminded Kusanagi and my rage monster, who were now straining to connect to each other. *Let it go, let it gooo....*

"However, I don't approve of the path he took," Kim-un-kamuy said with a sly twinkle in his eye. "So while I am not at liberty to reveal his whereabouts, I hereby grant myself the liberty to let you find those whereabouts yourselves!" He clapped his hands, and three luxurious red velvet curtains appeared around the platform. "Three curtains, three challenges. Succeed at any of them, and the path to the one you seek will open up. Fail all three, and you go back from whence you came. What do you say?"

It seemed fair enough. Kusanagi's energy subsided a little. *Whew.*

"Excellent!" Kim-un-kamuy threw his head back and bellowed, "Time for the first challenge! Pikata-kamuyyyy! Come on down!"

One of the three curtains opened to reveal a tall, gray-eyed woman with wavy black shoulder-length hair and a long, flowing cloak that billowed behind her as if she were standing in front of a giant fan.

"Introduce yourself to these fine folks!" Kim-un-kamuy said.

The woman smiled at us. "Delighted to meet you, children! I am Pikata-kamuy. I control the winds around here."

The winds? I felt Kusanagi's energy vibrate through me.

This is not a fight. This is not a fight, I told it.

Pikata-kamuy turned her gaze on me. Her face was pleasant, but there was a glint of suspicion in her eyes. "I detect something . . . special about you. I wonder what it is?"

"Nothing!" Niko yelped before I could even open my mouth. "Nothing special about her at all! She's as common as they come. Just an average adolescent with no derring-do, no wondrous weapons, and not a single skill to speak of. Helpless as a haystack. Boring as a bag of ballpoint pens. Isn't that right, Momo?"

"That's right," I said. Although seriously? Ballpoint pens? That was a bit much.

"Pikata here is your first challenge," Kim-un-kamuy said. He stepped to the side and swept his arm toward her. "Take it away, sister!"

Pikata-kamuy smiled. "As the kamuy of the wind, I love to dance. If you can match my moves, I'll take you wherever you like. But if you can't, I'll send you off to wherever *I* like."

"No, no, no! They get two more chances after that!" Kim-un-kamuy interrupted. "You know the rules. Why are you always trying to break them?"

"I *like* blowing people off the island." Pikata-kamuy pouted.

"If they fail all three challenges and come out alive, I'll let you do it," said Kim-un-kamuy.

If we came out alive? I nearly groaned out loud. Plus, everyone knows that magical beings never, ever propose a head-to-head contest if they think there's even a slight chance they might lose. With the exception of that one song about the devil and a fiddle contest in Georgia, I haven't heard of a single human winning against a supernatural being and not getting punished as a result of the god being a sore loser.

"We accept!" said Niko with much more enthusiasm than I expected. To us, he said, "Don't pout, my pessimistic little peapods." For once, he looked energized at the thought of a challenge that was sure to end in disaster. "We might have a shot, especially if you put me in front. I am an excellent dancer, if I do say so myself. I won the 'Most Room for Improvement' award in the 1927 Foxtrot Follies." He stood on his hind legs and pranced in a circle.

"Okay, I don't know if Niko should go in front," said Danny. "But he's right that we could win this. Look!" He demonstrated by doing the running man, the Griddy, and the Carlton. "And Jin's a pro, obviously. Whaddaya think, Jin?"

Jin looked like he didn't know whether to laugh or cry. I bet you can guess which one I wanted to do.

Ryleigh rolled her eyes and said, "No offense, but Jin has to go in front of both of you."

Before Danny and Niko could protest, Pikata-kamuy clapped her hands for attention. "You can make your decisions in a minute. Right now, it's my turn!" She snapped her fingers, and a rock appeared in her hands.

"This is Alexa," she said. "She will play any music you ask for."

"Alexa?" I couldn't help blurting out.

Pikata-kamuy shrugged. "It's very convenient. Alexa! Play the Santa Ana winds!"

A hot, dry blast of wind swept down out of nowhere and carried a song that made no sense:

Can't stop, addicted to the shindig
Chop Top, he says I'm gonna win big . . .

Pikata-kamuy whirled and pranced and stomped her feet; she shimmied and shook, and her cloak swirled around her like it had a life of its own. I'm not gonna lie, it was kind of breathtaking.

"I don't think we can beat that," said Jin. He looked like he had decided how he felt, which is to say, he looked like he wanted to cry.

"But we have to try. Okay. Here's what we do," said Ryleigh, suddenly in full boss mode. "We're going to request a song from Straight 2 tha Topp. One that everyone knows the moves to."

"I don't know any Straight 2 tha Topp dance moves!" said Niko. "I don't watch YouCube or do TikkityTok or whatever it is that you call your silly social media sites."

"That's okay. Jin is going to dance in front and shine like heck. And I'll go next to him and the rest of you can dance behind us. If you don't know the moves, you can just go like this." Ryleigh did a little side-to-side step move and went, "Left, tap. Right, tap. Left, tap. Right, tap."

"This is a wildly irresponsible waste of my talent," Niko grumbled. But he shifted to the back, thank goodness.

A few months ago, all of this would have made me so mad—the way Ryleigh took over, the way she hogged the spotlight and shoved the rest of us in back. But now I was just thankful. Because I knew that Ryleigh wasn't taking over—she was taking charge. And I much preferred this Ryleigh to the one who'd been strangely upset for so much of this mission.

Pikata-kamuy finished her performance and took a bow. Kim-un-kamuy cheered and whistled, and we all clapped politely.

"Amazeballs as usual, Pikata!" Kim-un-kamuy said. "And now it's your turn, kiddos!" He made a grand sweeping motion with his arms. Another wind pushed us onto the stage. "Show us what you've got!"

"Put your powers to use!" Niko advised Jin. "This is no time for timidity. No silly scruples. Our lives are on the line!"

"Momo's dad's life is on the line," said Danny.

"The *entire world's* lives are on the line," corrected Ryleigh, and once again I wondered if she'd let me save Dad or if she'd insist on trying to destroy the jewel first.

"Great, thanks. No pressure," Jin muttered.

"It's a good thing I thrive under pressure," said Ryleigh.

"Alexa," Jin said, his voice shaking. "Play 'Imma Fight 4 Ya.'"

The opening bars played, and Jin lit right up. He shimmered and sparkled in his own personal spotlight and even sent a little of it our way. Ryleigh and I knew the dance by heart, and it turned out that Danny actually knew some of the signature moves: Jump, spin, twirl, dip. Slide, stomp, point, wink. I completely forgot about Pikata-kamuy, the contest, Dad, and the possible imminent destruction of life as we knew it, and just had fun dancing—that's how powerful Jin's magic was. And then the song was over and we all took a bow and stood back up, breathing hard.

Clap. Clap. Clap.

Pikata-kamuy's face was unreadable, but we all know what a slow clap means. My heart sank.

But Kim-un-kamuy smiled at Jin and said, "Well done, young man! What a brilliant performance! Where did you learn to dance like that?"

Jin bowed his head modestly. "Thanks. I have a choreographer and a dance coach. But I guess you could say I get my talent from my mom, Benzaiten."

"Ah, yes, of course! I thought you looked familiar. She's one of my favorite Shintō kami, you know. Such a kind spirit."

Jin smiled unconvincingly.

"Unfortunately, your performance as a group was a little uneven, to say the least. A little lacking in pizzazz, if you will. Entertaining, but . . . how can I express this delicately?" He stroked his beard for a moment, then shook his head. "I can't. It was terrible. Pikata? Your thoughts?"

Pikata-kamuy gave us a thumbs-down.

"And that, my dear children, is why I must declare this lovely kamuy the winner." Kim-un-kamuy held Pikata-kamuy's hand up and snapped his fingers. A blast of horns blew from the sky and a roar of applause rose around us, as if we were surrounded by thousands of invisible Pikata-kamuy stans. Pikata-kamuy took a deep bow.

"Don't feel bad," Kim-un-kamuy said. "She is the world's greatest dancer, after all, so you were bound to lose." (See what I mean about gods and contests?) "Anyway, you have two challenges left! Pikata, will you please bring on the next challenge?"

Pikata-kamuy spread her cloak and spun in a circle. A howling wind swept out of the cloak and swirled around us, just like on the beach. The second curtain went up, revealing two podiums and a giant grid of blue squares. A rope tumbled down from a bell that appeared to be hanging from an invisible hook in the sky.

"Look at that, kids!" Kim-un-kamuy grinned broadly. "You now have a chance to win big on the greatest game show of all time, *Jeopardy!* Otherwise known as No Silly Questions!"

Suddenly we were crowded behind one of the little podiums, and Pikata-kamuy stood behind the other one.

"Yes!" Ryleigh pumped her fist. "I am amazing at trivia."

"The first team to collect a thousand points will win . . ." Kim-un-kamuy paused dramatically before announcing, "This brand! New! BALLLL!"

The invisible audience burst into applause as he held out a grimy old tennis ball.

"Um, that looks super cool," I said. "But if you don't mind my asking—"

"There's no such thing as a silly question!" said Kim-un-kamuy with an encouraging smile. "See what I did there?" He winked and chuckled to himself.

There's no such thing as a silly question is something teachers say all the time, but I've definitely seen a teacher or two roll their eyes at a question they thought was silly, so I had to take a moment to gather my courage.

Danny, however, had never cared if his questions sounded silly, so while I hesitated, he asked for me. "What's so special about that ball?"

"Ahh, wouldn't you like to know?" said Kim-un-kamuy with a gleam in his eye.

"Well, yes. I would. That's why I asked," said Danny.

Kim-un-kamuy let out a peal of laughter. "What a cheeky monkey you are! I'm not going to tell you just yet, because I abide by a very strict no-spoilers policy. All you need to know is that if you don't win it, your quest will be over. Get it? Got it? Good! Now, on with the show!"

Ainu It!

"**Here are the rules.** Each column in this grid is a different category."

The row of squares at the top of the blue grid lit up. They were labeled from right to left: THAT BEARS REPEATING; ONE, TWO, TREE; YOU WANNA PIZZA ME?; and AINU IT! Under each category, the squares lit up in columns with numbers from top to bottom: 200, 400, 600, 800.

"Pick a category and a point value and I'll give you the answer to a question. Ring the bell, ask the question that matches the answer, and win the points. Ask the wrong question and you get no points. First team to get a thousand points wins the game. Ready? Go!"

Before we could even discuss which category to choose, Pikata-kamuy called out, "Ainu It for eight hundred points!"

"Oh, great choice!" said Kim-un-kamuy. "And the answer is, He was a member of the Marvel Comics' superhero team Big Hero 6!"

Pikata-kamuy dashed forward, yanked on the rope, and shouted, "Who is Fredzilla!" as the bell clanged overhead.

"Bingo! Eight hundred points to you!" Kim-un-kamuy

waved a hand and a golden number 800 appeared above Pikata-kamuy's head. "The Marvel character Fredzilla is a descendant of the Ainu people and grew up on a secret S.H.I.E.L.D. base on the island of Hokkaidō!"

We were still staring at each other as a round of applause came from our invisible audience.

"But that's not fair!" Ryleigh said. "We didn't get a—"

"Ainu It for six hundred!" Pikata-kamuy interrupted her, and Ryleigh's eyes went steely.

"You guys, it's just whoever picks first and whoever answers first," she muttered. "Be ready!" She went into a crouch.

"Sweet! I was born for this!" Danny got ready to run as well.

"But we hardly know anything about—" I started to say, but I was cut off.

"What famous spy spent time in an Ainu—"

Danny was ringing the bell and yelling, "Who is James Bond!" before Kim-un-kamuy even finished.

"No fair!" It was Pikata-kamuy's turn to complain this time.

"I never said you couldn't ring the bell before I'd finished talking," said Kim-un-kamuy apologetically. "Son of Ebisu, you are correct! According to the novel *You Only Live Twice*, the Ainu once hosted international superspy James Bond. Six hundred points for the mortals!"

A golden 600 sparkled above us.

"How did you know that?" I asked Danny.

"I didn't. I just heard 'famous spy' and guessed. Lucky, huh?"

"Ebisu must be looking out for you," said Kim-un-kamuy. "Unfortunately, the movie and the book were full of inaccurate and unflattering stereotypes, and also there is a ludicrous outer-space element, so I'm taking a hundred points off. Five hundred!"

The golden 600 changed to a 500, and we all groaned, except for Pikata-kamuy, who grinned and said, "You Wanna Pizza Me? for six hundred!"

"Pizza!" Niko's face lit up. "Oh, I am ready for this one!" He got ready to spring.

"It is commonly thought to be a kind of pizza, but—"

Niko howled in disappointment when Pikata-kamuy beat him to the bell and shouted, "What is Chicago-style pizza!"

Kim-un-kamuy shook his head. "I'm sorry, my friend. But that is not the correct question."

"What? But—"

"Yes, I know that there are people who feel the same as you, but the fact is, Chicago-style pizza is still pizza."

Pikata-kamuy looked mutinous.

"Do you have the correct question?" Kim-un-kamuy turned to Niko, who nodded eagerly.

"Hawaiian pizza!"

"NOOOOO!" Ryleigh fell to her knees.

"I'm sorry, fox, but that was not a question. Who can—"

"What is Hawaiian pizza!" Pikata-kamuy shrieked.

Kim-un-kamuy nodded at her. "Well done! That is, in fact, the correct question. Hawaiian pizza is delicious, but it is not real pizza. Six hundred points to you, which makes fourteen hundred! Pikata wins!"

The fake applause sounded again, and Pikata-kamuy danced

around with the disgusting tennis ball. Kim-un-kamuy shot us a sympathetic glance. "Tough loss. But hang in there! You still have once more chance."

Pikata-kamuy gave us a smile. "I hope you fail!" she said sweetly.

"Well, then!" Kim-un-kamuy said. "I suppose you'll be wanting to learn about your third and final challenge!"

He did his game show–host arm wave, and the third curtain rose to reveal four massive wooden doors on the grassy field beyond the platform. They appeared to have been plunked down out of nowhere, and they appeared to lead to nowhere, which, of course, was how we knew they were magic and that they *did* lead somewhere.

Each door was guarded by a different giant animal. There was a ferocious white wolf, a lumbering bear, a growling komainu like Alfie and Meggie, and weirdest of all . . .

"Is that a giant shrimp?" Danny snickered.

"Uh-huh." Kim-un-kamuy nodded. "If you had won the ball, it would have helped you get past the guardians. They're fierce, but easily distracted, if you know what I mean. They'll try to kill anyone who approaches their portals, but toss the ball, and off they go." He shrugged.

"Lemme guess," said Jin. "The guy we're looking for went through one of those doors."

"Correct! And each animal guard represents an old Middle Land culture," Kim-un-kamuy explained.

"There's a shrimp god?" Danny asked, gaping. "Is there a realm of shrimp people somewhere?"

"The Emishi!" Niko exclaimed. "It's a Middle Lands kingdom that Kusanagi helped to conquer, just like the other ones—I see it now! The white wolf represents the Ainu, the bear represents the Matagi, and the shiisaa represents the Ryūkyū kingdom way down in Okinawa."

"Shiisaa?" I repeated. "Isn't that a koma-inu? It looks just like Alfie and—"

"Shiisaa, my undereducated urchin, only look like koma-inu. Koma-inu are Yamato creatures, and shiisaa have always lived in Okinawa. They're like cousins."

"Oh." There was so much I'd have to study up on later. Especially since . . . "Also, did I just hear you say *conquer*?"

"Yes, indeed you did," said Kim-un-kamuy dryly.

Sigh.

"But we digress!" he said. "Let's get back to the challenge. All you have to do is choose the correct door and make it past the guardian!"

Maybe this wasn't so bad. We could use Danny's phone to show us the right door. And as long as the only other challenge was to fight a monster, I wouldn't have to worry about letting go or understanding or moving beyond destruction or anything like that. All I had to do was let Kusanagi do what it did best: fight.

"Let's do this," I said to the others. "We need to get going." And then I almost laughed. Who would have guessed that I, Momo Arashima, would be eager to start a fight to the death?

But alarm bells began clanging faintly somewhere in the back of my mind. Something wasn't right. What was it?

Danny took out his phone. Jin began humming "The Lion Sleeps Tonight" to himself—maybe he figured it would work on all apex predators. Ryleigh got busy sorting through her shuriken.

"Is it possible that the worst is behind us?" Niko said. "We can definitely defeat any of those animals if we collaborate in combat. Though it might be wisest if you led the way, Momo, what with your weapon and all. Or perhaps Danny or Ryleigh."

"Okay, I don't want to, like, alarm anyone? But uh . . ." Danny sounded nervous, and when I looked at him, I saw why. The flashlight on his phone remained dark, no matter where he pointed it.

"Are you sure you're using it right?" Ryleigh asked. "Or maybe the battery died."

"Of course I'm using it right! It's my phone!" Danny groused. "And you know the battery never dies!"

"You're meant to make the decision on your own, without magical instruments," said Kim-un-kamuy. "It's a human dilemma you face, and you must solve it with your human faculties, such as they are."

"But how do we choose?" Jin asked.

Kim-un-kamuy shrugged his shoulders. "That is up to you."

"What happens if we choose wrong?" I said.

"You'll be blasted into oblivion, most likely," said Kim-un-kamuy.

Pikata-kamuy scowled. "But you said if they survived, I'd get to—"

Kim-un-kamuy raised a hand. "I stand corrected. *Mostly* blasted into oblivion. There will be pieces of you left over to blow off the island, I'm sure." Pikata-kamuy gave a satisfied smile.

"Can you give us a clue?" asked Danny, ever hopeful.

"No can do."

I stared at the doors, my mind spinning. *Think, Momo, think!* Wolf, bear, lion-dog, giant shrimp. Did the right choice have to do with the animal? Or was it random?

"It has to be the door with the wolf. The wolf is one of the guardians of the Ainu, right? We're in Ainu territory. It's the only logical choice," said Ryleigh.

"But what if this isn't about logic?" I asked. "What if it's about character? What if we're supposed to choose the biggest, scariest animal to, like, prove our courage or something?" That was kind of how the Mirror of the Sun had worked. The only way out was to have faith in myself and to be committed to doing the right thing.

"But which animal is the scariest?" Danny asked.

"Bear," I said.

"Wolf," said Ryleigh.

"Shiisaa," said Jin.

"I think the shrimp is kinda terrifying, actually," said Danny. "I mean, I know I laughed before, but look at those beady little eyes, and those antennae waving all over the place! It's straight out of a horror movie! How does that not creep you out?"

"Maybe it's mad at you for laughing at it," I said.

Danny shuddered. "Let's not even talk about that."

"Or what if it's a trick?" Niko put in. "What if we *think* we're supposed to prove our courage, but really it's the opposite? What if it *is* the shrimp?"

"But the shrimp is scary!" Danny insisted.

"Maybe it's one of those scary-on-the-outside, cinnamon-roll-on-the-inside situations?" Jin said.

"Nope, every one of them will attack you for sure," said Kim-un-kamuy.

"So it doesn't even matter which one we choose," Niko wailed.

"We need to split up. That way, at least one of us will end up in the right place," said Ryleigh.

"We can't split up! We're a team!" Danny said.

"I agree. Momo's the only one who can destroy the jewel," Jin said. "So if we split up and she picks the wrong door, the whole point of the mission is ruined."

"But if we all go through the wrong door together, *no one* will find the guy with the jewel," Ryleigh said.

"And we'll all be blasted to bits," Niko added.

"But if none of us gets the jewel, then at least Izanami can't get it, either," said Jin.

"You don't know that. We don't know if we can trust the guy in the brown robe," Ryleigh insisted.

"Ryūjin trusted him," I pointed out.

"And he also tried to trick us into staying at the palace," Ryleigh said.

"I don't want to die!" Niko moaned. "Can't we just determine the right door so we don't die?"

"There's no way to figure it out except to guess," Ryleigh said, exasperated.

"What's wrong with guessing?" Danny asked.

"By the way!" Kim-un-kamuy said. "Did I mention that your time is limited?"

"What?" I spun around to stare at him. "What do you mean?"

"Your time is limited," he repeated.

"We don't need to panic just yet," said Jin. "How much time do we have?"

"I'd say you have about two minutes."

"WHAT?" all five of us shouted at once.

"I think now would be an appropriate time to panic," I said.

"I agree," said Kim-un-kamuy. "Panic to your heart's content!"

"We have to maximize our chances of picking the right door," said Ryleigh. "We have to split up."

"We can't split up!" Danny said again.

"Which is why we need to figure out the puzzle of the doors, you bullheaded bozos!" Niko barked.

"One minute, forty seconds left!" Kim-un-kamuy called out. Next to him, Pikata-kamuy clapped her hands and whistled.

The wolf paced back and forth, his snowy white hackles raised and his pale blue eyes fixed on us. The bear stood with his feet planted, swaying from right to left, his lips drawn back in a snarl. The shiisaa crouched as if getting ready to spring. The shrimp stared at the sky and waved its antennae around. Creepily.

"Jin can fly over one of them, and the rest of us with weapons can fight each of the others," said Ryleigh. "Niko, I'll give you my invisibility hat and you choose who you want to go with."

"We have to go together!" Danny insisted.

"No, we don't!" Ryleigh practically spat the words out.

"One minute, twenty seconds left!" Kim-un-kamuy bellowed. Pikata-kamuy began taking what looked like warm-up breaths. Wind swirled around us.

"Ryleigh, come on," Jin begged her. "If any of us could do this on their own, it's you, but the rest of us need help. Hey—how about you pick a door and we go with you? You can be in charge! But we should do this together. We're a team. We're friends."

"No, we're not."

"One minute left!" The wind grew stronger.

"What? Of course we are!" Danny said.

"Stop lying. Just go and be besties and save the world together if that's what you want, but leave me out of it. I'm done being part of your little club."

Everyone gaped at her. I felt like my head might spin right off my shoulders, I was so confused. "What are you talking about?" I said. "We don't have time for this!"

"Thirty seconds left!" Kim-un-kamuy roared, as if to prove my point.

Let me fight! Kusanagi buzzed under the commotion, and suddenly I knew what I had to do. We were here because of me. It was my father's life we were trying to save. I was the only one who could destroy the Jewel of the Heart.

I pulled Kusanagi out and concentrated. *Tell me where to go,* I begged it. *Now, while they're busy fighting each other.*

Ryleigh was nearly in tears now. "I'm a loser, okay? I know you're all thinking it. All I do is let you down. I'm not even a good friend."

I caught Pikata-kamuy's eye, and then I nodded at my friends. I hoped the goddess would understand what I wanted her to do.

"Five seconds!"

"Now is not the time to air our anxieties!" Niko howled at the same time that Danny shouted, "Someone pick a door or I will!"

But it was too late. Pikata-kamuy summoned a gust of wind that blew my friends backward, and with a yell, I followed Kusanagi's energy toward the shrimp.

The shrimp whipped around, its antennae waving and its big black eyes staring. It looked less like a potentially delicious tempura item and more like a huge alien monster now. It opened its mouth wide and made a sound like a thousand jackhammers. (Yeah, that's right. Look it up. Shrimps have mouths, and those mouths are just as scary as you'd think.)

I didn't hesitate. That monster was keeping me from finding the only thing that would free Dad. It was keeping me from the only way to stop Izanami once and for all. And here I was once again, fighting for my life, for the lives of everyone I loved, against my choice, against my will. As I ran, I felt Kusanagi's power—*my* power—surge. *GET THAT MONSTER.*

But as I drew Kusanagi back, those alarm bells started going off again, and a bunch of questions rose up inside me. What had Kusanagi done to the shrimp people—the Emishi? And the Matagi? The Ryūkyū? What stories had been erased by its blade? If I killed the shrimp, would I be helping to keep those stories in the dark? Did that make me just like Prince Takeru and Mokugon-bake?

Whoosh. At the last moment, I redirected my swing down and to the right. It still cut an ugly gash in the shrimp's side, which streamed black oil and smoke. A few shrimp legs flopped around on the ground.

I felt another rush of fury: There was a *full-on monster trying to kill me* and I wasn't allowed to do the same to it? Unfair!

The jackhammers started again as the shrimp reared up and waved its antennae, roaring like some kind of shellfish Godzilla. Its remaining arms flexed and clawed at the air as it lumbered toward me.

That shrimp is the enemy! Let's go! my rage monster shouted at me. *It wants you to die! It wants Dad to die!*

The shrimp bellowed again. Kusanagi and my rage monster were right. That monster was ugly, it was cruel, and it was in my way. I needed to get rid of it.

Instantly, I was filled with furious, violent hatred, and Kusanagi's enormous power thrummed through me. *Ahh.* I'd forgotten how good this felt. How could it be wrong to wield this much power? This had to be the only way I could defeat Izanami.

"Momo! We're coming!"

What the . . . I glanced behind me and saw my friends struggling forward against a powerful wind. They could barely stand up straight, much less defend themselves or me. "Get back!" I screamed at them. "I can handle it!"

But as I turned to slice that shrimp to bits, I caught a glimpse of Danny's face and heard his voice in my head. *I know you're good. I know you're not violent. I believe in you.*

Time seemed to slow. My sword was suspended midstab. I couldn't let Danny down. I couldn't become like cruel Prince

Takeru, a monster addicted to the power of my anger. I thought of the Tsuchigumo, sacrificed to Takeru's thirst for power. The question rose up again: *What happened to the Emishi?* I looked at the shrimp, the god of the Emishi, who had probably lost their homes and their land, just like the Ainu and the Tsuchigumo. *What's your story?* I wondered. And weirdly, for a split second, I saw a person instead of a monster.

KILL! roared Kusanagi. It drove forward.

No.

The effort of wrenching my sword off course threw me sideways. As I struggled to regain control, I saw a hundred arrows fly through the air as Jin's voice sang,

Ah-weem-a-way, ah-weem-a-way
Ah-weem-a-way, ah-weem-a-way

"No, don't hurt it!" I shouted, but I couldn't tell if anyone had heard me, because a second later I was flying backward through the air. Then a deafening crash and a burst of light obliterated everything.

The Menu Options Have Recently Changed

My eyes fluttered open to bright white light that slammed into the headache that was trying to drill a hole in the back of my skull. I squeezed my eyes shut again. "Ughhh."

"Momo." Was that Danny's voice? It sounded muffled, like it was fighting its way through layers and layers of thick wool blankets.

"Danny?" I opened my eyes again, just a crack, but the light sliced in like a knife, and I had to shut them again.

"Just stay still for a while, Momo." It was Jin's voice, also wrapped in wool. "You hit your head pretty hard."

Hit my head? The memory of the fight with the shrimp came flooding back and pulled me out of my daze.

"Where are we?" I rasped. "What happened?" I struggled to sit up, but the headache, which seemed to have a life of its own, promptly smashed an iron sledgehammer up, down, and all around, and I had to lie back down, groaning.

"He said to stay still, you fidgety ferret," Niko's distant voice said crossly.

"What happened?" I asked again.

Danny's voice came through next. "Okay. So, first of all, you ditched us and tried to fight Shrimpzilla by yourself." I felt a stab of guilt. "But we can talk about that later. Anyway, some kind of wind barrier held us back, but we broke through and got that shrimp before it got you."

"But you went flying anyway, and you hit a tree," said Ryleigh. Aha. That would explain the headache. "I think maybe it was Kusanagi that did it," she added.

"Jin sang to calm Shrimpzilla down, and I tied Yasome's spider thread to one of my hundredfold arrows and shot it."

"And when the arrows split up, the threads did, too, and Niko used his telekinetic powers to loop them around the shrimp and back to us," Ryleigh said.

"And Ryleigh used her root-kata to anchor the end of the silk to the ground and trap the shrimp," said Jin. "But you'd told us not to hurt it, so I used some of Toyotama-hime's healing serum to fix its wounds. And then the door opened up!"

Everyone's voices were growing slowly clearer and closer, as if the layers of wool were being peeled away one by one.

"Why didn't you want us to hurt the shrimp?" Ryleigh asked.

"Because . . ." I thought about how I'd seen the shrimp glitch into a person, and how I'd managed to derail Kusanagi's bloodlust. How had I done it? If the door had opened up after Jin had used the healing serum on the shrimp, did that mean we never should have fought it in the first place? If we'd managed to kill it, would we have failed? I wished my head were a little clearer. I felt like the answer was hovering just out of reach.

The pain had subsided enough by now that I risked opening my eyes again. I was lying on my back in the middle of a grand hall with gleaming white marble walls. The air seemed to shimmer with faint pinkish light. Ryleigh sat at my feet, and Niko and Danny sat on my left and right. Jin sat at my right shoulder, holding a green bottle in his hand.

The serum. "You used Toyotama-hime's healing potion on me, too? Is there any left?"

Jin shook his head. "I used most of it on the shrimp. There was just enough left for you."

I struggled to my elbows, wincing at the pain. "Why? What if we need it in Yomi?" *What if we needed it for Dad?*

Niko harrumphed. "Don't be a ding-dong! You told us not to hurt the shrimp, so we healed it, and that got us through the gate. And of course he used the rest of it on you. Your skull was as fractured as a fortune cookie!"

My hand strayed to my head, but Jin caught my wrist and guided it back to my side. "You'll be back to a hundred percent in a few minutes, probably," he said.

"Okay, but as soon as I'm better, we need to find the guy in the brown robe." I could feel my thoughts getting clearer now, and the clearer they got, the more anxious I was to get going. "How much time do we have left?"

"Two days," said Danny.

"Two days? Okay, no, I have to get up." I tried to sit, but Jin pushed me back down.

"Not so fast. You have to finish resting," he said.

"And as long as you're resting, you can answer some questions," said Danny. "Like, for example, why don't you trust us to have your back? First you don't tell us about Izanami, then you volunteer to be executed without even asking us if we have an escape plan—"

"*Was* it a plan, though?" Niko interrupted.

"Whatever." Danny waved this away. "And now you try to sneak out on us and fight Shrimpzilla all by yourself? Why? We're supposed to be a team!"

"I know." My head pulsed. It was less painful than before, but somehow I felt worse. "I guess I didn't want you to keep having to risk your lives to help me."

"So you risked your own life and almost died. When we could have been there helping you all along," Danny finished. "You're just lucky we broke through when we did."

"I know," I said again, miserably. He was right. Hadn't they essentially taken down the shrimp kami without my help? At least Danny hadn't mentioned that I'd made them use up the healing elixir as well.

I stared at the domed white ceiling and reached for a better reason. "But it's my dad and my sword, so it's my responsibility."

"I already *told* you we all want to save the Middle Lands. Our parents could die, too." Ryleigh fumed. "But I guess you don't care what I say."

"Oh." Of course. I'd forgotten all about that in my worry that Ryleigh would want me to deal with the jewel before saving Dad. "I'm sorry."

But Ryleigh wasn't done. "Whatever. I don't care. Obviously, you don't want to be friends anymore."

"Okay, that's it. What is *wrong* with you?" Danny asked.

"Where is this even coming from? You have to tell us what's going on."

Ryleigh let out a forceful breath. "What's *wrong* with me is I've been the weak link ever since we started off on this mission, and I know you hate me for it." She glared at us, as if daring us to argue.

"What?" I said. "You have not."

"Seriously? Like, okay, with Mokugon-bake at the library. I didn't do anything useful."

"You nailed a ton of those little fire demons!" said Jin.

"But it didn't even slow them down!" Ryleigh said. "And I forgot all about the time bubble when we were at Ryūgū-jō, *and* I didn't realize that Toyotama-hime was taking us the wrong way until way too late. And I should have seen the snare that caught Niko! I should have warned you ahead of time not to panic and run if one of us got caught in the forest. I should have seen Yasome coming before she attacked. I started a fight instead of choosing a door, and that's why we didn't notice when Momo snuck out. Whatever. I never asked to be friends with any of you, anyway." Ryleigh buried her face in her arms as the rest of us looked at each other in astonishment.

"Uh. What are you talking about?" I asked. "Why would any of that make us drop you as a friend?"

"Oh, *and* I tried to be friends with Kiki again," Ryleigh blurted, lifting a tearstained face. "Remember how I said I couldn't come over for movie night on Thursday because I wasn't feeling well? I lied. Kiki said she wanted to hang out, so I went to her house instead. Now do you hate me?"

Strangely, that hurt much more than all the other mistakes

Ryleigh had listed. How could she have gone behind our backs like that?

But I took a deep breath. I thought about how Danny had betrayed me by recording and posting a video of my humiliation at the seventh-grade dance last fall, and how Niko had lied about putting my life at risk so he could earn his magic back. And how I'd tried to drown Danny only a couple of hours ago. And how he still believed in me. How we were still friends.

"But you're sorry, right?" I said.

Ryleigh nodded.

"Then it's fine."

"You're not mad at me?" Ryleigh asked.

"I'm mad that you lied to us," I admitted. "But friends don't stop being friends just because one of them messes up. They work it out and keep going."

"And we're not friends with you because of what you do, good or bad. We're friends with you because of who you are," Danny added.

"In my old friend group, people were always mad at each other," Ryleigh said. "People were always having to pay for messing up." It was true. Ryleigh's old friend group was always freezing someone out for reasons that made no sense to me.

"Well, that's not us," I said.

"And anyway, even if you make a mistake once in a while, you're still much better at strategy than the rest of us," said Jin.

"I absolutely agree!" said Niko.

"So as long as Momo doesn't make any more banana-pants decisions, we're all good," said Danny.

"Yeah, banana-pants decisions are your thing," I joked.

"Yeah, that's right! Danny gets us going. I calm us down." Jin began listing us on his fingers. "Momo inspires us—"

"And trusts us to have her back," Danny interjected.

"Right. Niko keeps us in line, and Ryleigh, uh . . ."

"I execute strategy," she said with a smile.

I'd been so worried about how much we'd been fighting. But when Jin talked about our differences this way, I felt better.

"Yes!" Danny said. "It's all about trusting each other to come through, and we do! Teamwork makes the dream work, amirite?" He and Jin cheered, and by now I felt good enough to sit up and join them. Even Niko barked a couple of foxy barks. Maybe we *could* actually work together. Maybe we always had.

A few minutes later, the effects of the healing elixir had me back on my feet and feeling better than ever. I was confident that I was on the path to whatever it was that would help me defeat Izanami, even though Daikoku had said I had to *move beyond* destruction, not just *avoid* destruction, the way I had with the shrimp. And we were one step closer to finding our mystery man. Which meant we were one step closer to saving Dad.

Even better, we didn't have to worry about where to go, because there was only one way out of the hall: a large wooden door in the middle of the far wall.

"What do you think is on the other side?" I wondered out loud.

"Only one way to find out," said Danny. He reached for the

massive iron handle, but paused before he touched it. "Isn't anyone going to tell me to slow down so we can figure out what to do after I open it?"

"Yes! Yes, you noodle-noggin! I think you should all wield your weapons!" Niko said. "Safety first, I always say!"

He had a point. We pulled out our weapons and stood on either side of the door, like cops about to raid a bad guy's apartment.

"On the other hand, we don't want anyone to think we're belligerent bullies. Perhaps a more amiable attitude would be appropriate," he mused.

"How about I just open it?" Danny said, and before Niko could say anything else, he gave the handle an energetic yank.

The door swung open to reveal a walled garden bathed in golden sunlight. Fruit trees dotted the landscape, some in bloom with fragrant pink blossoms, and some drooping with oranges, persimmons, and peaches. A narrow gravel path meandered around a sparkling lake, through low, round shrubs, crooked pine trees, and craggy boulders. The path turned into stepping stones over velvety stretches of moss, then led under a torii and across an arched wooden bridge to a rocky island with a single tree in its center.

The door we'd walked through had vanished, and all that stood behind us was a whitewashed wall so high that the only thing I could see beyond it was the bright blue sky. In fact, there were no doors or gates to be seen in any of the walls around the garden.

"Whoa," Danny breathed.

"Where—what is this?" Ryleigh whispered.

Niko shook his head and said, "I'm beyond baffled."

"Can we start searching for our guy?" I asked. I couldn't look at those fruit trees without feeling anxious about how little time we had left.

"But there's no one here," said Ryleigh.

"There's a little house over on the other side of the lake." Danny pointed to a tiny building that looked more like a shed than a house. "Maybe he's in there."

We walked in single file along the path in the direction of the house, or the shed, or whatever it was. The path took us around to the other side of the building, where a pair of white canvas slip-ons sat at the bottom of three wooden steps that led up to the wraparound veranda. A rough brown cloak hung on a peg, and the sound of someone snoring softly drifted through the sliding paper doors.

"This has to be him!" Jin said.

My heart began to beat faster. We were so close. What would I say? How would I ask for the jewel? Why hadn't I thought about this earlier?

A thick purple rope dangled from a golden bell that hung in the eaves. "Gently!" Niko cautioned Danny as he reached for it.

The bell jangled cheerily, and Niko called out, "Hello, O gracious garden dweller! Please forgive our frightful forwardness, but we would be awfully appreciative if you could make an appearance!"

Silence. More silence. Then, just as I was about to give up, the sound of someone moving around. A flash of light made us all step back. When our eyes adjusted to the brightness, we saw a tall, broad-shouldered, square-jawed man standing in the doorway. He was dressed all in white, from his hoodie to his joggers to his pure white socks. Flowers sprang up around his feet, even on the wooden deck. All the scents and sounds of the garden intensified: fresh earth, rich moss, sweet fruit blossoms. Humming bees and chirping birds.

I knew who it was even before Niko whispered in awe, "Izanagi the Creator," and none of us needed to be told to drop to our knees as he smiled down at us, his dark eyes crinkling at the corners. This was even better than I could have hoped. Izanagi was the only kami whose magic could match Izanami's. It was probably even stronger, since he was the one who'd cast the spell to keep her in Yomi in the first place. He would help us. Thank the kami-verse.

Izanagi spread his arms and said, "Welcome, friends." I felt like I was floating in a sea of light—safe, strong, and full of joy. "Congratulations. You have proven yourself worthy of entering my garden, a new pocket dimension in the Aum created by me, Izanagi the Creator. I am currently experiencing an unusually high volume of calls and cannot appear before you in person. Please select an option from the following menu. Please listen carefully to the menu options, as the menu options have recently changed."

What? We stared at each other, and then at Izanagi, and then back at each other again in disbelief.

Like, seriously. *WHAT?*

Izanagi held his hand out, palm up, and continued. "If you wish to leave a voicemail for me, Izanagi the Creator, press one. If you wish to leave an offering, press two. If you wish to return from whence you came, press three. To repeat this menu, press four. To end this call, press zero."

My chest felt like it might cave in on my heart, which was pounding so hard I could hardly think. Was this some kind of joke?

Danny took a few steps forward and cleared his throat. "Sir? Mr. Izanagi? Are you real, or—"

"I'm sorry. I didn't catch that," said Izanagi in a voice as smooth and comforting and sweetly bland as vanilla pudding. "If you wish to leave a voicemail for me, Izanagi the Creator..."

I couldn't take it anymore. I ran up the stairs—I didn't even bother taking off my shoes—and shoved him. My hands met with soft, fleecy fabric across a warm, solid chest. His brown eyes blinked down at me in almost comical surprise, and he stepped back. So he'd been faking!

"I'm sorry, I know that was rude," I said. "But I didn't know what else to do. Please, you have to listen to us! It's a matter of life and death, and we've come all this way!"

"I'm sorry. The voicemail box is full. Please try again tomorrow."

"Are you freaking *kidding* me?" Danny shouted. "We can *see* you! We're literally right in front of you!"

"Thank you for calling. Goodbye."

Izanagi stepped backward and closed the sliding doors.

For a moment, we just stood there, too stunned to speak or move. All I could think was *Did that really just happen?* Had Izanagi the Creator seriously just tried to convince us that he was a *voicemail message?*

Should we go in? I mouthed to the others, but before they could answer, there came the sound of a wooden door sliding along its tracks—on the other side of the house. Then the creak of the veranda. And then, very clearly, the sound of someone running away down a gravel path.

This Definitely Crosses a Boundary

"Hey!"

"Stop!"

"Come back here!"

We ran around the building and tore after Izanagi. He moved with incredible power and grace past the boulders and the peach trees, past the shrubs and the pines. He was heading toward the bridge to the island, and he probably would have gotten away from us, except he was wearing flip-flops, and just as he reached the bridge to the little island, one of them folded under and tripped him up.

"Yaaah!" Danny launched himself into the air and slammed into Izanagi's knees just as he was getting back up.

"Oh, come *on*!" The exasperated kami who stood and plucked Danny off his legs like a kitten had a very different vibe from the dignified being who had greeted us at his little house down the path. "Did you have to get your grimy little handprints on my nice white joggers?" He waved his hand, and the dirt stains on the joggers faded away.

"You're the one who tripped," Danny said, and Niko

immediately threw himself on the ground and began babbling apologies for Danny's disrespect.

But Izanagi didn't seem too offended. "I suppose you're right," he conceded with a rueful smile. He sighed and took us in. "How did you children get in here, anyway? I left very strict instructions that I was not to be disturbed."

"We were in Ainu Moshiri," said Jin. "And Kim-un-kamuy gave us three chances to come through the portal."

"I knew it!" Izanagi groaned. "Don't get me wrong, I'm impressed that you made it. But he wasn't supposed to give anyone the opportunity."

"He said he didn't approve of what you were doing," I ventured. "Maybe he wanted to send a message?"

"What *are* you doing?" Danny asked. Behind him, Niko moaned softly.

"Retiring."

I blinked in disbelief. "But—you can't!"

"Why not? I've worked long and hard and I deserve a rest." Izanagi crossed his arms. "But I'll tell you what. It can't have been easy for you to get here, and I'm sure you have a good reason, or you wouldn't even have tried. So tell me what you need from me, and I'll see what I can do. How's that? Though do be quick about it because I really am on my way out. In fact, you're lucky you arrived when you did. Ten minutes later and you would have found nothing but Aum."

"You go," Danny said to me. "This time it really is up to you."

I took a deep breath, crossed my fingers, and began. "Sir,

we really need your help. Izanami is holding my dad hostage in Yomi. And she says she won't let him go unless I bring her the Jewel of the Heart. But if we give it to her, she'll use it to take over the Middle Lands, and then who knows what else she'll do. So I was wondering . . ." I took another deep breath and tried not to worry about the fact that Izanagi's expression was growing darker and darker. "Would you consider coming with us to set my dad free?"

Izanagi looked thunderous now, and my knees were shaking so badly, I wasn't sure how much longer I could remain standing. But I couldn't back down now. *Think of Dad. Dad, Dad, Dad.* Dad talking about his marine biology field research, his eyes sparkling with excitement. Dad making me a giant ice cream sundae for dinner. Dad singing along to Sailor Twist as he folded laundry. I forced myself to look up at Izanagi. *Please,* I begged him silently. *I just want my dad back. Please help me rescue him.*

But Izanagi shook his head firmly. "No. I will never, ever go back down to that pit of filth."

I felt like I was drowning, grasping desperately at anything that might help me keep my head above the surface. "Okay," I said, "what if—what if you gave us the jewel?"

Izanagi burst into laughter. "Oh, no, no, no! As if I could allow anyone but me to even touch such a precious and powerful item! Oh, dear me, but that is too funny." He wiped a tear from his eye. "It's for that very reason that I'm taking it with me to the World Beyond. I simply can't trust anyone else to handle it properly. And this way, it will be forever out of Izanami's reach and the Middle Lands will be safe."

"But—but you have to help us! We only have—"

I opened my hands to find that the branches were in full bloom.

Danny looked up from his phone. "Today's the day."

I looked back at Izanagi and begged him, "Please. You're the only one who can help us."

"I'm sorry, my dear, I really am," Izanagi said. "But I've been working on my boundaries, and this definitely crosses a boundary for me. So if you'll excuse me, it's time for me to go."

He crossed the bridge to the island and turned to face us. Behind him stood the small, squat tree we'd seen from the other side of the pond. "Okay, then. Goodbye!" he said, and took a step back. "Have a nice life!"

The tree closed around him and he faded away, leaving behind something red and comma-shaped that pulsed with light at the center of the foliage.

My knees finally gave out, and I knelt on the ground. My heart squeezed tight. I could feel the tears rising. What were we supposed to do now?

"I think I might legit hate that guy," Danny grumbled.

Suddenly, Izanagi reappeared inside the tree, looking slightly translucent and very puzzled. "What's wrong? Why isn't it coming with me?" he muttered to himself. He reached out and grasped the pulsing object, but his hand went right through it. He turned to look at us. "Did you cast a spell?" he demanded. "Are you doing something to keep my jewel here?"

Dumbfounded, we shook our heads. Izanagi's face turned violet. "But I want it! I need it to create a nice new world of my own!" He tried again to take it, and again it eluded him. "No!

No! This isn't fair!" he shouted over and over as he scrabbled and grabbed, but his voice and body grew fainter and fainter until finally all that was left was the jewel, still pulsing gently in the middle of the tree.

"What the . . . ," Jin said softly.

"We're doomed as dust bunnies," Niko moaned.

"No, we're not. It's ours to take now," said Ryleigh. She crossed over the bridge and reached into the leaves of the tree, which shuddered as if in warning. "Or maybe it would be more respectful to ask the tree to give it to us," she said, stepping back. "Jin, could you ask?"

So he did. "Please, tree, could we have the jewel? It's for a good cause."

I didn't hear any magic in his voice. I held my breath. The tree tilted itself, like it was considering Jin's request, and the jewel glowed even brighter. Then it rose out of the branches and split itself into five new, identical jewels. Each mini-jewel drifted down toward a different person—one to me, one to Niko, one to Ryleigh, one to Jin, and one to Danny—and hovered in front of us for a moment before emitting a burst of light and—*zoop!*—getting sucked right into our chests.

"WHOAAA." Danny's face glowed, and he looked down at his chest in wonderment.

And then we were all looking down and poking ourselves in the sternum to see if the jewels had left holes as they'd entered (they hadn't), and saying things like "What just happened?" and "I feel all warm inside. Does anyone else feel all warm inside?" and "That was much easier than I thought it would be."

But as everyone else was exclaiming and smiling and practically levitating with excitement, it dawned on me that unless all five jewels came out and surrendered themselves to Izanami of their own accord (and somehow I doubted they would), that meant that in order to free Dad, we would have to surrender *ourselves*. And if I wanted to destroy the jewel so that Izanami couldn't use it to take over the Middle Lands, I couldn't see a way to do it that didn't involve me plunging Kusanagi into my friends' hearts and then throwing myself onto the sword.

Why couldn't the jewel have hung itself on our necks? Or was that the point? The jewel had once belonged to Izanami. Was it trying to go back to her? Had it gone inside us because it knew I might use Kusanagi to destroy it, and this was how it was protecting itself? *At least this solves the problem of Ryleigh wanting me to destroy it first,* I thought grimly.

The warm feeling in my chest leaked away and was replaced with cold, gray dread.

What would happen when my friends figured out what it meant for them to be carrying the Jewel of the Heart inside themselves? Would they want to keep going, or would they want to quit? What did *I* want? How far was I willing to go to save Dad? Or to save the world?

What is wrong with you? I wanted to shout at everyone. *The jewel is inside us! Don't you know what that means? It means if we want to save ANYONE, we have to die! Like, for sure!*

All at once, I saw shock on my friends' faces as they turned to stare at me.

"Did you . . . say something?" Ryleigh asked.

I shook my head.

Did you think *something?* said Ryleigh's voice in my head. This time *I* stared at *her.*

Omigosh, are we reading each other's minds? Now it was Danny's voice. *Whoaaa.*

It was a very cool side effect of having a jewel in my chest, I had to admit. Except we still had that one major problem.

"I hate to ruin the party, but did you actually hear what I said—I mean, what I thought?" I said out loud. Then I had to watch everyone's faces change as the reality of my words sank in. No one said or thought anything. Even Niko was silent—no blaming anyone for our situation, no proclaiming that we were crunched as Cronuts or mashed as mangoes, no wailing about how much he had to put up with as our guardian.

"There has to be a way out of this," said Danny. Of course.

"I really don't think there is," I said.

"No, there has to be," he insisted. "We just have to think. It'll come to us."

As it turned out, though, we didn't have time to think.

"Um . . . ," Jin said, "is it just me, or is this place dissolving?"

Sure enough, everything in the garden—every rock, every leaf, every bit of gravel on the path we stood on, even the lake and the sky—was breaking into tiny, glittering pieces that popped and fizzed and faded into darkness.

Izanagi's words came back to me: *Ten minutes later and you would have found nothing but Aum.*

The same thought must have occurred to Niko, because he howled, "The garden is returning to the Aum!"

"What does that mean?" Ryleigh asked.

"Everything eventually returns to the Aum, and this garden is doing just that! So we will either remain as we are but be stranded in the Aum, or we will dissolve into it just like the rest of this place!"

I went cold from head to foot. I'd only been in the Aum once, and it had been terrifying. Even if we didn't turn into a million billion sparkles, we'd spend the rest of our lives floating in infinite black space with nothing to hold on to and nowhere to go.

"Goodbye, kami-verse!" Niko wept. "Oh, tragedy of tragedies, to expire this way, unable to fight, unable to resist, cut off in the flower of my youth . . ."

"Danny, your arrow. The one that takes people anywhere they want to go," Ryleigh said. The Aum was larger than the garden now, and I felt like we were on a tiny island, watching a tsunami approach from every direction.

"Huh? Oh, right!" Danny dug into his backpack and pulled out the arrow as the memory came back to me: Before she'd sent us to fight Tamamo-no-mae on New Year's Eve, Amaterasu had given Danny an arrow that would take him and whoever he wanted to any destination he named. I'd forgotten all about it. Thank goodness for Ryleigh.

"Where should we go?" he asked, drawing his elbow back. The sky was entirely black. I screamed and leaped away from a hole that opened under my left foot.

"We need to go to Yomi. Tell it to take us to Yomi," Ryleigh said.

"To Yomi!" he said, and released the arrow just as the darkness closed over us. Then I was a million molecules flying through space, following the arrow to Yomi.

Do You Think We'll Meet Elvis?

"I didn't know Yomi had beaches," said Danny. We had tumbled onto the black, sandy shore of an oily, slow-moving river that smelled like mud and dead fish.

"This isn't Yomi," said Niko. "This is the Sanzū River, the border between Yomi and Meido. And you can bet your boots and buttons we will never cross it on our own."

"But I told the arrow to go to Yomi," Danny protested.

"No one can cross the river without paying the toll," Niko said. "I suppose even Amaterasu's arrow couldn't break through the boundary."

"Then how are we supposed to get across? It doesn't look safe to swim in." Jin looked dubiously at the dark water.

"Hello, children." We turned to see a short, kindly-looking man with a face that looked old and young at the same time. He wore a bright red bib over his monk's robes and a jaunty red beret on his round, bald head. "I'm Jizō. You look like you need to cross the river."

"Yes, please!" said Jin. "That's exactly what we need."

Everyone knows who Jizō is, but just in case you don't, I'll tell you: he's the kami who protects children on their journey into the afterlife. As long as he was at our side, we'd be safe. I felt better immediately.

Jizō was frowning at a little tablet in his hand. "That's odd," he said. "I don't see anyone on my list who looks like any of you. Are you sure you're supposed to be here?" He raised his head to get another look at us and gasped. "Wait!" His eyes brightened in recognition, and his face broke into a delighted smile. "You must be Momo! I talked to your mother just a few hours ago!" He pointed at everyone else in turn, saying, "And you're Niko! And Danny and Jin and Ryleigh!" Then he looked at me again and his brow furrowed with concern. "Your mother is very worried about you. She was convinced you'd already crossed over, even though I assured her that I'd know if you had. But I gave her a special tourist visa anyway so that if you did cross over, she could find you."

So that vision of Mom crossing Meido had been real. I *knew* it. I was overcome by a sudden wave of intense longing for her. Even after what I'd said to her, she'd still come all the way down to the land of the dead to try to find me. *I'm sorry, Mom,* I thought. Maybe I could use my new telepathic powers to communicate with her. I reached out with my mind. *Mom, can you hear me? If you can hear me, send me a sign.*

Nothing.

My scalp tightened with fear and anxiety. *Please let her be safe.*

"Are you all right?" Jizō asked gently.

I nodded and mumbled, "I'm fine."

"Mm-hmm." He obviously did not believe me—big surprise. In the same gentle voice, he said to all of us, "I'm very sorry, but it's against the rules to take living souls across the river."

"But we need to cross," said Danny.

"We have to rescue my dad," I said. "We have to do it today. And no one can do it but us."

"My poor child," Jizō said. "I wish I could help you."

"How did my mom cross over? She's a living soul."

"Oh! Well, she paid the fare, of course. I can't refuse a paying fare. But I doubt you have the proper—"

"What about this?" Ryleigh thrust out a gold coin—the coin that Sen had given her.

Jizō stared at it, flabbergasted. "Where did you get that?"

"It doesn't matter," said Ryleigh. "Will you accept it?"

"Yes, I suppose I must," said Jizō, taking the coin with a reluctant sigh. "Have a seat in my boat, children. Prepare yourselves to visit the land of the dead."

He waved his hand at the shore, and a long wooden boat glided out of the reeds that choked the river a little way upstream. We climbed in, and soon we were drifting down the river with Danny and Jin in front, Ryleigh and me in the middle, and Niko next to Jizō at the stern.

To our right was a sort of blank, silvery nothingness, like someone had pulled a curtain down along the riverbank. The Yomi side was shrouded in mist, too, but I could still see shadowy figures wafting aimlessly along the shore and emerging from the mist to stop and stare as we floated by. Here and there, the spindly branches of dead trees reached out like bony fingers. The river lapped hungrily at the boat, and I was afraid to look over the edge, for fear of seeing actual grasping hands reaching up to pull us into the water.

We passed under two bridges. One was old, decrepit, and unused, probably because of the giant boulder blocking the way to the silvery side of the river on our right. The other was crowded with people of all shapes and sizes. Snatches of conversation drifted down to us:

"But I can't be dead. I have a very important meeting in ten minutes!"

"Do you think we'll meet Elvis?"

"I hope the food is good on the other side."

"This line is taking forever! Isn't there some kind of VIP fast pass?"

Jin turned to Jizō, his eyes wide. "Are those people . . ."

"Dead," said Jizō. "Waiting their turn to be checked in."

"Where do we get checked in?" Ryleigh asked.

"You're not dead, my dear, so you won't be on the lists."

"So, ah, Your Benevolence, if you don't mind my asking, where are we going?" said Niko, who was looking more nervous with every passing minute.

"Patience," said Jizō.

We drifted on for a while, and Jizō leaned over and whispered to me, "May I give you a word of advice?"

I nodded. "Yes, please. I don't know what I'm doing. I'm on this mission that I couldn't refuse, and I have to make a choice, but every choice leads to someone dying. And then there's . . ." I hesitated, but Jizō looked at me with such compassion that I decided to be honest. "My sword, Kusanagi. Daikoku said I couldn't defeat Izanami unless I figured out to connect to it in a new way, but I haven't yet, and—"

Jizō laid his hand on my shoulder, and I stopped talking. "The source of your power is not good or bad. It just is. What you do with it is up to you."

"What if the source of my power is, oh, let's say anger? Or something else destructive and violent?" I asked.

"Anger is powerful. It can be a valuable tool for alerting you to things that wish you harm, and you should embrace it and be glad for it. But you are bigger than your anger. And there is something in you that is more powerful than your anger, that will allow you to go beyond the urge to destroy. It can transform everything if only you make room." That sounded a lot like what Daikoku had said.

"Is that thing love, by any chance?" I said sarcastically. Not to be rude, but I'd failed over and over to solve this mystery, and I was scared and frustrated. And whenever people talked in these vague riddles about the most powerful thing in the world or whatever, the secret answer was always love. But I happened to know that Mom's love hadn't saved me from Izanami the first time I met her as a baby, or the second time when I met her on the Island of Mysteries, so I was skeptical.

"It could be," said Jizō. "It depends. I don't know you or your situation well enough to say for sure. You'll have to figure it out for yourself, I'm afraid."

Had someone given him and Daikoku the same script to memorize or something? I sighed in frustration. "Why can't all you supposedly wise kami just tell me what to do? Why does everything have to be a riddle for me to solve on my own?"

In response, Jizō only chuckled and patted my shoulder. "I have faith in you, my dear. You should, too."

Seconds later, he pointed at a lonely little dock on the Yomi side of the river. He stepped out of the boat and stood on the surface of the water next to us and said, "We've arrived. Are you sure you want to get off on this side?"

For some reason, I'd assumed he'd take us all the way to Izanami, wherever she was. The thought of entering Yomi without his protection threw me into a panic. "But there are no oars! How are we going to get there? What do we do when we get off?" I babbled.

Danny, of course, only wanted to know, "How are you *doing* that?"

Jizō simply said again, "I have faith in you! You'll be fine." With that, he gave us a shove in the direction of the dock, waved goodbye, and walked across the water into the mist.

Without Jizō in the boat with us, the air felt colder and thinner. The water seemed darker, and the silence felt like a presence, like a monster hidden in the gloom, holding its breath, watching and waiting as we drifted to the fog-draped shore.

I thought of Izanami waiting for us, smiling her empty black smile. My heart began to race, and my breathing grew quick and shallow. *Slow down, slow down,* I begged, though I wasn't sure if I was talking to my heart, my breath, or the boat, which kept moving steadily toward the shore.

Momo, are you okay? It was Ryleigh's voice in my head.

I'm fine.

I knew Ryleigh could tell I was lying. But she didn't call me out. She just scooted closer to me until we were sitting shoulder to shoulder. She took my hand in hers, and her thought floated into my head. *I'm scared, too.* Somehow, that made me feel a little bit braver.

Around us, the darkness grinned, the mist sighed and swirled, and the cold wrapped itself around us and sank into our skin, and we kept gliding, gliding, gliding toward the dock until finally we bumped gently up against it. We sat in the boat in silence; no one seemed to want to be the first one out. Least of all me, even with Dad's and Mom's lives on the line.

"We have to get going," said Ryleigh, finally. "We don't have a choice."

"Actually, we do have a choice," said Niko. "We could stay right here instead of waltzing into the jaws of death like a bunch of naive little ninnies."

"You wouldn't do that, though, would you?" said Jin. "You wouldn't stay here when so much depends on us going ahead."

Niko sighed heavily. "No, I wouldn't," he conceded. "It's a real character flaw."

"And we've come this far. We can't give up now," Danny added.

I nodded. There were so many ways that this could go wrong. But we were only here because my friends had decided that saving Dad's life—and the lives of the rest of the world, I reminded myself—was worth risking their own. We were here because we thought there was a chance. I owed it to them to put my fear aside and get out of the darn boat.

"So, let's go, then! Hands in," said Danny brightly, as if we were his old sports bro friend group. He extended his hand, and one by one, we put our hands (and paw) on top, and for a moment, I felt a flash of the old guilt and worry: *I wish the jewel had gone into my heart alone. I shouldn't make everyone come with me to help me solve my problem.*

"'Together' on three," Danny said. "One, two, three!"

"Together!"

I looked to my right and to my left, at my friends who'd chosen to come for me *and* for themselves, who'd stuck by me when I'd tried to run away and who made me feel brave when I was afraid. *No. No more leaving people behind. Just be grateful they're here with you.*

I felt a tiny glimmer of hope, like a candle in my heart. Maybe it was foolish. It was definitely foolish. There was no way we could beat Izanami because literally no one can defeat death. But Dad was out there, and Mom was out there, and my friends and I were going to save them—and the world—together.

We walked off the dock and onto the shore, where something swooshed at our backs, like a heavy velvet curtain had swept shut behind us. Startled, we spun around to find that the boat had disappeared. We turned again to see an army of skeletons rising out of the ground—hundreds of them, maybe thousands, all lined up in rows, wearing tarnished armor, bearing rusty swords and spears and torn battle flags. Beyond them was a massive iron gate, and beyond the gate, a stone wall—no, wait, not stones. Skulls.

In the center of the wall, one giant skull stared at us with empty black eyes, its mouth stretched in a wide, broken-toothed grin. Instinctively, I reached out for Kusanagi, which appeared in my hands, shimmering and buzzing. An ocean of vengeful fury surged through me, catching me off guard. But it wasn't coming from inside me. It was rolling in giant waves off the skeleton army. I had flashes of bitter rivalries and betrayals, vengeance for fallen friends and burned villages. I was channeling their rage somehow, the bitterness of a thousand soldiers killed on the battlefield and beyond. But it had nowhere to go—their enemy wasn't here—and it churned and boiled inside me, begging me to take it to the World Above, where it could be unleashed on the living, who had the life energy these dead soldiers had lost, who didn't deserve it, who had squandered it on their pointless, meaningless, petty little existences.

Just as suddenly as it had come, the anger dropped away, sucked into a black hole, and all I was left with was my own anger, which now seemed puny and weak by comparison—because what did I have to be angry about, anyway? Nothing, compared to what had just flowed through me—death, betrayal, that bottomless thirst for revenge. That was what powered this army.

What confused me—and scared me—was the way the rage and the power had vanished so suddenly, as if someone had snapped their fingers and issued a command. I had a feeling I knew who that someone was. Was she just showing off? Letting me know in advance that we were doomed? Because if this was what we were up against, we didn't stand a chance. Not Dad, not Mom, not my friends, not me.

But even more terrifying than the prospect of fighting this army of death—so terrifying that I couldn't bear to think about it—was how I'd felt when all that power had coursed through me. It felt like the times when I rode Kusanagi's wave, focused and channeling its energy, letting it amplify my rage monster's power—but a hundred times—a thousand times—faster, higher, and stronger. I'd felt unstoppable. Was that how it felt to be Izanami?

Momo! Momo! Danny's thoughts called to me. I shook my head dazedly. Where had he gone? He'd been right next to me just a second ago.

Momo! he called again. His thoughts were jagged with fear. He was in trouble. I whirled to face whatever monster had him in their clutches, sword at the ready.

Danny, Ryleigh, Niko, and Jin stood in a row, tied to each other with a glowing blue cord. Next to them stood Shuten-dōji, the demon king I'd defeated way back in the fall, and Tamamo-no-mae, the nine-tailed fox demon I'd beaten on New Year's Eve. They sneered at me, Shuten-dōji's yellow lantern eyes glowing with hate, and Tamamo-no-mae's coldly beautiful lips curled in a snarl.

"Welcome to Yomi," Shuten-dōji said. That voice—at once hollow and brimming with evil—made me shiver.

Tamamo-no-mae smiled a saccharine smile. "You really *must* pay better attention."

I'd beaten them each once before, and I was stronger and more powerful now. I could beat them again. I planted my feet and balanced Kusanagi in my hands. "Let them go," I said through gritted teeth. I hoped they would take the trembling in my voice for anger instead of nerves.

"Hand over your weapon," said Shuten-dōji. Slowly, he brought his sword to Niko's throat.

Tamamo-no-mae smiled. "Or this dear little fox becomes a permanent resident."

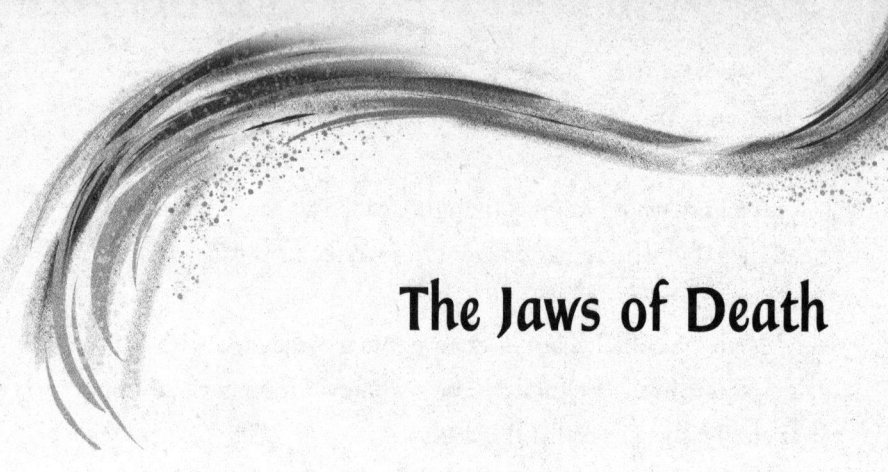

The Jaws of Death

Niko's eyes were wide with fear, and he trembled like a leaf in the wind, too scared to say a word.

How had things gone so wrong so quickly?

Think. Think, think.

You and Kusanagi can take Shuten-dōji, right? Danny's voice said in my head.

Yes, I replied.

Then go for it. You attack, Jin will save Niko, and Danny and I will grab our weapons and take Tamamo-no-mae, Ryleigh's voice said.

That seemed really risky. *But what if—*

It's all right. I will be a willing sacrifice. Niko's words were noble, but his face looked terrified.

I can't do it, I told the others.

If this was the decision that eventually caused the world to fall under Izanami's power, it would be my fault for not risking Niko's life for the greater good. Was that wrong of me? Probably. But I couldn't let my friend die.

At first, my hands wouldn't let go. Inside me, my rage monster screamed, *NO! Do not give away our power! We crushed him before; we can crush him again!* But I managed to throw Kusanagi to the ground. I shut my eyes and tried to believe what Jizō had said: *There is more to my power than just my anger.*

The blue rope that bound my friends together shot out and coiled itself around my hands. "What a good, obedient girl," Tamamo-no-mae purred. "I like you much better this way."

Shuten-dōji lowered his sword and laughed—a sound like rocks in a blender. "I thought you'd come around. Still as soft as ever, aren't you."

All five of us were yanked forward toward the wall of skulls in the distance. The skeleton armies rematerialized and crowded along the road, jeering and rattling their bones at us as we passed. Their bitter, hateful fury crashed around us like boulders, like trees falling in a forest fire. I felt like we might be buried in it.

It seemed like miles before we passed through the iron gate to face the wall of skulls. I couldn't bear to look at it, with all those eyes staring back at me. The giant skull at the center was the worst. Cold air drifted out of its eye sockets and its mouth—air that smelled like rotting meat and decaying leaves, thick and sweet-sour and choking. I recognized it as the odor that accompanied Izanami's attendants, the shikome—the odor of death. It penetrated my clothes and made my skin prickle. It dragged skeleton fingers through my hair. Breathing through my nose meant that I smelled it, but breathing through my mouth made me feel like I was drinking it. I wished I didn't have to breathe at all, though that would mean I was already dead. Ha.

The mouth of the giant skull began to speak. "Izanami the Destroyer, Queen of Death and Ruler of Yomi, welcomes her visitors," it hissed. Its jaws yawned to reveal a set of wide stone steps that descended into its throat, and the blue ropes that bound us fell away.

"The jaws of death," Niko whimpered. "Remember what I said about the jaws of death?"

"We can't turn back now," said Jin.

"We absolutely can," Niko said.

"Nope," Danny said. "We can't destroy the jewel anymore, but we can still free Momo's dad. It's the only thing that's still in our power. So we have to do it."

Besides, maybe having the jewel inside us gives us powers we haven't unlocked! Danny added silently. *I've been experimenting and I haven't found any, but you never know.*

I wanted to throw my arms around him and wrap him in the world's biggest hug. But that felt a little over the top, so I just smiled at him and said, "Thanks."

"'For Momo's dad' on three!" said Danny. "One, two, three!"

"For Momo's dad!" we shouted.

"And for the Middle Lands!" said Ryleigh.

"The Middle Lands!"

"You humans are such a bunch of weaklings," said Shuten-dōji. "You disgust me. So soft and sentimental. Like squishy little worms."

"Love isn't weak," Jin said. "It's the most powerful force in the kami-verse."

Tamamo-no-mae let out a peal of laughter. "Silly, silly child! I'd like to see you fight Izanami with *luuv* and see who wins.

No amount of love will keep a human from dying. Izanami always wins in the end." She prodded me in the shoulder and said, "Isn't that right, Momo?" as if she'd seen my doubts.

"Wrong," I said. I really wished I believed myself.

"Izanami won't win this time," said Niko. "Come on, my courageous companions! Into the dark and dangerous depths we go!"

I looked at him in surprise. "I thought you said we could turn back."

"I said no such thing," Niko lied. "Do you take me for some kind of coward? Ha! I laugh in the face of death!" And he herded us forward. I noticed that this conveniently allowed him to hang at the back, but whatever. If that's what it took for him to be brave, then fine. And to be honest, I was glad for the push.

We entered the gaping mouth and stood on the top step. The jaws creaked shut behind us.

"Can we hold hands?" Niko's human girl voice said. "I tried to fake it till I made it, like Danny does, but I failed. I'm scared out of my socks."

"I'm scared, too," said Danny.

"Let's all hold hands," said Jin.

The stench of death howled up from below and wrapped itself around us. I felt Jin's hand grip mine as Niko took my other hand. And we stepped down into the dark.

It felt like miles. I tried counting steps, but I stopped after a thousand. All around us, the darkness whispered things that made me want to give up with every step: *Let go. Join us. You'll never win.*

If we hadn't been holding hands, I would have started to doubt that I even had a body, or that anyone else was with me. I would have sat down on the steps and cried right there.

Then the darkness started murmuring, *There is no hope. Your mother has already surrendered. Your father, too.*

It was lying. It had to be lying. *Don't listen,* I told myself. *Don't listen.*

I focused on Danny, who said out loud every few steps, "I'm sure we're almost there," and Jin, who sang softly,

> *As long as I've got you, as long as you've got me*
> *Even when it's dark and cold, we will be all right.*

Down, down, down we went. When I finally saw a pinprick of blue light, I thought I might be hallucinating. But as we got closer, the dot became a splodge, which sharpened into the outline of a rectangle, which grew into the light creeping through the cracks around an enormous door. Which, when we stood in front of us, rumbled open.

Still holding hands, we walked through.

Happy Hinamatsuri!

We stood in a cavernous room with gleaming black walls that reflected the dim light of a chandelier lit with silver-blue onibi. The walls were lined with shelves that held a collection of ornate boxes, vases, and thick, leather-bound books. From somewhere across the room came the irregular *plip . . . plip . . . plip-plip* of water dripping. It put me on edge. I almost wished a horde of yōkai would bust through the walls and attack just so I wouldn't have to hear it.

I shivered, not just from fear, but from the cold, which now more than ever felt like it was alive, like it was hungry and we were its favorite meal. It draped itself around me, leaned its head on my shoulders, and blew its icy breath on my neck. *Welcome,* it said. *I've been waiting for you.*

No, wait. That was Izanami.

She was right in front of us, slightly hidden in shadow on the other side of the room. She started to glow, like she was turning on an internal dimmer switch, and soon I saw her every awful detail: the coal-black hair, the burning black eyes, pale skin, long, tapered fingers, and gruesome finger-bone crown.

She was holding an enormous book and standing in front of the basin of water I'd seen in my nightmares. This was where she'd confronted Mom and forced her into that awful bargain when I was a baby—twelve years of my life with Mom in the Middle Lands in exchange for the rest of my life by Izanami's side. This was where I'd seen myself in the Mirror of the Sun, standing next to Izanami and staring into that very same basin. I wanted to run and hide, but my legs seemed to have turned to wood, and my feet felt as if they'd been nailed to the ground.

"I believe it is customary, when someone welcomes you to their home, to bow and return the greeting," she said. She laid her book down on a nearby table and bowed her head. I felt myself being forced into a deep bow. Next to me, the others bent stiffly at the waist. I could hear Niko panting in fear and Ryleigh doing her box breathing.

"That's better," Izanami said. "I can be a bit old-fashioned, I'm afraid. But I ask you, where would we be without our manners? Happy Hinamatsuri, by the way!" She laughed delicately—the sound of glass scratching glass. "Don't worry. I won't hold it against you. In fact, I have a special treat for you! I am told that the answers to the mysteries of death are among the most sought-after in the Middle Lands. Would you like to take a peek?" She tapped her book and winked. "Don't be afraid. I don't bite."

"I'm not so sure," Danny muttered, to which Niko, back in fox form, responded with a sharp, "Shush, you ill-mannered imp! Do you want her to kill us?"

"We're literally in the land of the dead," Danny argued.

"But we're still alive, and I'd like to remain in this state as permanently as possible," Niko snapped.

"Goodness, but you *are* on edge, aren't you!" Izanami said, looking amused. "I suppose imminent death does that to people."

"See? Imminent. Death. Please, let's try to prevent that from coming to pass," said Niko.

"Silly fox. As if you had any choice in the matter." Izanami crooked her finger, and we were jerked forward until we stood right in front of her. Now that I was here, I could see the source of that dripping noise. Drops of water were falling from the ceiling into the basin, sometimes one by one, and sometimes a bunch at a time. *Plip, plip-plip-plip . . . plip. Plip.*

"I see you're admiring my collection of souls. But in order to appreciate it properly, you'll need to see this as well." She opened her book. "It's the book of the dead. By yours truly. It's a masterpiece, if I do say so myself."

It must have been thousands of pages long. The pages were so thin, they were almost translucent, and they were filled with columns of names written in elegant cursive, each one accompanied by a date, a time, a place, and a short description like *car accident, illness, war,* and in a couple of cases, *murder.*

Plip. Plip. Plip-plip . . . plip. Five more drops of water fell into the basin, and a breeze flipped the page to reveal two empty sheets. Five names, places, and causes of death appeared, as if being written by an invisible hand.

"Those people . . ."

"Brand-new citizens," Izanami said. "Which is to say, they've just died."

Then I saw something that nearly made my heart stop beating.

"What's that?" I asked, pointing.

I mean, I knew what it was. It was my name. And Ryleigh's name, written in pencil on a bit of paper that stuck out of the book a few pages farther on, like a bookmark.

"Oh, you recognized it!" Izanami clapped her hands like a little kid. She pulled the bookmark out and showed it to us. All of us were on it. And so were the names of Danny's parents, Jin's dad and his partner, and Ryleigh's parents and brother, written in the same flowing script that was in the book of the dead, like a VIP list.

"Think of it as a to-do list."

More like a to-die list.

"So they're still alive," Danny murmured, and I was reminded of what Ryleigh had said—that I wasn't the only one whose parents' lives were in danger. We were in this together all the way.

"Mm-hmm." Izanami nodded her head. "For now, anyway. But I have agents following them, ready to act on my command." She smiled her horrible, black-toothed smile. "I can do it now, if you like. Then you could see them in person." When we all begged her not to, she laughed. "Oh, my dear children, I'm just joking. My, but you are gullible! The reason they're on the list—the reason all of you are on the list—is because you are the ones I will spare when the Middle Lands fall to me. If you cooperate, it's the least I can do to thank you for your troubles."

I didn't even know how to feel about that. Grateful? Horrified?

"Oh, except for your mother, Momo. She was wandering around Yomi like a lost soul, and finally my guards took pity on her and captured her. She's here! In the palace! Can you believe it?"

My heart lurched, though whether it was with hope or dread, I couldn't tell you. "Where is she? What have you done with her?" I sounded shrill and panicky, like a scared little girl crying for her mommy. Only the steady pressure of Ryleigh's hand on my arm kept me from flying completely off the handle.

Izanami shook her head. "You know I can't tell you that. It would ruin all the fun. All I can say is that she's here somewhere, and I highly doubt that she'll be coming out to meet you anytime soon." She stepped forward, pushing us back and away from the basin and the book. She said briskly, "Now. Enough formalities. Let's move on to business. You are here in my realm, so I can only assume that you have brought me what I asked for."

I felt like I was still blundering around in the dark, trying to wrap my arms around this news about Mom, but the jewel began pulsing faster and heating up my chest, as if it knew what was coming. *Pull yourself together!* I heard Ryleigh say in my head. *Stay on topic!* That helped me calm down. Maybe Mom was here somewhere, but right now I had to focus on saving Dad.

Ryleigh announced, "We have what you want, but you said you would release Momo's father in exchange for it. We demand a simultaneous exchange of assets." Her voice only shook a little bit.

What are you doing? I asked her. *You could die!*

We'll figure it out, she answered. *Right?* She turned to the others, who looked as scared as she did. They all nodded. I had the bravest, best friends in the world.

"How adorably human of you." Izanami chuckled. "Bargaining to the bitter end, even though you have nothing to bargain with." She reached over and patted Ryleigh on the cheek and cooed through pursed lips, "Aren't you just the cutest thing." Irritation flashed through the terror on Ryleigh's face for just a moment, and I almost laughed. There was nothing Ryleigh hated more than being called cute.

"Well, my darlings, I don't like to compromise, but I think I can afford to indulge you just this once," Izanami said, and the mockery in her voice was so sharp and fine I could practically feel it making little paper cuts in my soul. She had so much power over us, she wasn't even worried that we might betray her and go back on our deal. Too bad she was right.

"Follow me." Izanami strode past us and did that finger-crooking thing, and my legs started walking of their own accord. There was no backing out now—literally.

She led us into a room with a huge tank of cloudy water in the middle. Floating inside the tank, anchored in place by yards and yards of cord that glinted even in the murk, was a whale. He was thin and listless, and scarred all over from those hateful cords. *Dad.*

"Dad, I'm here!" I called.

He was too big for me to see more than one sad, fatigue-dimmed eye, but it lit up at the sound of my voice, and his entire body strained toward me.

I flew across the room and threw myself against the tank—and fell into the water. It was icy cold, and I reeled backward in shock, soaking wet and gasping; the water was being held in place not by glass, but by magic.

The ends of the cords, I now realized, stretched through the water's surface and were held by creatures who looked like their skin was made of crawling insects. On seeing Dad wake out of his stupor, one of the creatures screeched and yanked on his cord, which caused my dad to thrash weakly as a plume of red curled out of his body.

"No!" I plunged my hand into the water and managed to brush the rough edge of one of Dad's fins with my fingertips. "I'm here! I'm here, Dad! It's gonna be okay!" I said, even though I knew that was nonsense. Because, really. Was it going to be okay? Probably not.

"So touching," said Izanami. "Nothing like a reunion between a girl and her long-lost father." I glanced at her, and she pretended to wipe away a tear. Something inside me growled. How dare she make fun of me and Dad.

"You think I'm cruel." She frowned. "But I assure you, my dear, sweet girl, I am not. I love a good family bonding moment, I really do. Would you like to see him in his original form so you can hug him properly?" she said, and without waiting for me to answer, she clapped her hands. "Here you go." Everything in front of me evaporated, leaving behind a man I wasn't sure I recognized.

He looked nothing like the way I remembered. He used to have thick, rough black hair, big shoulders, and a wide, smiling mouth. This man was thin, pale, and stooped, with long gray hair and a scraggly gray beard. He looked hollow, like a man whose spirit had been scraped out of him bit by bit, leaving nothing but an empty shell.

For a moment, the world felt upside down. I was used to seeing Dad as the strong one. He had never needed rescuing. He was always the one who'd rescued me. It didn't make sense. But when he looked at me, his eyes were the same as always—kind and gentle and full of love—and I forgot everything else. "Momo," he rasped. He stumbled forward, and I fell into his arms for real this time. I felt his ribs through the back of his ragged shirt, and his collarbone jutted out and pressed uncomfortably into my forehead. But he was warm, and his arms held me to him, and then I felt a pair of paws on my leg and looked down to see Niko wagging his entire body and making happy fox noises. Dad laughed and we knelt down to gather Niko into our hug, and just for a moment, it was like we were inside a snow globe, inside our own tiny, sparkly, happy little world.

"See?" Izanami said, and our little bubble shattered. "I told you I love a family moment. Now then. Momo, my child, do you remember the terms of our agreement?"

I felt like the pulse of the jewel was driving my own heartbeat.

What do we do? I thought to the others.

I don't think she knows we all have it, came Danny's voice.

Whatever you do, don't tell her, Ryleigh said.

"As I recall," Izanami continued, "I said that I would release your father in exchange for the third Sacred Treasure, the Jewel of the Heart. I have upheld my end of the bargain with, I think you will agree, the utmost integrity." She smiled a smile that made me feel like I'd been turned into an icicle. "And I expect that you, an upstanding, principled young woman, will now uphold your end."

"Momo, what have you done?" Dad whispered. His already pale face was even paler, and I had to turn away because I couldn't stand to see the look of disappointment and horror in his eyes.

"Momo?" he said again.

I opened my mouth to answer, but no words came out. Because what could I say? *Dad, in exchange for your life, I agreed to give the Queen of Death the final item she needs to escape Yomi and take over the kami-verse. You're welcome! Oh—did I mention that the tool lies inside my own heart? I meant to find a way out of this, but I couldn't, so now I'm about to become a tool for Izanami to restore her powers, and the kami-verse is doomed, but oh, well. That's life, amirite?*

"I'm *waiiiting*," Izanami sang. Her voice was sweetly melodic and laced with threat.

Now would be a perfect time to reveal those new jewel-related powers, Niko whined in my head. *Anyone?*

I'm working on it! Danny said.

"I can't give you the jewel," I said to Izanami, stalling for time.

Izanami inclined her head and pouted, like she was confused. "But how can that be? Surely you haven't come all this way just to cheat me out of my prize? Whyever would you do such a thing?"

"I—"

"Ohh, I see!" Her face brightened. "You mean you can't give it to me like an espresso machine or a bottle of perfume!"

Then her smile disappeared, and she snarled, "Child. Do you take me for a fool? I know where the jewel is and how it works. It is mine, after all." She pointed at me, and as if in response, the jewel pulsed even more powerfully. I looked down to see a red glow emanating from my chest. I could even hear it humming.

Izanami held out her palm. "All you have to do is tell it to come to me," she said.

"Momo! Tell me what's going on!" Dad pleaded.

Give it to me.

I blinked at Danny. *What?*

"I'm going to count to three, Momo," said Izanami. "And then I'm going to take it from you."

She said all you had to do was tell it to go to her, right? Try telling it to go to me!

"One . . . two . . ."

I concentrated on the glow in my chest. *Go to Danny,* I told it.

"Three."

Zoop. The warm glow disappeared, and out of the corner of my eye, I saw Danny smile just before Izanami thrust her hand forward and pain exploded in my chest, with alternating bursts of fire and ice, light and darkness. I gasped for breath but couldn't take in any air. And just when I decided that this must be the end, that I was going to die, I felt her let go, and the pain dissipated.

She stood before me, her eyes dark with rage. Dad's arms were wrapped protectively around my shoulders.

He began pleading. "She's just a child! You can't do this. Have mercy!"

"You sweet, innocent, ignorant man," Izanami said. She flicked her fingers and he crumpled to the floor.

"Dad!" I screamed.

"Calm yourself, child. He's fine," Izanami snapped. "He's just being quiet for a while. Now." She leaned down and put her face close to mine. "Where. Is. My. Jewel." It was more a threat than a question.

I shook my head, still woozy from the pain. "I don't have it."

Izanami spun around and narrowed her eyes at my friends. "Do any of *you* happen to know where it is?"

Let's play Keep Away! Danny called out in our minds. *Everyone, give your jewels to me!*

Almost instantly, Izanami looked at Danny, whose chest had been glowing half a second ago. "Give it to me," she said.

"I don't have it."

She blinked at him in confusion. He *didn't* have it.

Jin's chest was glowing now. Izanami whirled on him. "Give it to me!"

He shook his head, and it was gone.

With growing fury, Izanami turned from one to the other of us while we tossed the jewel back and forth, each time just before she could reach in and grab it. Finally, she seemed to give up. She looked at Niko, who had the jewel, and said, "I see that you're playing games with me. And while I do love a game, I don't have time just now. So I'll just have to—"

Give it to me! I called to Niko, and felt the warm glow spread in my chest just as Izanami thrust both her hands out. And through another burst of pain, I heard everyone else crying out along with me.

A few awful seconds later, she let us go again. She stood before us empty-handed, looking truly puzzled. "I should have been able to take it," she murmured. She fixed me with a dagger-sharp stare. "Why can't I take it from you?"

I shook my head. "I don't know anything about it, I promise! It just kind of split up and went into us when Izanagi went to the World Beyond."

Izanami held up a finger. "I'm sorry. What did you just say about my ex-husband?" Her attitude was calm, almost polite, but her voice was so full of danger that I stumbled backward a few steps.

"I—I said he went to the World Beyond."

Izanami's red lips pressed themselves into a line, and she closed her eyes and took three deep breaths, like maybe she was trying to calm herself down. But on the third breath, she threw her head back and screamed. It was so loud, so bursting with vicious rage, it became my entire world: the floor I stood on, the air in my lungs, even my actual spirit.

When she stopped, her eyes blazed, and her body still trembled with the power of that scream. She began pacing in a furious circle. "That coward! That disgusting slug!" she hissed. "I will not allow him to deprive me of what is rightfully mine. I will have justice!" Then she stopped, took three more deep breaths, and turned to me with a venomous smile. She appeared to have made up her mind about something.

She snapped her fingers and said, "Nighty-night, dears. I'll call you back when I need you," and Niko, Ryleigh, Jin, and Danny slumped together on the floor. Then she stretched out her arm, and a velvet bag materialized in her hand. "Recognize this?" She loosened the drawstring and pulled out an octagonal piece of bronze that shone with a different color on each edge: the Mirror of the Sun. "Let's see . . ." She turned it around in her hand. "I think I'll choose the side that shows me in my best light. I must admit, I am a little vain."

Izanami tapped the blue side of the mirror and turned her head back and forth to get all the angles. "Get ready with me as I prepare to use the collective power of the Three Sacred Treasures to escape my prison, dispense justice, and take over the Middle Lands!" She simpered and preened like a Pixtagram influencer, then looked up at me. "Oh, my. That will never do. Time for a makeover!"

She snapped her fingers again, and my jeans and jacket were replaced with a soft white robe and a red sash. My hair came out of its ponytail and hung down my shoulders and back.

"Look! Twinsies!" Izanami glided over to me and twirled. She was now wearing the same outfit I wore. She held out the mirror. In our matching outfits, we did look a lot like a mother-daughter pair, and I thought I saw Izanami's cold smile soften for just a moment. But it hardened right back up before I could be sure, and she said, "Oh—one more touch for me." She tapped the mirror again and placed it on her chest, where it spread into a gleaming bronze breastplate. My reflection smiled and waved at me, but I couldn't smile or wave back.

"Now, Momo, don't fret. I promised I would spare the lives of the ones you love most in the world so you can feel safe and happy for eternity. All I ask in return is that you accept your place at my side and help me bring about a new age of peace and equality by giving me back my jewel." Izanami's voice was warmer this time, persuasive, almost gentle.

"In the World Above, everyone fears death. But when I come into my full power, there will be nothing to fear. When everyone is dead, everyone is equal. There will be no suffering, no striving for useless material goods or power. No one will be hungry. No one will have to leave the people they love, and no one will be left behind. Don't you see, Momo? We want the same thing! You've dreamed of a world in which there is no stifling social hierarchy, where you're surrounded by friends. I am going to create that world. And you will be at my side, helping me and enjoying the fruits of our labor."

"But it'll only be peaceful and equal because everyone will be dead!"

"You say that like it's a bad thing." Izanami wrinkled her forehead and pouted.

"It is! Because . . . because when you're alive, you—you feel things! And, I don't know, some of those feelings are bad, but a lot of them are really great. And you can smell flowers, and catch snowflakes on your tongue, and—and taste chocolate." I felt like I was making it up as I went, but the more I said, the more I believed in what I was saying.

"You can listen to music. You can sing. You can dance. And yeah, sometimes I think I was happier when I was little, and I wish things hadn't changed, but there are so many things I love now that I wouldn't have gotten to experience if my life had stopped when I was young. Like my friends. And my favorite books. And going to a SttTopp concert. And so—so the more you live, the more you grow, and the more things you can find to love."

Izanami shrugged, seemingly unmoved by my speech. "You say potato, I say potahto."

"Huh?"

"One person's 'death' is another person's 'peace.' Where do you think the expression 'rest in peace' comes from?"

I felt like that was twisting things, but I couldn't say exactly how.

But Izanami had moved on. "I'll ask you nicely one last time, Momo. Please give me the Jewel of the Heart."

But after all that talk of death, I realized that I had some bargaining power. The jewel was inside me. And Izanami couldn't get the jewel without killing me. But if she killed me, then not only would Kusanagi go back to Susano'o, but who knew what would happen to the jewel?

So I squared my shoulders and said, "No."

Izanami's face twisted with rage for a moment before settling back into icy dignity. "Not even to save the lives of the ones you love? How very disappointing." She let her gaze wander to Dad and my friends, who had begun to regain consciousness, and tapped a long black fingernail on her chin. "Who should I take first?"

Oh, no. Why hadn't I thought of that? This was why she'd spared their lives—so that she could use them as bargaining chips! Danny, Niko, Ryleigh, Jin, and Dad looked at me. They didn't say a word, but I could see in their eyes that they'd heard what Izanami had said.

"Don't," I begged her. "Please."

"I'd *like* to keep everyone alive, of course. I did say I would, and I do want you to be happy! But I will do what I must to get the jewel. So. Who dies first? Hmm." She swept her gaze across the people I treasured most in the world.

"Eeney . . ." She pointed at Danny as he staggered to his feet.

I couldn't let her kill everyone I loved. But I couldn't help her conquer the Middle Lands, either.

"Meeney . . ." She pointed at Ryleigh, then glanced at me. "You can stop me anytime, darling. Just say you'll give me the jewel."

"Miney . . ." She pointed at Niko. Her fingertip strayed in Dad's direction, and she took a deep breath.

"*NO!*"

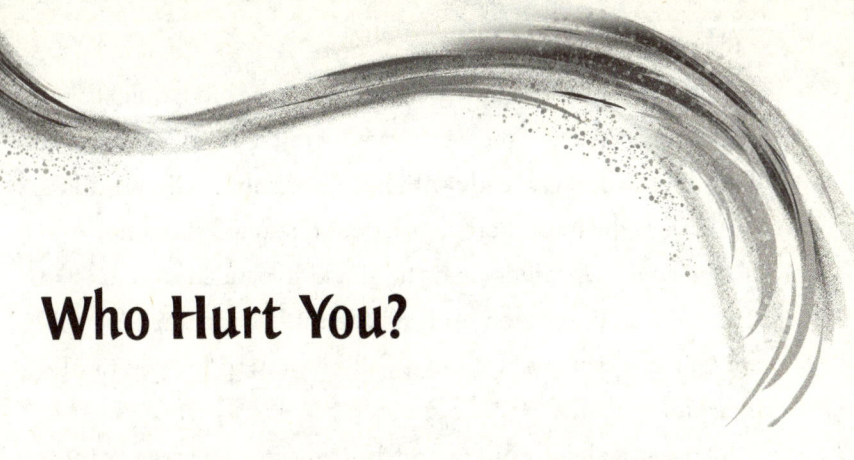

Who Hurt You?

Mom burst out of Izanami's armor and deflected the blast that came from her fingertips with a shield of silver light. She was dressed in off-brand yoga pants, a zip-up hoodie, and running shoes, but she looked every inch the goddess that she was. She gave off a bright white light, and her eyes flashed with a fire I'd only ever seen one other time, when she rescued me from the shikome in front of our house last fall.

"Get behind me!" she shouted.

I was overcome with relief and gratitude: Mom had been inside the Mirror of the Sun and come out again, which meant that she'd chosen to risk death to save me and Dad in this life rather than be reunited with us in that other life on the Island of Mysteries. She was back, and she was taking charge. She was acting like the mom I'd always wanted—the mom I'd always needed.

"Mom!"

"I said get behind me!" Her voice rang with power and command, and when I hesitated, she reached out and yanked me behind her like I was a toddler. She extended her other hand and, without taking her eyes off Izanami, drew Danny, Ryleigh, Jin, Niko, and Dad behind her with a flick of her wrist.

Izanami looked genuinely shocked, but she hid it quickly behind an expression of regal calm and pointed a narrow finger at Mom. But Mom was ready with her silver shield. She stumbled a little from the impact of the blast but remained standing.

She spun her hands, and the shield expanded over us like an umbrella. "Go to the bridge," she said. "Izanami can't follow you across it yet. Daikoku will be waiting for you on the other side."

Danny, Ryleigh, Niko, and Jin rose to their feet, a little dazed. But Dad was focused entirely on Mom.

"Takiri," he said, and touched her shoulder. "Is that you?"

Mom's shining aura wavered just the slightest bit. Izanami must have noticed, because she gave a sardonic smile and said, "Go on, have your reunion. I'll wait."

"I'm here," Mom said to Dad, without turning around.

"I looked for you everywhere," he said.

"And I looked for you." Her voice trembled with emotion, but she kept her gaze on Izanami.

"Momo," she said next. "Thank the kami-verse you're all right. I was so worried about you."

I thought about how angry I'd been the last time I'd seen her. I was still angry, if you want to know the truth. But here she was, risking her life for me. I couldn't bear it if we died and that anger was the last thing she got from me. My chest tightened and my throat closed up over a giant rock that seemed to have lodged itself inside. "I'm sorry I was mean to you, Mom," I choked out. "Before I left. I didn't mean any of it."

"I know," she said.

"I don't want you to die."

"Go. I promise I won't die."

But I was pretty sure she would. She was no match for Izanami.

"All right, kids, I know I said I'd wait, but Momo and I do have some important business to take care of, so can we wrap it up, please?" said Izanami. Her voice was breezy and cool, but the threat in it was unmistakable. She pointed a finger at us, and Mom's shield deflected the magic just in time.

"GO!" Mom shouted. She began pushing forth rays of light with such speed and power that Izanami was forced to pay attention to her. Mom was giving us an opportunity to escape.

Dad refused. "I'm not leaving you," he said firmly.

"Niko, get everyone out of here!" Mom commanded.

Niko was fully conscious by now, and he was more than happy to cooperate. "Yes, ma'am!" he barked. He began nipping heels and yipping, "You heard her! Don't dawdle like a bunch of sluggish sloths!" Danny, Jin, and Ryleigh stumbled ahead of him, protected by Mom's ever-expanding shield, and they disappeared behind me. But I wasn't about to leave Mom's side, and apparently, neither was Dad. The battle was costing her more and more effort, and Izanami did not seem to be tiring.

"All right, I've had enough of this." Izanami threw her arms forward, and Mom and Dad froze. Dad's mouth formed an O; I could almost hear him saying "Momo!" as his body turned to black smoke and drifted away. Mom turned into a two-dimensional version of herself, a faded, transparent, empty-eyed line drawing. Then she drifted slowly out the door.

It felt like someone had flipped a switch and put my entire life on pause: as if time had stopped and my body had turned to stone—no blood, no breath, no brain. Just a statue staring in disbelief at the spot where my parents had been only seconds ago. She couldn't have killed them. They couldn't be dead. This had to be some kind of trick, some other bargain she was setting up.

Izanami sighed, and a draft of wintry-cold air swept around me. "What a sweet man your father was, refusing to leave your mother's side! I must admit, I'm a little jealous," she said to me. "But we've wasted enough time already, and I don't have any to spare for sentimentality. I bet you wish *you'd* been a bit more sentimental. It would have saved your parents' lives."

She looked at me as if she expected some kind of response, and when I didn't speak, she said, "Don't be afraid, Momo. I won't hurt you. You're my daughter, remember? We have a bond. We're the same, you and I."

My mind creaked to life with thoughts of Mom, who had risked everything to come to rescue me in spite of all I'd said to her; and Dad, who had refused to leave us in danger. I managed to whisper to Izanami, "I'm not your daughter. We're not the same."

Izanami leaned over me. "Do not deny the undeniable. We have both been abandoned and rejected and misunderstood. We share the same pain and the same power. The same thirst for justice in an unjust kami-verse. How else do you think you've been able to connect to the power of the Sword of the Wind?"

What was she even talking about? I couldn't answer my own question, so I tried to answer hers. "Susano'o?"

Izanami scoffed. "He tried to *kill* you. And I *rescued* you, remember? And your mother pledged your life to me. In honor of our bond, I came to your rescue twice more: once when you tried to use Kusanagi against Shuten-dōji before you were ready, and once when you fought Tamamo-no-mae. You were only able to defeat them because of me. At the very least, you owe me for that." She smiled at me and held out her hand. "Help me, Momo! Give me the jewel, and we can bring justice and peace to the kami-verse."

"But you want to kill everyone." My voice sounded small and unsure.

Izanami sighed another icy sigh. "I wish I didn't have to. But it's the only way to make Izanagi pay for what he did to me."

"But he's gone."

"Even more reason. It's the only way justice can be served."

Justice. She kept saying that word, but it didn't feel right. Why not? As cruel as she was, I supposed Izanami deserved *some* kind of justice for what Izanagi had done to her, didn't she? And what was justice if not making someone pay for hurting you?

Maybe the problem was that she wanted to make Izanagi pay for hurting her by hurting him back. That was fair. But . . .

That was it. It was *fair*, but it wasn't *just*.

Izanami wasn't really interested in peace. She wasn't interested in justice. All she wanted was revenge. Izanami was the ultimate vengeful ghost, just like the Taira emperor Antoku's grandmother and the ghost samurai crab army. Maybe like the Tsuchigumo. But much scarier.

"I—I can't give you the jewel," I stammered.

Something cruel and dangerous flared in her eyes. "I want

you to know that even if you refuse to hand over the jewel, it will not stop me from moving into the Middle Lands. With Kusanagi, I can destroy the boulder and break the spell that has locked me in Yomi all these years. The only thing the Jewel of the Heart changes is the speed with which I can complete my mission and build my new kingdom. Instead of wiping out the Middle Lands in one fell swoop, I will be forced to destroy it city by city, town by town, forest by forest.

"People, animals, and Middle Lands kami will suffer. They will experience pain, loss, terror, and despair. Perhaps you will be able to take solace in your prideful insistence on your principles, on your pointless refusal to cooperate. But at what price? My armies are infinite, and they are relentless. My shikome are hunting down your friends as we speak. The Middle Lands will be mired in endless wars, epidemics, and natural disasters. And eventually you will lose hope and hand over the jewel, and you'll have to live with the fact that you could have saved countless people pain and suffering if you had simply done as I asked to begin with. So I encourage you to consider your options carefully. You cannot win. If you really want to do what's right, you will accept your fate and save the Middle Lands from immeasurable suffering."

My brain seemed to have gotten itself tangled in the spokes of an endlessly spinning bicycle wheel, and my thoughts flapped uselessly around and around. What was there to say? What was there to do? I couldn't let her win without a fight. But I had nothing to bargain with, no clever plans.

You have me!

The message sputtered in my head through a prickle of static, like it was coming through a bad cell phone signal.

Kusanagi? Little bursts of electricity shot through my arms, and I realized with a sudden shock that I was holding it in my hands. It had come to me in my moment of need.

Fight! What . . . have . . . lose?

Good point.

She wants . . . She'll kill . . . How dare she.

I was out of options. Daikoku had said that I couldn't beat Izanami the Destroyer at her own game, that I had to embrace the source of my power and move beyond destruction. But my rage monster only made Kusanagi's dark, destructive side more powerful. Trying to understand my enemies helped keep me from destroying them, but I *had* to destroy Izanami. As for being bigger than my anger, the way Jizō had said, I didn't see how that could be. How could I become bigger than the most powerful fighting force I knew, bigger than the thing that gave me the strength to fight monsters?

All I had left in the kami-verse was my sword and my anger, and the tiniest spark of hope that maybe it would be enough after all.

I closed my eyes and summoned my rage monster. *She killed Dad. She killed Mom. She's going to kill my friends. She's taking away everything I love just so she can satisfy her need for revenge.*

A torrent of anger at Izanami poured through me, and I let it meet Kusanagi's energy. The hilt sparked, and I felt the familiar thrill of connection as its dark, bloodthirsty power thundered through me. Kusanagi twitched in my hand as my pain melted into anger that took root and twined up through my legs, into my heart and head, and out to my fingertips. When I opened my eyes, a red haze descended over my vision. I was back. Now I could fight.

Izanami stood before me looking amused, which should have made me pause, but I was beyond backing down. In fact, I felt grateful to her, because she was the one who had taught me how to do this.

Who hurt you?

Izanami.

GET HER! my rage monster and Kusanagi boomed together.

I raised Kusanagi and swung with everything I had.

Through the roar and the haze, I saw Izanami smile. She raised her hand and flicked away the blow like it was nothing. My entire body vibrated as I staggered to regain my balance.

"Tsk, tsk, tsk." Izanami clucked her tongue in mock disappointment. "Try again, Momo. Concentrate."

This isn't fair. This isn't right. She needs to pay.

I swung again, and was deflected again.

"Are you sure you don't want to rethink this?" Izanami said. "You're only prolonging your own suffering and the suffering of everyone you know."

Stop, I told myself. *Stop this now. You can't win.*

But I couldn't stop. Dad and Mom were dead. My friends were as good as dead. It was her fault. I swung wildly, without looking, without aiming. It didn't matter what I hit. I just wanted the pain not to be mine. If I couldn't hurt Izanami, then at least she would know how I felt, which was broken. I hacked and chopped, and Izanami redirected and deflected until finally I lost my balance and crashed into one of the shelves on the wall.

The sound of something smashing to the floor. The smell of incense. A bloodcurdling scream.

I opened my eyes to see white smoke pouring out of a jar that lay in pieces on the floor. Izanami knelt next to the broken jar, alternately screaming curses at the smoke and at the pottery as she tried in vain to gather the broken shards and put them back together. She saw me staring, and with a wild-eyed shriek, pointed a finger at me. I went cold and stiff as marble. And then the smoke became mist that shrouded a tiny little island in a gray and choppy sea. At the center of the island was a pillar of stone. A beautiful young woman emerged from behind it. Was that . . . could it be . . . ?

It's Incredibly Toxic

I glanced at Izanami, who had stopped screaming and was now staring in silence at the scene in front of us with an unreadable expression on her face. She noticed me looking at her and said in a voice as flat and far away as the horizon, "Yes, child. It's me. I was a beauty, wasn't I?" She lifted a wasted hand to her face and stroked her hollow cheek. "I was so innocent. So eager to please." I couldn't tell if she was feeling nostalgic or bitter.

A man came around the other side of the pillar. He was tall and handsome, with broad shoulders and a loping, athletic gait. He had long, glossy black hair tied up in two man buns, and a neatly trimmed beard. Merry brown eyes and an easy smile lit up his face when he saw Izanami in front of him. Her own face lit up too, and she spoke to him.

"Izanagi and I were charged with creating everything in the Middle Lands," said the real Izanami in that same flat, faraway voice. "But no matter how hard we tried, we failed at first."

The fog thickened and then melted away to show Izanami placing a basket in the waves that lapped at the shore. There was something in it wrapped in cloth, and young Izanami sobbed as she watched it drift into the mist.

I knew without having to ask that it was Ebisu. I clearly remembered his story: He was their first baby, but he'd been born all blobby. Izanami had put him out to sea in a basket, and he was later found, rescued, and raised by the Ainu kamuy. That was why he had a soft spot for adoptees like Danny, and why the Ainu kamuy had let us into their realm.

"When we asked our elders from the World Beyond, they said it was because I always spoke first. 'Let Izanagi be the first to speak,' they said, 'and your wish will be fulfilled.' So I did what I was told." Her voice became as black and bitter as tar. She sighed, and the bitterness faded a little. "I must admit, though, I was happy for a long time."

The mist closed around the island, and when it cleared, there was Izanami again, rosy-cheeked and pregnant, with a dozen fat children tumbling around her feet. Izanagi stood next to her, and they looked at each other and at their kids with eyes full of tenderness. Maybe she hadn't liked having her voice and her opinions shoved behind Izanagi's (who would?), but she'd still loved him. They'd been happy together.

A few of the bigger kids splashed out into the water and turned into islands. The others jumped onto the islands and became mountains, and then I was watching a time-lapse video where Izanami had more and more children and the islands were populated with more and more mountains, then forests, lakes, rivers, and animals.

Time slowed down again, and Izanami was squatting on the floor of a hut, holding her big pregnant belly and breathing through puffed cheeks. There was a burst of fire, and suddenly she was writhing in pain, her legs engulfed in flames. It was horrible to watch, but I was still made of stone, and I couldn't look away. The fire grew and filled the hut, and Izanami disappeared. Izanagi roared in and hacked the fire into eight pieces with his sword and hurled the pieces across the sea. He watched as they landed and were absorbed by eight different mountains scattered across the islands, and then he fell to his knees and broke into sobs.

I snuck a peek at real-life Izanami. Her face was still impassive, but I was pretty sure I saw a tear trickle down her cheek.

The mist lowered and then parted again to show memory-Izanami limping painfully, wrapped in rags and bandages. Her burned face was haggard and tear-streaked, and she looked small and scared. In the Middle Lands, where Izanami and Izanagi had lived, it had always been light. Here, it was gray and dull and dark. She crossed a bridge over a broad river and was met on the other side by a shadow. The shadow embraced her and led her through a bleak, barren landscape, through a gate, and into the jaws of a giant skull. On the bridge behind her lay a gently pulsing red jewel.

Not long after, Izanagi appeared with a sword in his hand, his hair held in its man buns by shining ivory combs. His eyes darted randomly here and there, and I could tell that he couldn't see a thing and it scared the bejeezus out of him. But he was here anyway, searching for Izanami, so I had to give him credit. He paused on the bridge to pick up the jewel and examine it; it seemed to give him courage. He threaded it onto a necklace of similar jewels and picked up his pace. When he reached the gate in front of the giant skull, he stopped and shouted out her name. Izanami appeared in the mouth of the skull in a hooded black robe and answered him. His face lit up, and although he was looking slightly in the wrong direction, it was very sweet. And then he looked sad and worried—she'd just told him that she wasn't allowed to leave. She would send a message asking permission from the shadows who ruled the place, but it would be a long time before that permission was granted.

"Wait here. I'll wait with you. But promise you won't look at me. I'm not ready for you to see me yet."

Izanagi laughed. "It's too dark to see you anyway. How long do you think it will take?"

"I don't know," she answered. "Be patient."

The mist fell and rose again. Izanagi sat near the wall, drumming his fingers on his knees and muttering to himself. His beard had grown scruffy, and his hair was disheveled. He stared into the shadows where he had last heard Izanami's voice. His face was full of longing. He looked away, and then at the mouth of the giant skull. Down at the dusty ground, and then back again toward the skull. He stood up. He sat down. He tapped his toes. He sighed. He drummed his fingers some more.

Finally, he pulled out one of the ivory combs that held his man buns in place and broke off a tooth. He blew on it, and it turned into a flaming torch that he raised above his head as he looked one last time toward the mouth of the skull. His face contorted in fear and disgust, and he gasped out loud.

In the flickering light of the torch lay not the smooth-skinned, youthful wife of his memory, but a rotting corpse, crawling with maggots. Huddled in a half circle around her were eight skeletal figures dressed in torn black gowns. They had gray skin, patchy hair, white eyes, and red, red lips.

I don't know whose scream was louder and more horrified, Izanagi's or Izanami's. Izanami scrabbled at her cloak and threw the hood over her oozing face and wailed, "No! I told you not to look until I was ready!"

Izanagi was up and staggering backward away from her, shaking his head and breathing hard.

"Stay!" Izanami begged him. She gathered her cloak around her and stumbled toward him, her corpse-hand outstretched. "Please! Don't run away! If you can just wait—"

Izanami's jewel began to shine and pulse. Izanagi immediately clasped his hand over it, but not before she noticed.

"You found my jewel! Please, bring it to me. I need it!"

"I can't. I—" He put a hand to his mouth. "I think I'm going to be sick."

"Give me my jewel! It will heal me. I won't look like this when I return. You'll forget!"

"I won't. I won't ever be able to look at you again without seeing those . . ." He gestured at the maggots squirming out of her abdomen. "And that . . ." He pointed at her face.

"But I need it!"

"I can't give it back to you." Izanagi looked at her and shuddered. "Sorry. I have to go." He turned and sprinted at top speed across the plain, holding his torch ahead of him to light the way.

Izanami's face went from slack-jawed confusion to despair to incandescent rage. She threw her head back and screamed, "He has wronged me! Bring him back!"

The eight shikome rose up, and with a collective shriek of fury, they tore after the fleeing Izanagi. The chase was on, with the advantage switching back and forth between Izanagi and the shikome until Izanagi came across a peach tree. He picked three peaches and tossed them at the shikome, who of course stopped to devour them.

While they were distracted, Izanagi bounded back over the bridge, rolled a boulder across the end of it, and murmured something under his breath. A misty silver curtain fell along the riverbank.

Izanagi was still bent over his knees and panting from the exertion when Izanami appeared on the opposite bank, borne by eight creatures made of black smoke.

"Where are you? Come back!" she called. "It's not too late!"

"I can't." Izanagi's voice was kind but firm. "I can never see you again."

Izanami began to cry. "But why? Why are you leaving me here?"

"Because you're a corpse!" he said. "I can't be married to a corpse!"

"I told you I'm changing back! You just have to be patient! And you won't be able to create life without me!"

Izanagi held up the jewel. "I will, though."

Izanami stared. Her bones showed through her skin here and there, and her chin was falling off, but I could see pain and betrayal written all over her face. She screamed, and he took an involuntary step back.

"Give it back. It's mine!" She rushed across the bridge but got entangled in the silver mist, which reached out and pushed her back to the Yomi side.

"You don't need it anymore."

Another scream. "If you don't give it back, I'll—I'll—"

"You'll what? Kill all the people I create?" Izanagi seemed to have gained confidence and courage after seeing that his spell had worked. He held up the jewel. "I'll just make more!"

She screamed again. "Give it back!"

He shook his head. "I'm sorry, but I really can't talk to you when you're like this. In fact, I can't be with someone so angry. It's incredibly toxic. We're over. Forever."

Izanami let loose a shriek that made the ground shake, and just for a moment, I felt what she felt. I was rocked by a violent spasm of grief, like a dark, bleeding gash, vast and black and empty. And then I was overcome by a towering fury fiercer and wilder than anything I'd ever felt—biting, burning cold, and ravenous for destruction. An avalanche, a tsunami, a wildfire, an earthquake. Nothing would satisfy its hunger for revenge. Nothing would fill the chasm gouged by that betrayal.

On the other side of the bridge, Izanagi twitched, and a shadow of nervous anxiety flickered across his handsome face. Then he ran off without a backward glance.

The mist fell and washed away the memory, and all that was left were the broken shards of the jar that had contained it.

Neither of us said anything for a long time. I stole a glance at real-life Izanami. Her face was as still and empty as a frozen lake.

"He abandoned you here," I said at last.

"He did," she said. Her voice was hollow.

"And you were so sad."

She looked at the shards of the memory jar and said quietly, "I loved Izanagi. I gave up my voice to be the mother of his children. But after all I gave him, after all I did for him, he couldn't see me for who I really was when I was at my lowest. He stole the source of my power and ran away. And to cover up his shame, he told the world that I intended to kill him from the moment he saw what I had become, and that I had tried to drag him down to stay here forever.

"I was young and pure and full of life. I birthed the world! I didn't even know that Yomi existed, that death was a thing that could happen. And suddenly I was rotting away in a strange, dark land, with maggots crawling out of my belly. You can't imagine how terrified I was. Could *you* face an eternity knowing that the one who should have loved you and saved you had instead run away and left you to face all of that alone?" She looked at me, and I was filled again with the pain she had felt when Izanagi left. It was unbearable.

"He should have waited for you."

"Ha," Izanami spat. "He never would have survived down here. He never questioned his right to eternal youth and power, and when the sight of my ruined body challenged that idea, he fled and locked me away so he would never have to think of it again. He took the last of my hope with him, as well as my life-giving jewel. And he renamed it so no one would know it was mine. All I had left was my grief, my fear, my pain, and my anger. It was my anger that saved me. It gave me the strength to continue. Without it I would have collapsed in on myself."

I remembered what she'd said to me once before: *Anger is*

your friend. It is your ally. Anger hears the call of the weak, the frightened, and the injured, and rushes to defend them. It is your protector and the source of your power.

"I know what I have become. My rage has made me powerful, and I know that I am feared and reviled for it. But who can blame me? Without hope, without light, what choice did I have?"

It was so confusing. I should have hated her for the pain she had caused—and would continue to cause. Part of me did hate her. But she hadn't deserved the terrible things that had happened to her. All she'd ever wanted was to feel safe and loved and accepted for who she was. Wasn't that what *I* wanted? What anyone would want? Who could blame her for feeling betrayed and angry over Izanami's selfish cowardice? She might be bloodthirsty and cruel, but it came from her grief and her loneliness. Was it fair to cast her as a vengeful murder queen who would stop at nothing to destroy the world as I knew it? It was like all the other stories I'd heard on my journey here: Sen, the Tsuchigumo, the Ainu. Someone else had told it, twisted the facts, and left out her side.

I finally understood why I would never defeat Izanami with Kusanagi as long as I was trying to destroy her, as long as my power was fueled by my anger and my pain. She had so much more of it than I had to draw from. So how was I supposed to stop her? Telling her that I understood her pain hadn't solved her problem, and it sure as heck didn't solve mine. What else was left? Hug it out? Tell her to breathe in peace and breathe out love? Sing "Let It Go" together?

While I stood there dithering, Izanami snatched Kusanagi

out of my hand. Instead of morphing back into a guitar, like it did with everyone else, the sword retained its form—another reminder of the depth and power of her anger. She grasped my empty hand in her icy fingers. I was too surprised to fight back, and I'm not even sure I could have if I'd tried. The room faded away as the cold crept from her hand to mine, up my arm and through my body. I began to wonder if this was what it felt like to freeze to death. But then the sensation went away, and we were standing at the entrance to that old, empty bridge I'd seen from the river.

Behind us lay Yomi, all misty and gray and—Oh, no. The landscape was covered with demons lined up like an army on the march. There were gaki, the hungry ghosts with distended bellies and skin stretched so thin over their bones that they might as well have been skeletons; there was the rage-filled skeleton army itself; there was a squadron of shikome, with their garish makeup and milk-white eyes, and their hair peeling off their skulls; and hundreds more I couldn't even name. They drooled and smacked their lips and breathed in raspy, putrid gasps. There were animals, too: the kasha, those corpse-eating humanoid cats; korōri—tiger-striped badgers with wolfish snouts and poisonous breath; and a pack of hundreds of slavering wolves. Bitterness and rage and hatred poured out of them in rivers. I turned to see what they would be marching toward and saw only the other end of the bridge, blocked by a huge boulder. Everything behind and beyond it was obscured by that veil of silvery, shimmery light that Izanagi had pulled over the shore all those years ago.

"I warned you," said Izanami. "You've lost everyone you

love. Soon you will lose the Middle Lands. You can make its destruction quick and easy, or slow and painful."

She raised Kusanagi and pointed it at the boulder at the other end of the bridge. There was a great CRACK and the rumble of falling stone. Behind me, a howl went up, and the bridge shook under the weight of a thousand dead soldiers marching across it toward us, toward the portal she'd opened.

On the other side, the silver curtain that had obscured everything beyond the riverbank fell away, revealing—thank the kami-verse—another army on the other side. At its head was Susano'o, swinging a brand-new sword.

"Come at me, bro!" he bellowed. "You come for my fortress and my power, you come for me! ARGHHHHH!"

Susano'o was flanked by Daikoku, holding a gleaming gold hammer, and Bishamon, his backpack of flames on full blast, with his spear ready to fly. Ebisu's fishing pole had morphed into a mace, and even jolly Hotei had tied his bathrobe and put on a pair of sneakers. He held his bag open and was rooting around in it. I hoped he'd find something better to throw than pizza and In-N-Out burgers; though I had once been saved from a shikome by a bag of Auntie Anne's pretzel bites and some peach gummies. Benzaiten strummed a chord on her guitar that filled me with hope, and the two grandfather gods, Jurōjin and Fukurokujū, held up their scrolls, which shone with golden light.

Among the hundreds of earthly kami who ranged behind them, I recognized Momotarō, who had saved us from the yōkai attack in Chicago. Itsuma-hime and Yasome astride Stripey and Jojo led a battalion of Tsuchigumo soldiers and spiders. The

Gemini aunties were there, too, still wearing their puffy jackets and sparkly deely-boppers; next to them a regiment of foxes lined up smartly. Among their ranks—I almost shouted with relief when I saw them—were Niko, Danny, Ryleigh, and Jin. They'd made it after all. Not only that, but Danny and Ryleigh held brand-new shining weapons, and even Jin seemed to have a new set of silver wings.

The vanguard of the army of demons and ghosts reached the end of the bridge and crossed into Meido, the empty space between the Middle Lands and Yomi. Susano'o met them with a roar and a mighty slash of his sword. The battle had begun.

Is That Me?

It was everything you'd expect from a battle between the kami and yōkai of the Middle Lands and the demons of Yomi. The Tsuchigumo cast magical nets over skeletons, who got tangled and stuck in the sticky webbing. Momotarō and his cousin Kintarō clashed with Shuten-dōji and Tamamo-no-mae. Multi-tailed foxes (and one small, orange, single-tailed fox) sprang forward and sank their teeth into the flanks of snarling gray wolves. Benzaiten played a wild musical accompaniment for Jin, who flew above the battlefield and encouraged the Middle Lands fighters with "Eye of the Tiger." Danny and Ryleigh stood with the Gemini aunties, nailing the skeletons and hungry ghosts with their arrows and shuriken; the aunties, meanwhile, hurled golden shooting stars with amazing accuracy, shouting "Shame on you!" and "You should know better!"

At first it seemed to be going well for our side. But then a number of shikome who had stopped to gobble down a vat of chocolate pudding (courtesy of Hotei) finished their snack and charged the Gemini aunties. A platoon of skeletons had crumbled under the onslaught of arrows and shuriken, but thousands more were pouring over the bridge. The flesh-eating kasha joined the wolves.

"You should know," Izanami said, "that my disease and famine demons are making their way to the World Above while the kami of the Middle Lands are busy fighting. And for every living spirit in the Middle Lands, there are a thousand demons in Yomi."

She watched with grim satisfaction as one Gemini auntie's light faded to gray, and then another's. The skeletons had surrounded Ryleigh and Danny. Niko saw this and rushed to help, and all three were lost in the cloud of dust that rose around them. I listened for Jin's song, but the din of the battle made it increasingly difficult to hear. I wanted to cross the bridge to help them, but what could I do to help? I didn't have a weapon.

"You can put an end to this, Momo," Izanami said. "All you need to do is give me my jewel." She held out her hand.

I couldn't win. I would never beat her. She had everything. I had nothing.

Wait. That also meant . . .

I had nothing to lose.

"No," I said. And this time, I meant it.

Any guesses as to how Izanami took that?

If you guessed "not well," congratulations. You were correct.

Her body burst into flames, and she grew until she was taller than a house. "I'm sorry. Did you just say *no*?" she hissed.

"Yes. I mean, yes, I did say no."

Izanami's eyes were glowing embers, and her hair was on fire. In a voice like grinding metal, like a swarm of angry wasps, like a wildfire eating up a forest, she roared, *"GIVE ME THE JEWEL."*

She advanced on me, slowly and deliberately. I had no idea what I was going to do, but I stood my ground. As she got closer and closer, I saw myself reflected in the breastplate that used to be the Mirror of the Sun.

"Hello there!"

I almost jumped out of my skin. It was Yata-no-kagami, my reflection. "Come on in. I have something to show you." Yata-no-kagami extended her hand.

"GIVE ME THE JEWEL," Izanami boomed again. I could feel the blistering heat on my skin, and I could smell my hair singeing. A few more seconds, and I would turn into a char-broiled Momo-burger.

I grasped Yata-no-kagami's hand and she pulled me into the mirror.

Inside, it was strangely silent and blissfully cool. The mirrors to my alternate lives were still arranged around the room, as cloudy as I remembered them.

"I thought it might be helpful if you visited the other sides of the mirror," said Yata-no-kagami.

"The what?"

"The other sides. There are eight sides, remember?"

I did. "But why?"

"I'll just give you the tour and you can see for yourself.

Follow me." She held open a curtain and waved me over, and I followed her through the gap.

The first room had a softly carpeted floor, and walls covered with hundreds of old mirrors. "Regular mirror side. Nothing magical about this room," said Yata-no-kagami, and we passed through it without even stopping.

The second room was a fancy dressing room furnished with plush armchairs and low tables laden with crystal bowls of colorful candy. I couldn't help pausing in front of the single mirror placed on a low platform on one side; it made me look like a fashion model or a movie star. Yata-no-kagami gave me a little nudge. "Your best light. Fun, flattering, kind of a waste of time. Keep going."

The third room had several mirrors, all playing different scenes from my life like a bunch of monitors streaming different shows. "This is the side that shows your greatest strength," said Yata-no-kagami.

My rage monster, I thought glumly. The reason why I would never beat Izanami—because my greatest strength was also her greatest strength, and her anger and pain were bigger than mine. Sure enough, there I was on the shores of Lake Michigan fuming at Danny; fighting with Ryleigh in the Palace of the Sun; storming down a cinder cone to fight Tamamo-no-mae. I was on the bus, threatening Brad after he'd teased me; I was attacking the ningyo; I was screaming at Itsuma-hime and her spider court; I was raising my sword at Apasam-kamuy as they stood on the bridge protecting Ainu Moshiri.

"This isn't helping," I said.

Yata-no-kagami just cocked her head and walked on through the next curtain.

This room had to be the room of my greatest weakness. But it was the same as the one we'd just left: a bunch of screens playing a bunch of video clips. Some of them were even the same ones. There were a few extras: me telling Mom a couple of years ago that I didn't believe in the kami-verse; trying to tackle Brad after he threw a cup of punch on me at the seventh-grade dance; strangling Danny underwater; swinging Kusanagi around just a few moments ago.

"Are you trying to tell me that my anger is my greatest strength *and* my greatest weakness?" I asked Yata-no-kagami wearily. "Because that still doesn't help."

Yata-no-kagami gave me a funny look and then burst out laughing. "Don't be silly! Your greatest strengths are your burning desire for a just world, and your loyalty and sense of duty to those who depend on you. Your greatest weakness is your self-doubt—your belief that you aren't powerful on your own."

I thought about those scenes in the third room again, and now they seemed different. I'd been mad at Danny because he'd been mean to Niko; I'd fought with Ryleigh because I wanted her to know that her mean-girl ways were wrong; I'd fought Tamamo-no-mae so I could save all those kids' lives. I hadn't been about to attack Itsuma-hime; I'd been begging her to execute me instead of my friends.

As for my greatest weakness, hadn't Ryleigh been saying all along that I needed to believe in myself? Hadn't Danny told me that he believed in me, and that I should, too?

Finally, I understood what Jizō had meant about being more

than my anger, and that whole ninja-samurai thing about letting it go. And what Toyotama-hime had meant about not being ashamed or afraid of who I was. And what it meant to move beyond destruction. My rage monster wasn't my greatest strength or the source of my power. Kusanagi didn't make me who I was. Their power—my anger—was just a feeling. I didn't have to smush it down or try to control it like some kind of wild beast. I just had to let it be what it was. I could use it to serve my sense of justice and duty, or my fear and self-doubt. When I was afraid or in pain or anxious, anger gave me courage and made me feel more powerful. But because all I wanted was to get rid of the things that made me afraid or caused me pain, I destroyed them. Just like Izanami, who had allowed her anger and her pain to define her entire being and let it warp into bloodlust and poisonous vengeance.

I thought of Dad and Mom, and of Danny, Niko, Ryleigh, and Jin, who I might never see again. I missed them so much, the pain of it threatened to overwhelm me. But no amount of revenge—not even destroying Izanami—would bring them back or make me miss them less.

What would happen if instead of using my anger to destroy my enemies, I focused all that power on seeking justice?

Izanami had said she wanted justice. What would happen if, instead of revenge and destruction, she *actually got justice*? Was that even possible? Or was it too late?

"I have to go," I said to Yata-no-kagami. "What's the fastest way out of here?"

"We have to finish the tour," said Yata-no-kagami, and she rushed off. I followed her through a room full of pictures: a baby, a cowering mouse, a bear, a butterfly struggling out of a cocoon. "How others see you!" shouted Yata-no-kagami.

Then we dashed through a room that showed me struggling with a backpack that was way too big for me; wobbling on a tightrope; fighting with my rage monster, then shaking hands with it; and a cloudy image that I couldn't quite make out. "How you've changed!" said Yata-no-kagami.

That meant that the final side of the mirror would show my true potential. Inside was a statue of a warrior clad in gleaming armor and holding a glowing sword. She looked fierce, calm, and confident.

"Is that *me*?" I asked as we hurried past it.

"Potentially," said Yata-no-kagami. "But also, you know. Potentially not."

"Wow. You really know how to build up a person's confidence."

She shrugged. "That's not my job," she said, and held open the final curtain. "Tour's over." She beamed at me and saluted. "Good luck!"

I tumbled out of the mirror to find that the battle was still raging and Izanami's army was still marching relentlessly across the bridge. Izanami herself was a blazing column of flame and fury, urging her soldiers forward. They swirled past us like we were two boulders in a rushing river. When she saw me at her feet, the scream that came out of her mouth made every kami, demon, and monster pause for a moment to stare at her.

I knew what I had to do.

To guide Kusanagi beyond its desire for destruction, you must embrace your own source of power along with the power of the sword itself. If you succeed, it will transform everything.

Do not be afraid of what is inside you. Do not be ashamed of who you are.

You are bigger than your anger.

I remembered how hard it had been after Dad had disappeared; how Mom had also disappeared, in a way, and how maybe it wasn't her fault, but how it still shouldn't have happened. It wasn't fair to be mad at her about it, but I couldn't help it. And I was mad at myself for being mad at her. And *furious* at Susano'o for causing the storm that had swept Dad into the sea in the first place.

I was mad at the world for being the kind of place that made boys like Danny feel like they had to be tough all the time, that made girls like Ryleigh and Kiki feel like they had to be pretty or perfect to deserve friendship and love, that having power meant being mean and excluding people, that friendship was about trading favors and keeping score. I was mad that the world divided people up and made Danny feel like he didn't deserve to claim his heritage; I was mad at Benzaiten for lying to Jin, and at Jin's dad and Ryleigh's parents and Mom for making us feel like we were responsible for keeping our families afloat.

I was mad at Izanami for making Dad suffer to get my attention; for killing literally everyone; for causing so much pain and destroying the world just because she was mad at Izanagi. I was mad at Izanagi for being a coward and a liar, for pretending that it was all Izanami's fault that she had become Izanami the Destroyer, Queen of Death, when he was the one who had abandoned her here.

None of it was fair. None of it was just. And here I was. Having to make it right, all by myself.

No, not by myself. My friends had helped me get here. And they were out there fighting, too, trying to make things right.

It was time to do my part.

Here goes nothing.

A Million Fireflies

"KUSANAGI!" I called to it out loud, and there it was in my hand, blending its power with my rage monster's and filling my veins with lightning.

Who hurt us? it demanded. *Who do we attack?*

I opened myself to all my anger at the world, at the unfairness and injustice of everything. I was so full of anger and pain that I thought I would explode. I needed to attack someone, or smash Kusanagi into the ground and let the power out into the world to destroy everything around me.

But now I understood that destroying the cause of my pain wouldn't make the pain go away. I had to let myself feel my anger and then let it go—no, let it be—before I could use it to make things right and restore justice.

Slowly, something strange happened. I began to feel less furious and hurt, but no less brave. I was still bursting with the power—I mean, I could *feel* it. It was practically shining out of my eyes. The lightning in my veins was still there, but it was a whole different feeling, fueled not by despair but by hope. Not an overwhelming need to destroy the things that had hurt me, but a desire to build and heal.

I raised Kusanagi high above my head, and in the brief moment before I brought it down, Izanami broke into that same, smug smile that I'd seen when I'd tried to attack her earlier. But she didn't know what I knew.

The sword plunged into the bridge. The bridge swayed and bucked, and the skeleton army clattered into a heap of bones. Lightning flashed. The wind howled around us and drowned out the battle; I didn't know if the skeletons had reassembled themselves or if they'd been blown off the bridge completely. All I knew was that Izanami kept coming. She was in a towering rage. She seemed to fill the sky.

Yata-no-kagami. I held out my hand. *I need you.*

Izanami's armor melted away, and I felt the weight of the mirror in my palm. I activated it, turned it toward her, and said, "I know who you were. I know who you still are, deep down. You are Izanami the young goddess, who gave everything so that the world could come into being. You are Izanami the wife, who was wronged by a husband too selfish to face her suffering and too cowardly to face her anger. You are Izanami the mother, who should have returned to the land of the living but was abandoned and left for dead. You are right to be angry. You deserve justice."

But we'd been over this already, and it didn't stop her. Her eyes were fixed on me. She hadn't even glanced at the mirror.

Please, I begged her silently. *Look in the mirror.* I held it higher.

"You're someone who always wanted to give life, not take it away. It's not right that someone like that should be trapped here, and it's not right that you were robbed of your ability to be who you truly are." I kept the mirror up. "Look! Look at who you truly are inside—who you could become."

That stopped her in her tracks. Finally.

But I still didn't know if my gamble would pay off. What if her true potential had changed? What if her true potential was a vengeance-obsessed, murderous queen of death, and her greatest strength really was her anger, and her destiny really was kami-versal domination?

Izanami stared into the mirror. "What about Izanagi? How will he pay?"

This was the tricky part. "I don't know," I said.

"It's not fair that he should get away with what he did," she said. The flames on her body flared up.

"No, it's not," I said. Izanami was silent. My arm was getting tired from holding up the mirror, but I didn't dare put it down. What was she seeing in it? I felt like the entire kami-verse was holding its breath.

"You can use your anger to destroy everything that Izanagi made. But you'll also destroy everything *you* made. And he won't even care."

She nodded slowly and said, "I'm still angry at him."

I felt the jewel pulse once in my chest, and then it was in my hand. I said, "But you're more than your anger and your desire for vengeance. Just like me. You said you wanted justice. But justice isn't about getting even. It's about fixing what's broken and making things right. And this is the best I can do to make things right." I lowered the mirror and held the jewel out to her. There was no going back now.

The tower of fire in front of me died out, and in its place

was a moldering corpse. Dried flesh stuck to bone, and dull, lank clumps of hair straggled across a disintegrating linen robe. I tried not to gag. Izanami said quietly, "I still miss living. I miss the world above. The scent of flowers, the warmth of the sun. I miss my children."

"That's why I'm giving you back your jewel. Because Izanagi shouldn't have taken it, and now he's gone, and there's nothing any of us can do to make things right except to give you back what's yours. Because you deserve to be who you really are."

Izanami closed her eyes and brought the jewel to her husk of a chest, where it sank from view and then streamed out in golden sparks of light. The sparks danced through her, twining their way down her arms, threading through her hair, skipping, curling, swirling, and shimmering through her body, and even over the gown she wore like a million fireflies. For a few moments, the light was so bright, I had to close my eyes against it.

When the light dimmed enough for me to open my eyes, I gasped. The jewel had restored Izanami to a version of her former self—not as young as the one I'd seen in the memory, but not the gaunt, skeletal queen that I had always known, either. Her cheeks weren't as plump and dewy as they had once been, but her skin was still smooth and mostly unlined. Her obsidian hair was shot through with streaks of silver. I could see a row of white teeth where the blackened fangs used to be. Her eyelids fluttered and opened to reveal those same piercing coal-black eyes. But the vengeful hatred I'd come to expect wasn't there. Instead, they were filled with grief and remorse.

"Ah, Momo," she whispered. "I am so very sorry for all the harm I've done. You must be furious with me."

Once I'd broken open the memory of Izanami as a young life-giving goddess, I'd been so focused on her that I'd forgotten everything else. But now that I had a moment to relax, the images of Mom and Dad fading away, and of my friends being overcome by a skeleton army, slid into my mind, and the enormity of what I had lost finally landed. Tears clogged my throat and gathered behind my eyes. The prospect of a future without Mom, without Dad, maybe even without Danny, Niko, Ryleigh, or Jin yawned in front of me. It felt like walking into the mouth of that giant skull all over again, down into that long, dark, endless staircase. Only this time I would have to do it alone.

I wasn't sure if I could hold this much pain. Suddenly I understood in a whole new way how Izanami must have felt: completely hopeless, without any way forward except to rage at the injustice of it all. And I didn't want to become what she had been: obsessed with revenge, defined by her pain and anger.

It isn't fair. It isn't right. She has to pay for what she's done.

Justice. I needed to focus on justice.

What if there was no justice? What if Izanami was allowed to go back to her old life and I had to keep on going without the people and the fox I loved?

All I could do was tell her how I felt. And demand justice. And hope.

"I *am* furious with you," I admitted. "And you owe me more than an apology."

"Yes, I do," Izanami said, her voice low and sad. "And if you can wait, I will do my best to make it up to you."

She rose to her feet. Then she reached down and yanked Kusanagi out of the wooden span of the bridge, and our little bubble broke. The battle rushed back in with its deafening clangs and roars, and for a moment I was sure that Izanami had tricked me and was going to go back to her conquest after all. But she held the sword aloft and called out, "Stop!" and I almost fell over from shock.

She had a whole new voice. It sounded like bells and brass instruments. It sounded like gold. It sounded like sunlight on the ocean. Izanami herself was shining, not with brilliant golden rays like Amaterasu, the kami of the sun, but a deep orangey-pink glow like a sunrise. The shikome dropped their snacks, the kasha and the wolves let go of their victims; Susano'o and Momotarō let their swords drop, and Daikoku lowered her hammer.

Izanami lowered Kusanagi and handed it back to me. Then she beckoned to someone in the horde of demons on the bridge. A lone skeleton stepped out of the crowd and bowed. She whispered to it, and it rattled off into the darkness on the Yomi side of the bridge.

"Go back where you belong, and rest," she said to the others. Thousands of skeletons and shikome and hungry ghosts shuffled, limped, and drifted back over the bridge and into the mist.

Next, we went into Meido, stepping over the rubble of the boulder that Izanami had crushed with Kusanagi. A huge cheer went up, and everyone got to their feet. All seven of the Lucky Gods—Daikoku, Bishamon, Benzaiten, Ebisu, Hotei, Jurōjin, and Fukurokujū—emerged from the crowd and knelt before Izanami, followed by Ryūjin and Toyotama-hime, Momotarō, even Itsuma-hime and Yasome and her two siblings, and a bunch of other heroes I recognized from Mom's stories.

But there were plenty of fallen kami, too: faded, colorless versions of themselves, more like zombies than living spirits. It made me think of Mom, and I had to swallow a lump in my throat. And there was the awful, nagging fear. Where were my friends? I didn't think I could bear it if they had lost their lives. I couldn't see them from where I was, and I was both tempted and afraid to search for them in the crowd.

"Momo!" Niko burst through a clump of nine-tailed foxes, closely followed by Danny, Jin, and Ryleigh. A moment later we were locked in a giant, joyful group hug. I stopped caring about anything else—how momentous this was, what a tremendous victory we'd won. All I cared about was that my friends were okay.

"We were so worried you were dead," said Ryleigh.

"Not me," said Niko. "I was completely confident that you would come through."

"You were crying like a baby," Danny scoffed.

"Just like the rest of us," said Jin.

"Hey, where's your mom and dad?" Danny asked.

"They, they . . . um." I couldn't say it. I couldn't even bear to look at my friends' faces as they realized why I had stopped talking to wipe my eyes. As they folded me into another, quieter hug, we were interrupted by a thunderous shout.

"GUPPY GIRL! HA-HA-HAAA!" I couldn't help smiling just a little as Susano'o bounded across the plain, kicking up truckloads of dirt as he went. He skidded to a stop in front of us and gaped at Izanami before glancing sheepishly at all the other kami, dropping to his knees, and mumbling, "My lady."

I'd nearly forgotten about her. Izanami smiled at my

grandfather and looked around at the other kami like she couldn't quite believe she was here.

Some of the zombie-kami had begun to move toward the bridge to Yomi, where, I assumed, they would become officially dead. But Izanami held up her hand. "Wait," she said. "Come back."

She turned her palm up, and a rosy-red flame appeared. She blew on it, and it flew off her palm and landed on a collection of broken black plates. Instantly, the plates reassembled themselves and I was looking at Ise Ebizō, the lobster-samurai from Ryūgū-jō.

"Whoa," said Danny.

"My deepest, most humble thanks, Great Mother," Lord Ebizō said with a twirl of his whiskers and a deep bow. "With your permission, I will excuse myself and search for my troops." She nodded, and he retreated into the crowd.

Next, Izanami blew a flame at a zombified tree kami. Its scarred and peeling bark repaired itself, and color swirled back into its gray leaves. She touched the shoulder of a ratty gray cardigan under an ugly gray wig, and Pink-Haired Auntie from the ferry to the Sky Kingdom sparkled to life. "Oooh, Momo!" she cried after she'd bowed to Izanami and thanked her. "How lovely to see you! Here, have a candy." And she pressed one of her little red portal candies into my palm before bustling off to find her sisters.

Soon we were surrounded by a throng of kami whose spirits had been taken from them in the battle. Izanami moved through them, restoring one after the other. Wounds healed, broken limbs repaired themselves, and color streamed back into each one. Ryleigh grabbed my hand and whispered in my ear, "You should ask her to do your parents."

"Yeah. Maybe when she's done." I couldn't bear to ask her now and find that she couldn't, or wouldn't. If the answer was no, I wanted to put it off as long as possible.

Once Izanami had moved off to what Susano'o must have felt was a safe distance, he got to his feet and grinned at me. "What a battle, guppy girl!" he said as if nothing had interrupted him. "What a fight! I haven't had this much fun in a thousand years!" He swooped me up and swung me around so hard I thought he might be getting ready to throw me back over the river into Yomi. Eventually he put me down, and while I tried not to throw up from dizziness, he barreled through a recap of what he kept calling the Battle of Meido—which I soon realized was the fight between himself and Tsukiyomi.

"It was epic. Epic, I tell you! First, I went BLAM! and knocked his block off with a thunderbolt. But he recovered and tried for a sneaky stab with one of his silver knives—did you know he keeps knives in that fancy-schmancy suit of his? I told you he was a killer! But I was ready for him. I went YAH! and blasted him with a tsunami. Ha-HAA! That chump didn't know what hit him!"

"What happened to him?" I asked. "Where is he?"

"Ah, that sniveling coward slithered back to his safe space up there on the moon as soon as he realized the tide had turned," Susano'o scoffed. He paused and seemed to size me up. "And what did you do with Kusanagi? How did you use it? Did you do me proud? Did you slay a thousand demons? Ten thousand?"

"Um. Not exactly. I sort of convinced Izanami to call off her attack."

Susano'o's jaw dropped. "Well, blow me down!"

Danny, Niko, Jin, and Ryleigh looked just as surprised. "So that was you!" said Danny.

"What was me?"

"There was this big bang," said Jin.

"A crash! A kaboom!" said Niko.

"The manifestation of your powers, guppy girl!" Susano'o whooped.

Suddenly I felt bashful, on top of being totally bewildered. "I mean. I guess? I had Kusanagi—"

"Naturally," he said.

"And I kind of . . ." I made a stabbing motion at the ground.

"Of course!" He nodded his approval.

"And it all sort of . . ." I twirled my hands to mime the winds that had surrounded us. "And I held up the Mirror of the Sun and showed Izanami her true potential. And I gave her back the Jewel of the Heart."

"You *what?*" Ryleigh shrieked.

"It felt like—it *was* the right thing to do," I said. "It's a long story. I'll tell you later."

Susano'o shook his head. "Well, blow me down," he said again. Then he looked up and cheered. "That's my guppy girl! Kicking the butt of the most powerful kami in the kami-verse!"

"I wouldn't say I kicked her butt, exactly. I just, you know. Showed her who she really was, and I gave her the justice she deserved."

"Which means you kicked her butt!" Susano'o thundered

off, whooping and hollering and boasting to anyone who would listen that *his* granddaughter had used *his* sword to kick Izanami's butt. I watched him go and sighed. I'd have to make sure his version of the story didn't become the one that everyone told.

"He may never understand." Daikoku's voice behind me made me jump. I turned to see her smiling down at me. "Hello, Momo. Congratulations. You've done well."

"Thanks," I said. I wondered how much she knew.

And then she said gently, "You have sacrificed much."

I understood right away that she was talking about Dad and Mom. My throat burned and my eyes filled with tears. I didn't like the sound of that word: "sacrifice." That meant giving something up.

I ground the heels of my hands into my eyes to stop the tears, which kept trickling out anyway. But then there was a warm hand on my shoulder, and Izanami's new golden bell-like voice said, "I've finished my work restoring the spirits of the Middle Lands. Now it's time for you to come with me."

I opened my eyes, and she took my hand and led me back toward the bridge, with the Seven Lucky Gods following close behind us. As we crossed the span, I saw that the skeleton that Izanami had sent off earlier had returned with Dad's spirit and the zombie-kami form of Mom. They floated together on the far side, half shrouded by the mist and glowing a pale, unearthly silver blue. When I waved and called out to them, they didn't wave or call back.

But justice meant making things right. Hadn't Izanami agreed that apologizing wasn't enough? She'd restored all the fallen kami to life, and it made sense that she'd take care of them first, since there were more of them, and technically, it was the greater injustice. Now, finally, it was my turn. My heart, which had twisted itself into a tight, hard knot, loosened.

The skeleton led Dad and Mom onto the bridge, and we met them exactly in the middle. They smiled at me now in recognition but remained silent. But I wasn't worried. I could feel Mom's deep compassion and Dad's steadfast, loving warmth. Izanami turned up her palm and blew on the flame that appeared. Rosy pink tendrils swirled around us, and the eerie blue glow dissipated. Mom and Dad grew less transparent, more solid. Light sparkled in their eyes.

I smiled up at Izanami and squeezed her hand. "Thank you," I whispered, and ran into my parents' waiting arms.

I Want What I Want

It was a very, very long hug. When it was over, we stood around awkwardly, facing Izanami and the Seven Lucky Gods.

"Now what?" I asked.

"Now you go home," said Izanami.

"Sounds great," I said. Dad put his arm around me and I leaned into him. I couldn't wait to go back and start my life over with him in it.

"What happens to you?" Ryleigh asked. "Are you Izanami the Creator now? Are you going to live with us in the Middle Lands?"

Izanami touched her hand to her chest, which still glowed softly. She looked thoughtful. "I suppose I will resume my duties as creator. But Yomi still needs me, too."

"There's no one who could take your place?" Niko asked.

"I'm afraid that 'Queen of Yomi' is not exactly at the top of anyone's list of career goals," she said with a wry smile. "So I will take on the extra job and work extra hard, I suppose."

"As women always do," said Daikoku with a snort.

"But now that the spell that kept me in Yomi has been

broken, I can cross the bridge whenever I like." Her eyes took on a faraway look. "I think I will accompany you home. I would like to see the sun again."

So we started back over the bridge toward Meido and the Middle Lands. I found that my feet were placing themselves one in front of the other on their own, and I felt my eyelids getting heavy and my mind going pleasantly gray and foggy. I couldn't summon the will to fight it. I'd already fought so much.

I bet I would have kept going in that half-asleep state all the way across Meido, but the moment we stepped off the bridge, Daikoku said sharply, "Hey! Back off!"

"No! I won't back off! Ow! Lemme go! Momo Arashima, you owe me! You made a promise!" The voice was screechy and insistent and vaguely familiar.

A promise? Something inside me stretched and shook itself awake. I looked around for the speaker. Who did I owe? What did I owe them?

"Momo Arashima, it is time to keep your promise to Sen!"

That cut through my brain fog like a record scratch, and the memory came rushing back.

Sen. The crabby but courageous old crone from Ryūgū-jō. Oh, no.

"Who is this? What did you promise her?" Bishamon demanded. He had her sticklike arm in a firm grip.

"She's someone who helped me. And I promised . . ." I hesitated before saying more.

"What did you promise?" Mom's voice was uncharacteristically harsh. I wondered if she was thinking of her very first fateful promise to Izanami.

Miserably, I explained the situation. "This is Sen. We met her in Ryūgū-jō. She's the girl whose father gave her ningyo meat, and she's been cursed with eternal life. She got Ryūjin's memories of the Jewel of the Heart for us, and then she helped us escape and continue our mission. I promised that if she helped us and I managed to survive, I would . . ." I trailed off.

"She promised she would use Kusanagi to release me from my life in the Middle Lands," Sen butted in.

All seven Luckies recoiled, and one of Izanami's perfectly arched eyebrows went up.

"Oh, kiddo," Dad murmured.

Niko howled, "Holy halibut hash! How could you swear such an odious oath!"

"I had to!" I protested. "It was the only way to get the memory box. I never meant to go through with it!"

"I fetched the memories, you survived the mission," said Sen. She jutted out her wrinkled prune of a chin, and her eyes drilled into me. "You made a promise, Momo Arashima, and I demand that you keep it."

I glanced at the others, searching for a sympathetic face. "I can't keep a promise like that!" I looked at Sen, who now seemed small and sad, even though her arms were still folded and her mouth was still set in a defiant scowl. "I know it's not fair to make you keep living a life that's basically a punishment for something you didn't do. But you're a human, not a demon. And I just . . ."

"Just what? Traitor," Sen spat.

"I can't do it," I said. "In fact, I refuse. I don't want to use Kusanagi that way anymore."

"There must be something else we can do for you," said Jin. "You went through so much to help us, and you've suffered for so long."

"Nothing else," said Sen. "I want what I want."

We stood in silence for a while, clearing our throats and fidgeting and looking at the ground. Finally, Danny said, "Wasn't there some rule about how a spell can only be broken by the one who cast it? Isn't that what Niko said about Susano'o's spell around the Island of Mysteries?"

"And Kusanagi broke Tsukiyomi's curse on the Mirror of the Sun," Ryleigh pointed out. "Is that why you asked Momo to use it?"

Sen nodded. "It can destroy anything. Even curses and spells cast by other kami."

"But wait! If the person who cast a spell can break it, why not get Ryūjin to lift the ningyo curse?" Jin said.

"That's why I went down to his palace in the first place, remember? And he refused," Sen grumbled.

"But now he owes you a favor," Ryleigh said. "By helping us find the Jewel of the Heart, you helped save the Middle Lands and restore Izanami to her former self."

So Bishamon sent a Gemini auntie to fetch Ryūjin. When he arrived, he was not pleased to hear that he was being asked to revoke a centuries-old spell.

"You wouldn't let me put a protective curse on the other creatures of the ocean. 'The humans need them to survive,' you said. And look what's happened! Species after species is dying out. I refuse to revoke my protection of the ningyo. Without it, they'll be hunted to extinction, just like so many other creatures in my kingdom!"

"It would be a highly irregular solution, but we find ourselves in a highly irregular situation," said Ebisu. "And it would be just this once, for this one human."

"She has earned her freedom, dear brother-in-law," said Benzaiten.

"I've more than earned it! I've paid for it times a hundred! And it wasn't even my fault!" said Sen.

Ryūjin stroked his whiskers lazily and took us all in with his golden eyes, as if to gauge how seriously he should take this. But no kami, not even the dragon king of the ocean, stands a chance against the Seven Lucky Gods plus Izanami.

"All right," he said finally. "I suppose in this one very special case, I can lift the curse."

He made his way over to Sen and put one giant paw on each of her shoulders. He looked deep into her eyes and muttered under his breath as she swayed back and forth and stared wide-eyed at him. Abruptly, Ryūjin let go, and Sen crumpled to the floor. For one terrifying moment I thought she might be dead. But she stirred and said peevishly, "No need to be so rough, you rusty old bag of scales."

Niko gasped audibly, but Ryūjin waved off the insult and bowed to Izanami and the Seven Lucky Gods. "If there is nothing else, I will take my leave," he said, and when they bowed back, he slowly faded out of sight until nothing was left but a glimmering outline, and then even that disappeared.

Sen, meanwhile, was gazing at her outstretched, wrinkly hands.

"How do you feel?" Ebisu asked her.

"Old and creaky," Sen groused. Then she smiled a tiny, toothless little smile. "Mortal."

"What will you do? Where will you go?" asked Danny.

"We would be honored if you could live with us," Mom said. She looked at me and Dad and Niko. "Isn't that right?"

"Of course," said Dad.

"Ah. Well. Ahem," said Niko. "Do we have enough room? Surely Sen would prefer her previous palatial surroundings to our humble home."

"I'm not going back there," said Sen. "The folks at Ryūgū-jō are a bunch of snobs. And time passes so slowly there. I already said I didn't want to live forever!"

I looked at Sen's scraggly hair and her threadbare kimono and remembered how gorgeously dressed everyone had been at the Ryūgū-jō party and how they'd looked at her with their noses wrinkled in disgust. I thought about how she'd been confined to that dark little room. No wonder she hated it. She was a tough old lady, but without money or friends, she'd be helpless anywhere she went in the rest of the world.

"Will you please come and live with us?" I asked her.

Sen gave us a wary sidelong look. "I'm not cooking or cleaning for you," she said.

"Of course not! I'm a great cook," said Dad.

"And I can do my own laundry," I said.

"I'm not babysitting, either," she added, with a pointed glare at me.

"That's Niko's job," said Mom.

"It most certainly is not!" Niko spluttered. "I am a companion, not a nanny! And I refuse to be held responsible for any more reckless rule-breaking."

"I don't need babysitting, anyway," I said indignantly.

"The point is, *we'll* take care of *you*," Dad concluded.

"I don't need taking care of," Sen said. She jutted out her chin and folded her arms and glared at us. Then, apparently satisfied that she had made her point, she added, "But I'll come with you anyway."

Whatever's Right for You

This voyage home on the *Takarabune* was different from the last one we'd taken, when we'd slept the entire time and the Seven Lucky Gods had been busy distributing good fortune and returning missing children to their homes around the world. Now that the threat of Izanami the Destroyer taking over the Middle Lands was gone, and Izanami the Great Mother was on board with us, we could relax and take our time.

We spent the next few hours on the best world tour ever. We glided through tropical rainforests and played in waterfalls, navigated rocky canyons and touched down on snowy mountain peaks. We listened to the clink and crackle of ice in an arctic bay and the creak and rustle of redwood trees in an ancient old-growth forest. Everywhere we went, the kami in the area came out and waved and shouted, "Hello, Mother! Remember me?" and Izanami waved back and called, "Hello, children! I do remember you!" We passed through a thunderstorm, and Susano'o hurled a lightning bolt just over the bow and shouted, "Ha-haaa! Back in business again, I see! I'll be sure to tell Tsuki-dooky!"

"Bad-mannered boor," Niko muttered.

"He and Amaterasu and Tsukiyomi are the only major kami in the world who are not descended directly from me. You know that Izanagi birthed them by washing out his eyes and his nose after he left me, right? So technically they don't owe me any allegiance," said Izanami. "And I can understand how Susano'o must feel: born of snot instead of tears, full of all that chaotic energy when his older siblings are naturally regal and dignified and disdain him. I don't blame him for wanting to stir up trouble every once in a while."

Amaterasu had better manners than her little brother. She appeared in the face of the setting sun, and just before it slipped over the horizon, her three-legged crow, Yatagarasu, landed on the deck and announced, "KAAA! Her Royal Radiance, Amaterasu, Queen of the Sky, salutes you and welcomes you back to the land of the living. She offers you this small token of her respect and hopes it will please you in the years to come."

He dropped a tiny golden box on the deck and took off into the darkening sky with another "KAAA!"—though not before giving me and Ryleigh a beady-eyed glare. I guess he hadn't gotten over the way we'd tricked him into abandoning his post in front of the Hall of Mirrors on New Year's Eve.

Izanami opened the box, and a brilliant ray of light streamed out. "It's crystallized sunlight," she said, smiling. She held up a ball the size of a marble between her thumb and finger, where it shone so brightly it almost felt like daytime again. "What a thoughtful gift. I can take it out and look at it whenever I start missing daylight in Yomi." She put the crystallized light back into the box, and everything grew gray and dusky again. As the stars came out, they twinkled and waved cheerily at us.

Only Tsukiyomi, barely visible in the darkness outlined by the sliver of a crescent moon, seemed unhappy.

"Do you think he'll ever get over it?" Ryleigh asked as we gathered at the railing to wave at him.

Izanami shook her head. "I don't know. But here *I* am, so I suppose there's hope for anyone."

Jin used the voyage to spend some quality time with his mom. I watched the two of them sitting in a corner of the deck in a long, earnest conversation, and I hoped Benzaiten would hear him and start showing up for him regularly.

Izanami looked skeptical when I told her this. "Benzaiten is the kami of music and language," she said. "She's like flowing water. If you try to make her settle in one spot, she'll feel trapped, and she'll either find a way to leak out, spill, or evaporate, or she'll get musty and slimy and poisonous. You have to let her go where she wants to go."

"He doesn't want her to settle down in one spot," I said. "He just wants her to visit him every once in a while. To show him that she cares about him. I mean, she's an actual goddess. She can manage to drop in a few times a year, can't she?"

"Perhaps," Izanami said. "I hope so."

Meanwhile, Ryleigh seemed to have bonded with Daikoku and Bishamon. Bishamon worked with her on some new shuriken-throwing techniques, and Daikoku, once a goddess of darkness, seemed to be teaching her how to throw entire spaces into complete shadow. Every time I listened in, they were discussing leadership techniques, business and military strategy, and cutting-edge information-gathering technology. Ryleigh really was interested in all that stuff. I hoped her parents would see that and let her do things the way she wanted so that she would keep loving it.

Finally, Danny spent as much time as he could with Ebisu, quizzing him about his years with the Ainu, and who his Ainu parents were, and what it was like to be a Japanese kami who'd been brought up somewhere else, and whether Ebisu could maybe give him a little extra luck the next time he put together a fantasy football team. Hotei hung around the two of them, listening and laughing and handing out an endless stream of snacks. "It's not either-or, little dude," he said, digging around in his sack. "It's both-and. Sure, there's folks out there who wanna restrict who gets what, and sure, you'll probably change your mind every now and then, but there's plenty to go around, it'll always be there, and I say you get to choose whatever's right for you."

"Well said, little brother," said Ebisu.

"Wiser than you thought, eh?" Hotei winked and crammed a handful of seven-spice popcorn into his mouth.

At last, the *Takarabune* flew into the skies above the San Francisco Bay, and Ryleigh, Danny, Jin, and I leaned over the railing, pointing out familiar landmarks to each other. We were home.

Sen was supernaturally healthy for someone who was hundreds of years old, but she was still hundreds of years old, so the first thing she wanted to do when we walked in the door was to go to bed. Once she was snoring under her covers in the guest bedroom, I asked Dad, "Can we stay up a little bit longer and snuggle on the couch?"

Mom looked at Dad with some concern. "Dad's tired, Momo. We should let him rest."

"That's right. Don't be a babbling baby," said Niko. "You can wait until tomorrow."

"But I . . ." I didn't know how to express it. After years of missing and grieving Dad, I felt an almost physical need to be Velcroed to his side, to make sure he was really and truly *here* and not a dream or a hallucination. I felt like if I let him out of my sight, he might suddenly disappear again, or I'd wake up and all of this really *would* turn out to have been a dream.

"You don't have to explain," Dad said. And in spite of the dark circles under his eyes, he plopped down onto the cushions, held his arm out to me, and smiled. I sat and nestled into him. Mom sat on his other side, and Niko curled up in his lap. "I missed you all so much," Dad said. "I thought I'd never see you again. And I don't think I'll ever get enough of this, now that I'm home." He gave me a squeeze and kissed the top of my head.

I think it might have been the happiest moment of my life.

Hotei had given us a parting gift of a giant bucket of Auntie Anne's pretzel bites, and after a while, I fetched them and Dad and I dove in, even though Mom fussed about getting crumbs on the couch.

"I remember getting these at the mall with you the day before I left on my trip," said Dad.

"So do I. That's why they're my favorite," I said.

Dad smiled down at me. "And now they're mine, too."

Eventually he and Niko dozed off, and I decided that now was as good a time as any to ask Mom a question that had been simmering in the back of my mind ever since she'd burst out of the Mirror of the Sun in Izanami's palace.

I cleared my throat and gathered my courage and said, "Why

did you come back out of the mirror? Why didn't you stay in that perfect life on your island?"

Mom smiled at me. "Because I love you," she said. "And I wanted to keep you safe. Why would you think I *wouldn't* come for you, silly girl?"

I didn't want to accuse her of being a bad mom, because she wasn't. But I had been shocked that she'd come back. How could I tell her this without hurting her feelings or making it seem like I thought she didn't love me?

She seemed to understand my silence. "I know I wasn't there for you when Dad was gone. I wish I could have those years back and do them over again."

"But she came through when it counted, didn't she?" said Dad, who had apparently not been dozing after all.

But that was just it. That phrase: *when it counted*. I didn't hold it against Dad because he didn't know what Mom had been like without him. To him, she was the same heroic kami he'd always known.

And *when it counted* made Mom seem like just that: the big hero, the great goddess who came through in the clutch moment to save the day. And she was. But what about the other, smaller moments when she hadn't come through? When she could have saved me in more ordinary ways, like when I needed her to hug me after a hard day at school, or to notice that my PE uniform had grass stains on it, or that we'd run out of shampoo, or to help me figure out what to do when the refrigerator broke? Hadn't those moments counted, too?

I heard Izanami's voice again: *Anger is your friend. It is your ally. Anger hears the call of the weak, the frightened, and the injured, and rushes to defend them. It is your protector and the source of your power.*

I deserved to have had someone to take care of me, to hug me when I was sad, to help me get the stains out of my uniform, to buy shampoo and call the refrigerator repair company. And it was okay—it was *right*—to be angry that I hadn't. Even if it hadn't been Mom's fault.

So I told her everything, even though it was hard to do. It was especially hard when Mom's eyes filled with tears as she listened. I felt like I was hurting her feelings and making her sad, which was the last thing I wanted. But when I stopped to ask if she was okay, she motioned for me to keep going.

Once I'd finished, she said, "I am crying because your pain is my pain, and to know that I caused it makes it hurt even more. But I'm glad you told me. You've carried my emotions in your heart and on your shoulders for so long. It's time for you to let go and let me carry them again."

That made *me* cry. It *had* been exhausting and lonely, carrying all that weight by myself. I felt her arms around me, and as we cried together, I felt that weight lift off my shoulders. And when I said, "It wasn't your fault," I wasn't secretly angry anymore—not at her, anyway. I just felt sad for both of us—but now I had someone to share that sadness with. And a reason to feel hopeful that Mom was ready to be there for me in the small human ways, as well as the big magical ones.

And Now, for My Next Dance . . .

"**Three cheers for Niko and** his brand-new tail!" Hotei shouted, and everyone on the deck of the *Takarabune* burst into cheers and applause. All seven Luckies were there, along with me, Mom, Dad, Danny, Ryleigh, and Jin. Niko bowed and proudly swished his tails, the second of which he'd been granted in a ceremony a few hours earlier.

Our first week back from Yomi had been less chaotic than I'd expected, thanks to a few strategic emails about an extended Southern California vacation with Jin that Ebisu had cleverly sent to the school and to Danny's parents, who still didn't know about his secret kami life. Bishamon had sent a note to Ryleigh's parents, and Benzaiten had paid Jin's dad a visit, so while they had been out of their minds with worry, they hadn't bothered calling the police. And no one objected to us attending a party on the Ship of Treasures (or as Danny's parents believed, a party on Ryleigh's parents' yacht) a couple of weeks later.

"Friends and family, I have dreamed of this day for decades," Niko said. "And in honor of this occasion, I will now demonstrate the dance that won me 'Most Room for Improvement' at the 1927 Foxtrot Follies, and which, if I had performed it last month in Ainu Moshiri, would have gained us automatic access to Izanagi's pocket universe garden." He nodded at Benzaiten, who smiled and plucked out an old-timey tune on her guitar as Niko sashayed and pranced happily around the deck.

Everyone applauded at the end, though I think some of us were mostly just glad it was over. Niko bowed and said, "And now, for my next dance—"

"Nope!" Bishamon banged his spear on the deck. "That is more than enough, fox! It's time to move things along!"

Niko pouted, but he didn't object, because his new tail wasn't the only reason we were here. Danny, Ryleigh, Jin, Niko, and I had one last duty to carry out.

Mom and Dad went off to chat and feed snacks to the *Takarabune* dragons, and the Luckies gathered around us. Jurōjin pulled a scroll out of his sleeve and hung it in the air, where it unfurled in one long blank sheet all the way to the deck. Fukurokujū pulled a calligraphy brush out of *his* sleeve and sent it to the top of the blank scroll.

"Finally, we have time for you to record what happened for posterity," said Jurōjin. "Who would like to start?"

I told the story of Izanami's first nightmare visit, when she showed me how she'd imprisoned Dad and offered to set him free in exchange for the Jewel of the Heart.

"I still can't believe you didn't tell us right away," said Danny.

"I know, I know," I said. "If something like that ever happens again, I promise you four will be the first ones I tell."

Jin told the story of our battle against Mokugon-bake and

his fire demons at the library, and how the ningyo had almost ripped his throat out to get the song he was singing. Ryleigh picked up the story starting when we entered Ryūgū-jō, but I interrupted to make sure she included one thing.

"When Sen ate all our food and screamed at me to get out, Ryleigh was the only one who suspected she might be trying to warn us," I said.

"Yeah, that's true," Ryleigh admitted.

"If we'd listened to you, we could have saved a lot of time," said Jin.

"Speaking of which, I totally lost track of time," Ryleigh said.

"We all did," said Danny. "You're not perfect, but none of us are."

"Oh, and also speaking of which, we should tell Sen's story," I said.

It went on like that the whole way through, with each of us adding facts and details, trying to get it all in. When we finally finished, the brush and scroll clattered to the deck as if they were exhausted from all that writing.

"Thank you, children, for your courage and for your story," said Fukurokujū.

"*Stories*, actually," said Jin.

"Yes, indeed," Jurōjin agreed. "The Tsuchigumo's story was new to me. And of course, I'd never heard Izanami's story before."

"So now that they're all written down, can you spread those stories around?" Danny asked. "So that everyone else will know them, too?"

Daikoku shook her head. "That's not in our job description."

"We've got our hands full just spreading luck, courage, goodwill, and wisdom," said Ebisu.

"And snacks," said Hotei.

"I can provide inspiration, if you like," Benzaiten offered. "But that's all I'm allowed to do."

"What we're saying is, we rely on you mortals to do the storytelling," said Daikoku. "If you want to make sure that people hear these stories, *you* will have to make sure they get heard."

"Mokugon-bake and his fire demons are still out there," Bishamon said. "Not to mention hundreds of others like them. Just because Izanami the Great Mother isn't bent on destroying the world anymore doesn't mean evil doesn't exist."

He wasn't wrong. I thought about what had happened just the other day at school, when Kiki had tried to start a rumor that Ryleigh ate her boogers when she thought no one was watching. Not that Kiki was evil, but she sure hadn't been part of the transformation that Daikoku had promised would happen once I figured out how to use Kusanagi and my anger for justice instead of vengeance.

"Don't worry, bro. We got it under control," said Danny.

"Never call me that again, rodent" was Bishamon's only response.

But he didn't argue, because we did have it under control. Okay, maybe not totally. Mokugon-bake was unkillable, after all. And I didn't trust Tsukiyomi, and for all I knew, Susano'o might decide he wanted his sword back after all.

But no matter what happened, I knew that together, my friends and I would figure it out.

Author's Note

Dear Reader,

Wow. Here we are at the end of the trilogy. I can hardly believe it! I've loved telling Momo's story so much, and I hope you've loved reading it.

As always, I want to remind you that while the gods and monsters in this book come from real Japanese legends, folktales, and religious traditions, I wove my own experiences, opinions, and imagination into the fabric of this particular story. I also want to note that this book is a little bit different from the others in that I included a few Ainu gods, monsters, and stories. The Ainu were a whole different culture and people who were colonized by Japan in the 1800s. I encourage you to learn more about them, as well as the kingdom of Ryūkyū (now known as Okinawa), whose people and their descendants also have their own separate culture. The Tsuchigumo, Matagi, and Emishi, on the other hand, were clans who resisted the Yamato clan's expanding rule but who were ethnically and culturally similar to their conquerors.

And now I encourage you, dear reader, to find and embrace the source of *your* power, to fight for justice, and to always be on the lookout for the stories and storytellers that Mokugon-bake has erased or hidden away, so you can reveal them to the world!

Acknowledgments

Writing books (and especially book series!) is a lot like going on a long, arduous quest where you have to battle monsters and overcome seemingly impossible challenges: you get lost or stuck at key moments, giant plot holes open up, characters fall flat and lose motivation, and mistakes you make early on come back to haunt you toward the end. But just like Momo in this story, I was able to prevail because I had lots of help along the way.

I have such deep admiration for my editor, Liesa Abrams, who fights for justice by lifting up voices and stories that the world needs to hear. The openness, vulnerability, and empathy that she brings to the author-editor relationship are as unparalleled as her talent and her passion. Thank you, Liesa, for keeping the bar high, for letting me fall and get back up a thousand times, and for gently, patiently helping me figure out how to write a novel again (among the gazillion other things that editors have to do).

I've been extra lucky to have *two* editors on my team, and I am so grateful to Emily Shapiro, whose wisdom and encouragement helped me keep going when I was lost in the dark and led me to unlock key insights into my characters and their journeys. I suspect she also did a lot of behind-the-scenes work that I never saw.

Leigh Feldman has cleared the way and opened doors and cheered me along on my adventures from the beginning, not just in publishing but in "real life," like a cousin who's been through it already and *knows*. Leigh, thank you for insisting that Momo deserved three whole books. Thank you for always being ready to listen. Thank you for your honesty, sage advice, and sense of humor.

Vivienne To does not miss. Every cover she's illustrated for the Momo books makes me want to run around and show it to everyone I meet. And to the incredibly talented Sara Matsui Colby, thank you for bringing Momo and her friends and enemies to life in the audiobooks. I bow down to you and your talent as a narrator!

Speaking of the audiobooks, Tai Hofmeister, Baxter Houghton, Malcolm Huss, and Lex Kolody created a pitch-perfect boy-band sound for "Imma Fight 4 Ya" at the end of the *Momo Arashima Duels the Queen of Death* audiobook. The SttTopp world tour is waiting!

I got incredibly lucky with the team at Random House Children's Books. Everyone is top-notch, from the design team to the publicity team to the school and library, marketing, operations, and audiobook production teams. A special shout-out to my publicists, Cynthia Lliguichuzhca and Kristopher Kam, who have kept me in conferences and school visits, and to Rebecca Vitkus, Michelle Cunningham, Barbara Bakowski, Clare

Perret, Nicole Moreno, Jen Valero, Catherine O'Mara, Olivia Mackenzie-Smith, Lauren Klein, Katie Halata, Adrienne Waintraub, Erica Stone, and everyone else who made sure that the best possible version of Momo made it out into the world.

The longer I've been an author, the more grateful I am to have a group of local author friends to kvetch with, celebrate with, and just hang out with. Thank you to Joanna Ho, Stacey Lee, Parker Peevyhouse, Randy Ribay, Traci Chee, Kim Culbertson, Gordon Jack, Lisa Moore Ramée, Keely Parrack, Kristi Wright, Sonya Mukherjee, Evelyn Skye, Abigail Hing Wen, Kelly Loy Gilbert, Stephanie Lucianovic, Mike Jung, Christine Evans, and many more. Thanks also to my not-so-local Asian auntie crew (you know who you are) for the same.

Special thanks to the real-life superheroes who keep the book-burning demons at bay: the librarians, booksellers, and teachers who are out there fighting to ensure that kids have access to all the stories they need and want. An extra-special shout-out to Mary Sheila McMahon, Grace Lane, Audrey Mueller, and Chris Saccheri from Linden Tree Books; to Angela Mann, formerly of Kepler's Literary Foundation; to Joss Diaz from Kepler's Books; to Grace Li from Hicklebee's Books; and to Heather McDill at The Reading Bug.

I asked my aunt Jun Kuroda a random question about the source material in which one of my characters appears. Jun and Dr. Teruyo Ueki, professor emerita at International Christian University, managed to find Professor Emiko Hata of Shizuoka Eiwa Gakuin University, who not only had written a paper about this obscure seventeenth-century document but had actually *translated it into English*. At their request, Hata-sensei generously shared the relevant pages with me. Thank you to all three of you marvelous women.

Okay, it's family time. My sons, Tai and Kenzo, inspire me every day with their courage and their determination to keep going even when they doubt themselves. And then there's my husband, Tad Hofmeister. Not only is he smart and talented and handy around the house, but he always stands up for what's right, even when it's uncomfortable. I'm so lucky these amazing men are my family.

Finally, one last special shout-out to Mouse, our cat who thinks she's a dog. Who's a good girl? You are! (Mostly.)

Glossary

Ainu (aye-noo) The Ainu are the Indigenous people of the island of Hokkaidō in Japan, the far northern areas of the island of Honshū, and the northeastern coastal region of Russia, including the islands off the coast. Ainu language, religion, and traditions are distinctly different from those of ancient Japan. In the late nineteenth century, Japanese colonizers nearly wiped out the Ainu, but today there is a movement to revive and celebrate Ainu culture, language, and religion. I'm looking forward to the day when we get to read some cool Ainu stories by Ainu creators.

Ainu Moshiri (aye-noo mo-shee-ree) The Ainu term for the land where they live.

Amaterasu (ah-ma-teh-rah-soo) The shining kami of the sun and queen of the Sky Kingdom, and big sister to Tsukiyomi and Susano'o.

Apasam-kamuy (ah-pah-sam-kah-moo-ee) The Ainu deity of transitions. That's why they're on the bridge! They are sometimes depicted as female, sometimes as male, and sometimes as both (because transitions, get it?), which I think is very cool. They protect women in childbirth, and they also protect Ainu Moshiri against potentially unfriendly strangers.

Benzaiten (ben-zai-ten) The kami of music and writing (especially poetry), who is sometimes depicted as a kami of water because music and writing should flow like water.

Bishamon (bee-shah-mon) You should know him well by now! The fierce kami of warriors and righteousness, who loves to squash demons under his feet. He has a giant ring of flames around his head.

Daikoku (dai-koh-koo) Another old friend from the *Takarabune*. The kami of business and farmers, whose roots stretch back to Kali, the Hindu "black goddess" of death, darkness, destruction, and time. Daikoku is usually depicted as a man, but every once in a while we get to see her as a woman. She carries a magic hammer that conjures anything you want when you swing it three times. I gave her the pocket watch.

Ebisu (eh-bee-soo) The god of fisherfolk and luck was the first child of Izanami and Izanagi, but the stories say he was born without bones, so his parents tucked him in a basket and put the basket into the sea. Luckily, he floated north to the land of the Ainu, who rescued and raised him.

Emishi (eh-mee-shee) A fierce clan who lived in northern Japan and were finally conquered in the tenth century by the Yamato, who originated in one of the southern islands of Japan. The name can be translated to "shrimp barbarians," though it's not clear why. It may be because the men had long whiskers, like shrimp. Or it may have come from the Ainu word emushi, which means "sword." The bit about worshipping a shrimp god is my invention.

Fukurokujū (foo-koo-roh-koo-joo) One of the two ancient grandpa kami of wisdom and old age who hang out on the *Takarabune*. He carries a scroll with him, on which are written the stories and wisdom of the world. Or maybe it's just a bunch of memes—who knows? He has a gigantic forehead, which is how you can tell him apart from the other grandpa, Jurōjin. Long name, long forehead.

hime-uo (hee-meh-oo-oh) Their name means "princess fish" (or "fish princess," if you prefer), and they are the attendants and guards in the court of Ryūjin, the dragon king who rules the creatures that live in the sea. Hime-uo are beautiful and magical and perfect, which makes me think they might be just a little bit stuck-up.

Hotei (hoh-tay) A fan favorite, he's the kami of contentment. If you look up Hotei on the internet, you'll get a bunch of pictures of a smiling bald guy with a big belly, leaning on a giant sack of goodies. That's pretty much Hotei in a nutshell.

Ise Ebizō (ee-seh eh-bee-zoh) A nobleman in the court of Ryūjin, he is Ryūjin's trusted adviser. He is loyal, honest, and pure-hearted (though perhaps a little pompous).

Itsuma-hime (ee-tsoo-mah-hee-meh) Historically speaking, she was one of the leaders of the clan of people who lived in central Japan that the Yamato nicknamed Tsuchigumo, which means "dirt spider." I suppose it's easier to wage war against people when you pretend they're not really human.

Izanagi (ee-zah-nah-gee) With his wife, Izanami, he came down from the World Beyond (which is even beyond the Sky Kingdom), and the two of them created all the kami in nature. When poor Izanami went to Yomi, the land of the dead, Izanagi tried to rescue her but ended up running away, casting a spell to make sure she could never leave, and divorcing her. He seems like a nice guy, to be honest, but he's definitely not winning any awards for best husband.

Izanami (ee-zah-nah-mee) She gave birth to all the original kami in the kami-verse except for Amaterasu, Susano'o, and Tsukiyomi. She went to Yomi after giving birth to Kagutsuchi, the kami of fire. Izanagi bravely went to rescue her, and she told him if he was patient and waited for her to be ready, she'd be able to return with him. Long story short, he wasn't patient, saw her as a corpse, and not so bravely ran away before locking her in Yomi forever. Furious, she vowed to kill a thousand people every day. But he was all, "Oh, yeah? Then I'll *make* a *thousand five hundred* people every day!" And off he went to do just that. I can't be the only one who thinks Izanami got a bad deal, right?

Jewel of the Heart Its technical name is Yasakani-no-magatama, or the Eight-Foot Jewel, which really means "giant jewel" or possibly "necklace of jewels," but how boring is that? So I changed it. As far as I could discover in my research, the main characteristic it imparts is kindness, and it's shaped like a comma. Remember how Amaterasu hid in a cave because she was upset with Susano'o for ruining her palace? And how she saw her reflection in Yata-no-kagami, the Mirror of the Sun, and was tricked into coming out of the cave? Well, according to the story, this jewel/necklace was hanging next to the mirror. The thing is, no one knows where it came from. But pre-death Izanami is usually pictured wearing a necklace of comma-shaped jewels, and Izanagi continued to create life after he locked her away, so . . . you do the math.

Jurōjin (joo-roh-jeen) The other grandpa kami of wisdom and long life. The main difference between him and Fukurokujū is that he has a normal-sized forehead.

Kim-un-kamuy (keem-oon-kah-moo-ee) The Ainu god of bears and mountains. There are lots of stories about bears in the Ainu religion. Sometimes they're kind and generous, and sometimes they're deadly, which makes a lot of sense because bears feed humans with their meat, but they can also, ahem, kill you.

Matagi (mah-tah-gee) Would you believe it? Another tribe that the Yamato defeated in their quest to expand their southern empire across the islands of Japan. The Matagi lived in the northern regions of Honshū, the main island of Japan, and they had some cultural similarities to the Ainu of Hokkaidō. One is their reverence for the bear, an important Matagi deity. A few Matagi people carry on their hunting and worship traditions today.

Mokugon-bake (moh-koo-gon-bah-keh) One great thing about yōkai tradition in Japan is that you can discover new yōkai who reflect the evils and troubles of the times. There's even an annual competition on the island of Shōdoshima to see who can create the coolest new yōkai. Mokugon-bake is my creation, and he's the demon who makes people want to destroy or suppress books and stories that cause them discomfort.

Momotarō (moh-moh-tah-roh) The peach-boy hero who saved his lands by defeating an island full of oni, or evil demons. He's kind of like Captain America, but younger and with animal companions.

ningyo (neen-gyoh) Most kids think of mermaids as beautiful singing princesses who can breathe underwater and who have cute little fish tails and long, luxurious hair. But the Japanese version is *scary*-looking. Think giant fish with a human head, fangs, horns, and a taste for human blood. (*See the entry for* Sen *to find out what happens if you should be unlucky enough to eat the flesh of a ningyo.*)

orcas The Ainu sea god, Rep-un-kamuy, is often portrayed as a carefree and generous orca. Mako and Cookie, however, are two real-life orcas who live in the waters off Hokkaidō. Look them up online! And remember: orcas aren't whales!

Pikata-kamuy (pee-kah-tah-kah-moo-ee) She is the Ainu kami of the wind. She keeps the wind in her robes, and she used to get a kick out of causing ocean storms and blowing down villages, until one day the demigod Okikurmi challenged her to a dance-off—and she lost! She promised never again to use her powers to destroy people's homes. But it seems she's still allowed to blow intruders out of Ainu Moshiri from time to time.

Ryūgū-jō (ryoo-goo-joh) The fantastical enchanted undersea palace of Ryūjin, the dragon king. Life here is just one long, fabulous party, with music, dancing, delicious food, and sparkling conversation. But beware! A human fisherman named Urashima Tarō went down there with one of the princesses, and after a few days he returned home to check on his parents—and a hundred years had passed. Time flies when you're having fun, I guess.

Ryūjin (ryoo-jeen) This guy. He's usually kind, but he's also unpredictable, and he's at the center of all sorts of stories. At least three of his daughters married human men.

Ryūkyū (ryoo-kyoo) Not to be confused with Ryūgū-jō or Ryūjin. Today the kingdom of Ryūkyū is known as Okinawa, Japan's southernmost island prefecture. The Indigenous Ryūkyū people used to have their own separate culture and kingdom, with gorgeous palaces and temples and everything, but like the Ainu, they were colonized by Japan. After World War II, Okinawa became an important American military base as well. As with the Ainu, Ryūkyū people are now working to revive and preserve their language, culture, and traditions. I hope one day someone writes a Ryūkyū story, because there's a lot to tell!

Sen (sen) An unscrupulous fisherman caught a ningyo and showed off by giving pieces of the carcass to his friends. Most of them had the good sense to throw their portions into the sea, but one man fed his portion to his daughter (whom I have named Sen) because it was said that anyone who ate the flesh of a ningyo would become immortal. He thought he was turning his daughter into a kami, but instead the poor girl remained human and just kept growing older and older without ever dying. (*See also* ningyo.)

Shiisaa (she-sahh) These Ryūkyū/Okinawan lion-dog guardians are very similar to the koma-inu who guard Shinto shrines in the rest of Japan. But shiisaa were part of Ryūkyū culture even before the Yamato took over. In Okinawa, you will find shiisaa guarding the entrances not just to shrines, but to homes and businesses as well.

Shuten-dōji (shoo-ten-doh-jee) This guy was the number one most powerful demon in Japan until Minamoto-no-Raikō chopped his head off with the sword that became known as Dōjigiri, or Demon-slayer. He was about to rise to power again when Momo sent him right back down to Yomi, where he belongs. If he had one weakness, it would be his absolute belief that he is still number one, which leads him to underestimate the strengths of others.

Susano'o (soo-sah-noh-oh) The kami of the sea and its storms, he is Amaterasu and Tsukiyomi's younger brother and was born out of Izanagi's snot, thus giving a whole new meaning to the term "snotty little brother."

Takeru (tah-keh-roo) He appears in Japanese folklore as a hero of the Yamato clan, which spread from the southern island of Kyūshū to the rest of Japan. His story began when he killed his older brother, and his dad thought it might not be a good idea to have such an angry, violent prince hanging around court. He sent Takeru on a bunch of missions to put down rebellions in the far regions of the empire, hoping he'd be killed in the process. On one of these missions, Takeru used Kusanagi to harness the power of the wind to defeat a rebel clan. (That clan is not named, but I think it was the Tsuchigumo.)

Tamamo-no-mae (tah-mah-moh-noh-mah-eh) The meanest of the mean girls, she is a nine-tailed fox who turned to the dark side. She's said to have used her looks to make powerful men do her bidding. Her bidding was usually something like, "Kill a whole bunch of people!" I must admit I have Complicated Feelings about the way so many stories and legends feature evil, beautiful women who make men do terrible things.

Toyotama-hime (toh-yoh-tah-mah-hee-meh) The dragon princess (in her human form) fell in love with and married Ho'ori the Hunter, and went to live with him on land. She became pregnant and made Ho'ori promise not to watch her when she gave birth. But Ho'ori peeked anyway and saw a dragon holding their baby. Ashamed (or maybe infuriated?), Toyotama-hime fled into the sea and closed the border so that Ho'ori couldn't come after her. She eventually sent her sister Tamayori to take care of the baby, who grew up to become the first emperor of Japan.

Tsuchigumo (tsoo-chee-goo-moh) "Tsuchigumo" means "dirt spider," and the term refers to the people who lived in the regions slightly north of the Yamato territory and to the giant, evil spider-monsters who supposedly lived there as well. Most historians believe that the Yamato gave the people this name.

Tsukiyomi (tsoo-kee-yoh-mee) The middle child of the Big Three: Amaterasu is his older sister, and Susano'o is his younger brother. He definitely has middle-child syndrome, which is to say he wants to prove that he's worthy of his older sister's admiration and that he's superior to his younger brother. He seems bright and beautiful, but he has a dark side—just like the real moon.

Yamato (yah-mah-toh) Japan has had many names throughout history, and Yamato is one of the early ones. It was the Yamato who spread their culture and gods from the southeastern island of Kyūshū and onto the main island of Honshū. In fact, some historians believe that the story of the gods is actually the story of the gradual conquest of Honshū by the Yamato.

Yasakani-no-magatama (yah-sah-kah-nee-noh-mah-gah-tah-mah) (*See* Jewel of the Heart.)

Yasome (yah-soh-meh) A historical leader of the clans who banded together to resist the rule of the Yamato way back in the day. She was a woman, which I feel weird pointing out, but otherwise people might assume she was a man. *Sigh*. Why do you suppose that is?